Deviants

By the same author

One Small Voice

Deviants

SANTANU BHATTACHARYA

FIG TREE
an imprint of
PENGUIN BOOKS

FIG TREE

UK | USA | Canada | Ireland | Australia
India | New Zealand | South Africa

Fig Tree is part of the Penguin Random House group of companies
whose addresses can be found at global.penguinrandomhouse.com

Penguin Random House UK,
One Embassy Gardens, 8 Viaduct Gardens, London SW11 7BW

penguin.co.uk
global.penguinrandomhouse.com

First published 2025
001

Set in 12/14.75pt Bembo MT
Typeset by Falcon Oast Graphic Art Ltd
Printed and bound in Great Britain by Clays Ltd, Elcograf S.p.A.

The authorized representative in the EEA is Penguin Random House Ireland,
Morrison Chambers, 32 Nassau Street, Dublin D02 YH68

A CIP catalogue record for this book is available from the British Library

ISBN: 978-0-241-70723-4

Penguin Random House is committed to a sustainable future
for our business, our readers and our planet. This book is made from
Forest Stewardship Council® certified paper

For Mama. For Niya . . .

Amay bole boluk loke mondo, birohe taar praan banche na
Dekhechhi roopsagore moner manush kancha shona

Nabanidas Khyapa Baul

Let people call me a deviant if they will
I can no longer brook this isolation
I've glimpsed my person in the sea of beauty, and they're pure gold

Mambro's Manuscript

The man in your dream is the man of your dreams.

He is in his twenties, handsome in a Bengali sort of way, luminescent chestnut skin, effortlessly slim, bespectacled, not very tall, his hair flirting between wavy and curly, crowding over his broad forehead like kalboishakhi clouds on the horizon; his smile pricks perfect dimples into his cheeks, his chin has a cleft.

In this dream, you're a grown-up too. You and he are dressed in dhuti-panjabi; you're out and about in the Grand Old City; it is the best time of the year there, Durga Pujo celebrations, the annual worship of the mother goddess over five days. In a blur around his face are adverts in neon, heads of people, decorative facades of pandals. You and he walk, fingers intertwined, stand among the throngs with joined hands to witness the sandhya-arati at dusk.

You fell asleep on the lawn. Light presses down against your eyelids now as you wake, but you're still dreaming, one slipping into another, no friction. The young man is wrapped around your senses, face radiant, eyes playful, fingers stroking the hairs on your forearm. The sky is a smudged rainbow.

And even though you're only a boy of six, and everyone in your world is husband–wife–child, and you've never known a man to love another man, you feel love for this man, and feel his love reflecting on yourself, as though reaching across into the mirror, touching the face.

And that is how, still little, held up by the earth, illuminated by the gloaming, you know you're different, you're precious. It will be over thirty years before you feel this way again.

ENTRY ONE

Vivaan's VoiceNote001

You see, when it comes down to it, each of us really has only one story to tell.

That's what Mambro said, anyway, on his last visit. We were at the Coffee Plantations and having the chat. Yeah, THE CHAT. I'd just told him everything, no filter, and he'd handed me his manuscript. Then Mambro rested his head against the wall, looked up at the ceiling, took a deep breath and I knew he wanted a smoke. Man, I know the guy so well even though I hardly see him!

He turned to me. What would you name your story?

Love at first tap, I replied. It came out so quick, as if I'd given it a lot of thought beforehand, but swear to god I hadn't! Mambro laughed in my face. I acted offended. What? Isn't it smart? At least it'll sell!

Well, you should write it then, he said.

I was like, for real? Now I knew he wasn't joking.

Yes, he said, you should tell your story yourself as it happens. Otherwise, you will have to reconstruct your own life from scraps of memory later. Or worse, someone else will tell it on your behalf. They might even make loads of money from it!

So here I am, doing just that. I'm going the old-school way, voicenotes on my phone. Honestly, I could've just got ChatGPT to do it, my classmates do everything on ChatGPT, essays, slides, even programming! I could've given it talking points – it was love at first tap, then fun things happened, then dark things happened, then shit hit the fan and it all got real bizarre, now there, write it for me. But urgh, no thank you! No AI for me, especially after . . .

But but but, back up Vivaan! You're getting waayyyyyy ahead of yourself. Try to find a beginning to this story. Let's see, how about intros?

Right, okay, so, I'm Vivaan. I live in the Silicon Plateau, India's home of visionary tech and billion-dollar unicorns, not the animal, ha! Look it up if you don't know what it is. This is the twenty-first century, people, get with the programme! This place used to be the Garden City, but that was like, super long ago.

According to my birth certificate, I am seventeen years old. Of course, on the hook-up apps, I'm well over eighteen. On the dating apps, I can pass for twenty-one. And on the internet, I'm timeless. In this country, there is no Right to be Forgotten.

Turns out some of us don't even have the right to be remembered! But that's the whole point of this story, so stay with me.

As I said, it was love at first tap. About a year and a half ago, Zee tapped my profile on Grindr, I tapped him back, and we knew something had started right there. Love is nothing but unpredictable chemical attacks to further fuck up the already-fucked-up human brain. You're thinking, cynical much? Hey, but it's true, pure satya-vachan.

We didn't even chat for long. Zee was a no-time-waster, not like most guys on the apps who're like, hi hello, can I see more of you, and I'm like, you're fucking seeing my face bro, but they're like, oh I mean your dick, your ass, your right nipple, whatever, then you're sending them pics of parts of your body like you're a cadaver for a medical trainee, but they'll just go AWOL and you know they're chatting up other men, and when they've been rejected by the A-listers, they'll come back to you. By then, you've done your round of A-listers and got rejected yourself, so if they suggest sex, you'll be like, okay yeah I'm horny, let's get it done with.

But Zee! Now see, that man had class. I say MAN but he was actually only a year older than me, still is, I guess, unless he's dead in a ditch somewhere and I didn't get the memo.

Zee started with: You have nice eyes, when can I see them in person?

I was all gooey inside, no one had ever spoken to me like that. But I tried to hold my ground. I was like, Ooo do you only like the eyes, what about the rest of me?

Zee typed, I'd like to see the other parts too, but one by one, until I can stand back and see the whole of you.

I know all this seems really tacky right now, but if you've been on those apps and know how people talk, you'll know that someone bothering to type out full sentences without grammatical errors is enough to make you fall in love with them.

Anyway, so I invited Zee over then and there. I'm not supposed to invite strangers home. That's a rule. Mom and I had agreed it a while ago. She'd said, Listen, Vivaan, I know you're growing up and all that, so two things. One, always use protection. Two, never bring strangers home, only friends. I'd wanted to say, But Mom, who wants to have sex with friends? In any case, I'm not big on friends, never had any close ones, always kinda fish out of water, Mom says I'm an old soul in a young body. But I'd kept quiet. From then on, we had a don't-ask-don't-tell policy. She has this unshakable trust in me, which is cute but I totally took advantage of it. I was sixteen for fuck's sake!

So Zee came home. This must've been within half-an-hour of said taps. I'm usually home alone for a few hours after school. Not until last year though. During the pandemic, Mom and Dad were at home the whole frikkin time, being passive-aggressive in formal language on their phones and laptops. So when the CEOs of their companies forced employees to return to the office four days a week and began throwing free food and Thursday drinks in their faces, I was the happiest, I wanted to go to the OG Silicon Valley and kiss them, even if they're straight.

I have to say at this point that Zee isn't his name. On the app, it was Z. But when he said it while introducing himself, he said Zee and I had to reorient myself because in my head, I'd said Zed. I guess Zee was going for the American way. We're all half-American anyway, their accents, their TV shows, their politics, the amount of time we spend talking about America when they don't give a rat's ass about the rest of the world. My English teacher would be very disappointed though, she tries her best to teach us the Queen's English, even though by Queen she means Victoria and not Elizabeth II, who has also now died by the way. Yeah, that's how far back in history Miss Gibson is stuck.

Zee was really unassuming. I'd expected him to be the suave kind, you know the type, how some men can have their heads deep in their own asses. But Zee was confident without being overbearing. He was wearing jeans and T-shirt, and walked in quietly and sat on the sofa in the living room, like he was a guest and Mom was going to bring him sharbat or something. Most men just look for the bedroom the moment they enter.

I sat on the rocking chair opposite him and started rocking. That chair has been with us since I was a kid. It's so second nature that I don't even know how fast I'm going. This made Zee smirk, like he was observing someone he liked but also found amusing? I put my feet on the ground and stopped right away. I asked him what's funny.

Zee shook his head, said nothing, just that I was exactly how he'd imagined.

Some adjectives would be helpful at this stage, I said. Weird? Childish? Cute? Sexy? I knew I was reaching with that last one but hey, no harm trying.

Zee said, Adjectives are assholes. They try to classify us, put labels on us. We're so much more than the adjectives.

Then he started talking about himself. He lived not too far away from me, he went to the school right next to mine, the one we're locking horns with all the time, we're serious competitors. I was like, WTF! How have I not seen you?

Zee bobbed his head in mock surprise, There are only two thousand of us between both schools. Not gonna lie, that made me feel quite stupid.

Zee said he was an only child. I said I was too, we're expensive enough, if our parents had any more children, they'd have to move to the slums!

Zee laughed so hard at this, clapping his knee, his upper body flat against the back of the sofa. I just sat there and watched him, so genuine. We'd been talking for only ten minutes and he'd already told me so much about himself. And now he was laughing like he was with a pal. He had good teeth, a neat face, no acne shit like most people our age, his hair was straight and falling on his forehead all the way down to his eyebrows. And I have to admit this, in that moment, I thought – I'd be with this guy if he'd have me, I really really like him.

Then Zee stopped and caught his breath. I asked if he did this often, going to strangers' homes, he was quite young.

He said, Yeah sure, I mean, you can always tell the good ones from the fishy ones. Made me blush again.

He got up and walked around, peering at the photos. So Mom has this thing, our walls are covered from top to bottom with family photos. Wait, let me actually go to the wall and tell you what's on there . . . Umm, let's see, so here's Mom–Dad before me, trekking up the Himalayas and Kilimanjaro and whatnot, here's Mom–Dad–me, then Mom–Mambro–Dadu–Didu, oh I love this one, Mambro and me digging into a gelato. Okay yeah, so you get the gist, Mom's photo obsession, like we're some aristocratic raj gharana and our faces need to be memorialized in frames for our subjects. Who's this, who's that, Zee kept asking as he surveyed them.

Then he took out his phone and showed me pics of his parents. They looked fine, generic Indian corporate parents. I didn't want to lie like everyone does, say ooo they're so lovely, aww your mum's so pretty . . . all those stock phrases, you know? The worst is when they call old people CUTE! My classmates say that about each other's grandparents. I'm like, no, bitch, old people aren't cute, they've lived longer and seen more things than your bubble-butt ever will! Gets my goat. Just because they're stooped and soft doesn't make them fucking cute.

Anyway, so, with Zee, I was too aware of our shoulders and elbows touching, I even bent my head forward to catch a whiff of his scent, it made me want to dig my nose in his chest and stay there all day. This, after I've had enough sex to be a certified whore, I thought I'd skipped all this shi-shi-foo-foo for the real thing.

Zee asked if my parents knew about me. I clarified, You mean if they know I'm gay?

He re-clarified, I mean if they know you have sex with men. No one's gay or straight or bi, everyone's everything, you don't have to choose, defo not when you're just sixteen.

I taunted, Do you say these things for shock-and-awe, or are you like this only, slightly off the beaten path?

Zee laughed again, very loudly, so loud I was sure the

neighbouring aunty would want to ring our doorbell and ask what the joke was. This time, he ruffled my hair and patted my cheek. I was a bit offended. I said, You're the same age as me, don't give uncle vibes.

Zee leant in and our hair touched. It's weird, you can never feel your hair when it's on its own, but the moment someone else's hair brushes against it, you feel it standing. Zee kissed the tip of my nose, his lips were quite wet. He whispered, Well uncles don't do this, do they, unless they're pervs or something?

I had to smile. I brought my face forward to kiss his lips, but he withdrew, Let's not do everything today, Vivaan. Yeah, I'd given him my real name by then.

I then told him that my parents know I'm gay, or into men, or however he wants to anthropologically categorize me. My Mambro is gay, so it's never been a taboo in my family to talk about these things. A couple of years ago, Mom asked me point-blank if I found men attractive, I said yes, and that was that. By the way, Mambro's an author, he writes novels. I'm usually one of the first people to read his drafts! Honestly, although it was true, I threw the last bit in to show off.

Zee pored over Mambro's photo on the wall the whole time I was speaking. That's pretty cool, can I borrow one of his books?

Sure thing! They're in my room, signed first editions! I hoped this would finally get Zee to move to the bedroom.

But Zee didn't budge, kept running his fingers on the frames. Why do you call him Mambro?

Oh, like, because he's my mother's brother? When I was a child, they taught me to call him Mamu like everyone calls their maternal uncles, but when I was older, I wanted to come up with something cool, so Mambro! They all laughed at first, but you know what, it stuck. I gloated. It's clever, no?

Mam's bro is Mambro. I felt like my eight-year-old self had re-emerged, this is what I'd said when I'd come up with it. What was it about Zee that was making me show all my cards?

Mambro No. 5, Zee winked.

Well for me, he's Mambro No. 1 because he's the only uncle I have. But also, his Mamu, so Mom's and Mambro's maternal uncle, was also gay.

Zee raised an eyebrow. So you're a third-generation gay then!

I mean, technically that's incorrect because for that my parents would have to be gay, which would be quite cool but also borderline problematic? But yeah, my uncle is gay and his uncle was gay, so, in some fucked-up way, I am indeed third-gen. Never thought about it like that.

That is very cool, Zee seemed quite enthu about this. Do you have a pic of your Grand-Mamu on this wall, or somewhere?

I didn't, which was embarrassing but also natural, like, how many people have photos of their grand-uncles framed and hung unless for a specific reason? I said, Actually I don't even think we have that many photos of him, most are from my grandparents' wedding and thereabouts. I made a note to digitalize these photos next time I visited Dadu-Didu.

How much do you know about him? Zee was asking. I doubt he was openly gay, like, in the 1970s or 80s? The fact that you know about him surprises me!

Yeah, well, I don't really know heaps, I know he died quite young, not sure how. Mambro has said he'll tell me his Mamu's story when it's the right time, maybe when I turn eighteen.

Zee rolled his eyes. What's with everyone wanting us to turn eighteen first? Eighteen to drive, eighteen to vote, eighteen to fuck. You know, right, that they think we're stupid? Always moaning, oh Gen-Z this, Gen-Z that. They don't realize we understand the future better than they do, because, erm, we ARE the future!

Have you told your parents? About your fluid sexuality, or sexual fluidity, or whatever? I rippled my arms like a water acrobat.

Zee shook his head like an elephant with epic levels of disagreement issues. Nah! If straight-identifying people don't need coming-out ceremonies, why should we? But honestly, at this point, I think our parents would be quite happy if we're into humans, as in, that we don't want to fuck robots or aliens or pygmies.

Umm, PC Alert!! Pygmies are humans and totally fuck-able, I nudged Zee.

Touché, Zee put his hands up. But you'd have to trek into the African rainforests to fuck them, which would be quite the commitment. Not judging bro, if that's your jam, go for it.

Then we went out on the balcony and stood there, not saying much, staring at the greenery, red flowers popping out of the gulmohar canopies as far as the eye goes. Zee put his hand on mine, and I intertwined my fingers in his. His palm was fleshy, like a comfortable cushion, I wanted to dig my nails into it.

So no sex today? I asked. I was still getting my head around this, that a handsome boy had come home, we were alone, there was all this chemistry, and we hadn't even kissed! What was this, the 1970s?

Zee didn't laugh this time, he continued looking out, then said, I'd like to see you again, if that's okay with you?

Okay with me? I mean, my intestines were doing cart-wheels, but I tried to play it cool. Sure!

I gotta go now, but promise you won't disappear on me?

In that moment, Zee seemed vulnerable, like he'd lost something and had an innate fear of losing it again. I wanted to take him to my bedroom and lock him up and not let him leave, not in an S&M sort of way obvs! I just said, Well you know where I live, it's not you who can lose me, if anything it'll be the other way round.

That was when Zee properly touched me, he placed his hand on my chest, I could tell my heart was beating against his palm, and he seemed to want to calm it. We stayed like that for what felt like a long time. If neighbouring aunty was playing peeping-tom, she could go tell Mom or the whole housing block, I had no fucks to give.

After Zee left, I wanted to wank but I didn't. I know this is weird but something in me didn't want the pent-up energy of that afternoon to be released from my body. I wanted to hold it in there for as long as I could.

That night, I thought about me being a third-generation gay man. I'd never seriously considered it, it's just been this open knowledge in the family, I don't think I was ever told about Mambro, his sexuality has always been what it is, and about my grand-uncle, well I must've been told at some point, but neither Mom nor Mambro made it a big deal.

Not gonna lie, put like that, third-gen gay man seemed something momentous, I was almost ashamed that I hadn't felt the weight of it until then. Had my family normalized it too much? Wasn't it supposed to be normal, though? I wanted to call Mambro right away and ask him to tell me about his life, about his Mamu's life. But I knew he wouldn't do it over the phone, we'd have to meet in person for that, and he lives so far away, I'd have to wait until his next visit at least.

I just couldn't wait to get my hands on their stories, and add my own little fairy tale to the family literary canon.

Ooo, canon, nice one! Miss Gibson would be pleased as punch, as she herself says.

That's it from me today, folks. This is your host, Vivaan, signing off. Goodnight, shubh-raatri, shabba-khair!

Grand-Mamu's Story

The year was 1977. Sukumar was twenty-five years old, living in the Grand Old City, when he touched love for the first time.

That first touch of love was damp clay, patted down into an even mound, drying quickly in the autumnal heat, to be used for sculpting the divine frame of the mother goddess. And the love was for the young man who'd brought him here, to the Sculptors' Quarters. Let's call the man X; as in all clandestine love stories, the lovers shall go unnamed.

Sukumar had first met X outside the offices of the *Jugantor* newspaper, across the street from Sukumar's house. It had been a rainy afternoon, and a group from the art college stood huddled on the pavement under the eaves of the overhanging balcony, talking about volunteering with a Master Sculptor for the idols that year. Sukumar was on his way back from the tuition class where he taught schoolchildren, but slowed down. He'd never really got along with this crowd, these men who chain-smoked and slapped each other's backs and discussed communism in sure, deep voices. He'd always known he was different, his gait, his wrists, the way he let his dark curls caress his face like the locks of Suchitra Sen in the movies. As much as he was intrigued, accompanying these men to the Sculptors' Quarters was out of the question.

Until X had angled his body in a way that formed a bridge between Sukumar and the group. 'You coming?' he'd asked, as though he already knew Sukumar. The rest of the group turned to look, some might even have opened their mouths to correct X, *oh he's not one of us, he's not even at art college,* but there was something authoritative about X, even though his posture was relaxed, and when Sukumar found himself saying yes, X smiled and allowed smoke to roll out from the corner of his lips.

Of course Sukumar said yes! As far back as he could remember, he'd been in thrall to the divine frame, the perfect proportions of the goddess's ten arms, her fiery potol-chera eyes, the graceful slant of the trishul with which she entrapped the buffalo-demon. As a boy, when Sukumar went to the Sarbojonin Park to attend the annual festivities of Durga Pujo with his grandma and little sister and cousins, and everyone else was so taken by the lights and the rituals and the stalls of food that lined the rims of the enclosure, Sukumar's eyes would remain transfixed on the idol. 'Ma Durga', he'd utter her name, bewitched. What would it feel like to render her human for these five days of the year when she descended from heaven to bless the mortals?

On their way to the Sculptors' Quarters though, X had paid Sukumar no attention. He seemed to know everyone, and flitted from one subgroup to another, while Sukumar fell in step behind them all. They walked through the Northern Quarters, crossed the wide road to the river, before turning inland again. The bank of the river was sludgy from the rains earlier, their shoes got stuck in the muck, some took off their footwear to avoid slipping. But X bent down and picked up a handful of the clumpy earth with an uninhibited flourish, held it up for his audience. 'This alluvial soil of our land, ah!' X smacked his lips. 'This is the clay with which we shall sculpt our goddess!' Some of the men clapped their hands, chanted *sadhu-sadhu*, hear, hear; some hooted, *you should've been in the theatre, man!* Sukumar let a smile escape his lips in spite of himself.

When they started again, he caught a glimpse of X turning back to check on him, and was that a wink X gave him?

It wasn't until a few days later that Sukumar spoke to X. Sukumar had been here every afternoon since that first day, rushing after class through the snaking lanes, as though to fulfil a summons issued by the goddess herself. But X had been surrounded by the other art college apprentices. They'd been instructed to prepare the copious volumes of clay that it would take to sculpt the idols. After all, the demand was insatiable; every lane of the Grand Old City, every nook, every park would instal an idol to be worshipped. During those five days of Durga Pujo, the city fizzed with the heady energy of the devout. Even the atheists were out in their finest to partake in the extravaganza.

But that afternoon, a few days in, Sukumar found himself alone with X. The other men seemed to have vaporized, and Sukumar's lean, young frame trembled from the proximity.

'I would never have thought they'd etch the idol's eyes in first, even before the rest of her body is done.' Sukumar tried to sound spontaneous even though he'd obsessed about what to say for a long time.

X kneaded the putty, then sponged the sweat off his forehead with the back of his hand, leaving a streak just where his wavy hair ended. 'Isshh,' he exclaimed, 'so humid today.' Sukumar wanted to wipe the clay away, instead he added water to his mound.

X sat down, his body effortless on the unpaved ground, knees digging into his torso, not caring that his panjabi would get soiled. 'The goddess needs to see herself being created from the earth, that's why we do the eyes first.'

Sukumar was flattered that X had heard his question, had cared to answer. He gave his head a nonchalant jerk. 'Well, *we* aren't doing anything. *We* are just preparing clay for Master-babu.' Truth be told, he'd been disappointed at the menial nature of the task he'd been assigned. But there were too many experts here, people who'd sculpted for decades, people for whom this was family trade, their heritage. 'I'm going to tell Master-babu that I want to paint the eyes, I'm good with strokes.' He felt foolish the moment he said it. He stopped himself from telling X that he had spent his childhood painting the goddess's face on sheet after sheet of paper, the angle of her eyes, the curve of her chin, the spot at which the gold nath pierced the left side of her nose.

X leaned forward, his smoky breath on Sukumar's face. 'You know what I'm waiting for? When they put clothes on the idols. It's not easy, wrapping the heavy silk around a murti, but I'm good with folds.' He held his fingers out, flexed taut between imaginary pleats of garment. The fingers were long, the nails filed, and Sukumar had to fight the urge to entangle them in his.

'If you're so good at this, why do you have that job?' Sukumar mocked. He'd learnt from the others that X worked at the printing press of the *Jugantor* newspaper. He'd gone to art college, had wanted to be an illustrator, but since the newspaper already had two illustrators who weren't going to retire any time soon, X had had to start in a clerical role.

'And if you're so good with paintbrushes, why did *you* study commerce?' X teased back.

Sukumar wanted to tell X of the afternoon his father had taken him to Hare School to get him admitted into the commerce stream. His marks in science had been poor at the end of middle school, and he'd heard his parents' voices in hushed drones from outside the closed doors of their room. What were his options, what would give their son a good future? The next day, his father had told Sukumar that henceforth, he would study commerce; the prospects were looking good, he could become a chartered accountant. His mother had ironed his shirt and trousers, and father and son sat in the car and were driven to the gates of the school's overbearing colonial building, where he'd walked behind his father down the pillared corridors until they'd reached the principal's office. They were asked to wait, and as Sukumar stared out through the window at the grassy playground, he felt his father's palm on the small of his back. 'Stand straight, son,' his father said in a low voice, manoeuvring his fingertips as though to pile the discs in Sukumar's spine atop one another. Sukumar had slipped into his default stand-ing position, leaning on his right hip, curving it out, buckling the right knee to take his ample weight, pushing the left palm into his left hip for balance. It was how girls stood, he'd been scolded in school. That afternoon, having been exposed to his father, his face had flushed crimson. As they waited for the principal, he observed his father's posture; the man was short, Sukumar was already two heads taller than him, but he had a spine as straight as a pole, his chin pointed upward, his bushy eyebrows always equanimous, never betraying what he was feeling. His father had been one of the city's most promising young barristers, a self-made man, a low-ranking police con-stable's son who'd paid his way through law school himself and topped his class, set up a practice from scratch, raced ahead of a cohort that consisted only of lawyers' sons who'd inherited their family's leatherbound libraries and address books. His father was his hero. For the rest of that afternoon, he'd made sure his back was erect, his head steady on his long neck. He'd been thirteen then, two years before his father had suddenly fallen ill, then died within a few months.

But it was too early to tell X all this. Instead, now in the Sculptors' Quarters, he danced his eyebrows in mischief. 'That's because I love commerce so much!'

This got X giggling too. Master-babu frowned from the corner of his eye. The young men fell silent. Quietly, Sukumar extended his hand and patterned the clay on X's forehead into a design. The clay had dried a while back, and globs of it dropped on X's nose. Sukumar brushed them away with care.

'What did you make?' X mouthed, not wanting to disturb Master-babu again.

'The third eye,' Sukumar whispered.

X widened his eyes in a show of sacrilege. 'I thought only the goddess could have a third eye, to see what the rest of us can't.'

Well, you see in me what no one else does, Sukumar wanted to say, but he just blushed.

On days when Sukumar didn't teach classes or have an internship to go to, he positioned himself by the window, trying to study. The rows and columns on page after page of bound books rose above the print and floated before his eyes, the technical terms seemed garbled, the questions on profits and losses and taxes and liabilities irrelevant to how human life should be led. He'd graduated from college four years ago, and had been trying to train as a chartered accountant, taking the exams every few months, and failing every one of them. The paltry pay at the internship and the fees from the coaching centre hardly met his needs. The clock on his unemployment was running down a little faster every day.

Every few minutes, he'd pull the lever to part the wooden slats of the window, checking to see if X had stepped out of the office for a smoke. It happened often enough; X was an inveterate smoker, sometimes lighting a new cigarette with the end of the last one. Most times, he had a colleague or two with him, the men of the printing press, journalists, cartoonists, freelancers, men to whom Sukumar had nothing to say. What did one talk about with these people?

In the evenings, after work, X waited in front of the *Jugantor* office, his eyes on Sukumar's door across the street. Sometimes Sukumar delayed leaving home by a few minutes just so he could watch X, imagine X's accelerated heartbeat at the thought of seeing him. When he finally joined X, he never explained his lateness, nor did X ask. There was a comfort about their being together; no time kept, no promises made.

'Tell me,' X said one evening as they stopped for tea on their way to the Sculptors' Quarters. 'You're so obsessed with Durga, but you never care about Mahishasur.'

'What's there to care about?' Sukumar clicked his tongue. 'He's the demon the goddess is slaying. The whole of Bengal knows the story. He was running riot in the heavens, none of the male gods could kill him; so they joined forces and created Durga, bestowed all their powers on her. That's why she has ten arms, a weapon in each gifted by a different god. Then they sent her to fight Mahishasur. The guy hid inside a buffalo, but couldn't escape her wrath.'

X snorted dismissively. 'Do you know that's such a high-caste Brahminical version?' Sukumar had to shake his head. He felt out of his depth; this was the story his mother and grand-mother had told him since childhood. 'There are versions in which Mahishasur is a tribal king, a kind man, a tender of buffaloes. He's cast as a demon only because he was low-caste and dark-skinned.'

Sukumar bobbed his head in amusement. 'Uff, look at you, Mr Intellectual. High-caste, low-caste, how do you even know these things?' Then he wagged his finger. 'Don't say that to my grandma when you meet her. You won't make a good impression.' He tried to sound matter-of-fact, as though X meeting his family was the obvious next step.

'Oh no, you think she won't approve of our match?' X was clever with repartee. He narrowed his eyes and sipped his tea, the naughty smile pricking dimples into his cheeks. Then he broke the spell. 'I'll come say hello to your family one of these days. Who do you live with?'

'My mother and my grandma. My sister got married last year and moved out to the Garden City. Her husband works there.'

'And your father?'

'He's no more. I'm the man of the house now . . .' He wanted X to know everything – how his father had died ten years ago, the sudden illness had proven expensive and left them with very little money, how the family had had to give up their sprawling flat in the Lakeside Quarters and move back into the cramped ancestral home in the Northern Quarters where Grandma still lived, how he'd kept up the charade of trying for chartered accountancy only because his father had wanted this for him, though he knew he'd never become one.

But X had already put a hand on Sukumar's shoulder. This was the first time he'd touched him intentionally. Sukumar felt his body stiffen, currents cavorting around his nipples. He looked away so he wouldn't have to meet X's eyes.

'I'm the man of the house too. There's no running away from money, na?' X's voice was laced with kindness. 'I grew up in the District, my family still lives there. They're always asking for money – the house needs repair, the elders need doctors, on and on it goes.'

Sukumar changed the subject; he wanted to talk about happier things. 'You can come say hello to my family on Dashami.' He'd already plotted this out: on the last day of Durga Pujo, after the idols had been immersed in the river and people bid farewell to the goddess, youngsters visited elders, touched their feet, sought their blessings. It seemed like a plausible occasion to introduce X to his family.

But X was already shaking his head. 'Oh I won't be here for Dashami. In fact, I won't be here for Pujo at all.'

Sukumar felt his gut drop. He had assumed he'd be spending all five days of celebrations with X, going from one neighbourhood to the next, viewing the decorations, the artisanry, the different styles in which the idols were sculpted. He'd secretly hoped that X would stay back at his place one night. But of course, X had plans; X was smart, he had people to have fun with.

X brought his face close to Sukumar's, even though they were on a busy street. 'Disappointed, I see. Ki korbo bolo? I have to go to the District, spend Pujo with my family. Everyone returns home this time of year . . .'

'It's all right.' Sukumar was careful not to let too much on. 'I understand. You have to be where you have to be. I couldn't leave my mother and grandma alone for Pujo either.'

X seemed relieved that Sukumar had understood, and Sukumar was happy that his response had mattered to X at all. He wanted to hold X's hand, give him a kiss on his cheek, maybe on his lips . . . He'd felt this way about men for as long as he had a memory of himself, although he'd always believed he could conquer his tendencies, be like everyone else; but there was something about this man that was making him want to throw all that up in the air for the first time. Could it be that X felt the same way about him?

Sukumar forced himself back to reality. 'Achha, if we don't rush now, Master-babu won't even let us pat the clay. We're so late!'

It was the night before Mahalaya. Six days left to Durga Pujo. The household was ready for bed, dinner completed, lights switched off, a loudspeaker somewhere playing a devotional shyama-sangeet, when there was a knock on the door. Sukumar sprang to his feet, headed downstairs to check. He could hear his mother mumble prayers nervously. Since his father's death, she'd be gripped by paranoia at the slightest notion of the untoward.

When Sukumar opened the door, his heart soared then seized up. It was X, smiling his best smile, the rim of his turtle-shell glasses slipping down the bridge of his nose, level with his eyelids. Sukumar could smell the drink on him.

'Won't you welcome me in? I've come to say hello to your family.' X's voice was airy. It had rained that evening, and the breeze was cool, blowing straight in from the river. 'I leave for the District tomorrow . . .'

Sukumar opened the door wide to let X in. He wasn't sure of what he was doing, bringing a drunk friend into the house so late. The other friends he brought home were well-behaved, studious; they ingratiated themselves with the elders right away. As though reading his mind, X squeezed his arm. 'Don't worry, I won't make a scene.' Sukumar's face broke into an embarrassed grimace.

When they came up the stairs, his mother was on the landing, the anchol of her white saree draped over her head, as she did in front of strangers. Ever since her husband's death, she'd only worn white, the colour ordained for widows, lest they forget their grief, want to dress up and look pretty, lest they arouse the desires of other men, or god forbid, harbour desires of their own. There was a time when she'd loved colours, stacks of expensive silk and taant sarees piled up in her wardrobe; but as a widow she'd given them away to relatives, who came in droves to commiserate, and left with bags of balucharis and benarasis. Sukumar wished he could show X a glimmer of that woman his mother had once been.

Sukumar did quick introductions, then said X would stay here the night; they would take the room upstairs. His mother was curious but polite; Sukumar hoped she was too sleepy to suspect anything. She asked X if he'd had dinner. 'Yes-yes, Mashima, don't worry. I just came to say bye to Sukumar, but he insisted that I stay over. Your son is a very stubborn person . . .' X raised his hands in a gesture of helplessness; his charm seemed to be working on Sukumar's mother too.

Another flight of stairs up, past Grandma's room on the mezzanine, and they were on the terrace. 'This is a small room. It's usually used as a store, but I can lay a mattress for us . . .'

X put a hand on Sukumar's mouth to silence him. 'It's a pleasant night. How about we just lie under the stars?'

They lay side by side on the rough floor, the blanket fluttering at the corners, billowing up around their bodies from time to time like a cloud. The sky was overcast. 'You're a fraud,' Sukumar teased. 'Where are the stars you promised?'

X nuzzled Sukumar's shoulder, his chest, his hair. No one had touched Sukumar like this before; there was a swirling in his groin, familiar yet for the first time so intense. X rested his head on his palm, adjusted his glasses. 'Tell me something about yourself that no one knows.'

Sukumar felt his chest pushing at the seams. He wanted to tell X that he was in love, with him, that he had never felt this way about anyone else. But he only said, 'I miss my sister, a lot. She's only two years younger, so we grew up like twins. Now she's so far away. Her letters arrive once a month, and when we write back, my mother and I share an Inland Letter leaflet, so I get only one side. I can't even tell her anything.' He hadn't admitted all this to himself in the year since his sister had got married. His last image of her was at the station when he'd gone to see her off; he was struck by how grown up she'd looked, wearing a neat saree, the vermilion sindoor running deep through the parting in her hair, the bridal bangles of shankha and pola on her wrists. It was as though she'd transcended to a parallel universe of couplehood and home-making, a world Sukumar had no access to.

'You know,' he told X, looking up, his bent knees swinging like a child's, 'I used to joke about her favourite singer being Sandhya Mukherjee. She loves listening to adhunik music on the radio, and was so happy whenever they played Sandhya's songs. I would sing over them, imitating the shrill voice, and she'd get so annoyed.' He steeped in the memory of those warm nights when brother and sister huddled around the transistor, their mother some distance away, folding her last paan of the day after she'd served Grandma her milk and medicine, the three of them humming at their own pitches.

'Show me how you'd imitate Sandhya,' X begged. Sukumar quivered his voice and did a comical rendition of 'E Gaane Prajapati'. This made X howl with laughter, slapping his palms on the ground. 'You are so talented, Suku.' There, he'd even given Sukumar a name of his own!

Sukumar gloated, then turned away; he wished he could tell his sister everything right now, about himself, about meeting X, about this night on the terrace even as it was unfolding. He had never been a man of many friends, if any at all; his sister had been closest to him. 'Now I don't even know if she has a radio where she lives,' he wondered aloud, 'and do they even get Bangla transmission outside Bengal?'

He rolled over to regard X, who was drifting off to sleep, legs akimbo, arms over Sukumar's stomach. He listened to the light snores, wishing this could be every night of his life.

Sukumar felt X shake him awake. The sky was tinged with the promise of daybreak. 'Otho, wake up!' An urgency in

X's voice. 'It's time for the Mahalaya broadcast. Do you have a radio?'

Sukumar stumbled downstairs to get the portable transistor. X turned the knob to tune in to All India Radio. The broadcast had just begun. 'Ya Chandi', the choir incanted.

'Do you know about this recording?' X asked. As usual, Sukumar didn't. He knew it was broadcast every year early morning on the day of Mahalaya, to herald the countdown to Durga Pujo, but had never thought to ask more. Being with X was making him realize how naive he'd been, how little about the world he knew.

'This montage of songs and mantras and radio-plays, solos and choruses, was recorded for Akashvani in 1931. Imagine that! Our parents were just children then. Our country was still a British colony. It's *that* old! The voice that does the Chandipath is of Birendra Krishna Bhadra. He curated this programme and brought all the artists together.' X was brimming with emotion. 'He's given Bengal something that will be played for generations, centuries.' His breathing came in gusts, words trying to catch up to his thoughts. 'Sometimes people do these things, maybe they're just doing their work, or living their lives, but they have no idea that they're changing everything for the future . . . Nothing will be the same again.'

Sukumar took X's fingers and brought them to his lips, gave them a light kiss. 'You know so much.'

X snickered in a self-deprecating way. 'A little more than I should. I wish I could just go through life blinkered, like everyone else.' Then he turned and lay on his back. The two friends watched the first light of dawn crack, the first crow fly across the sky, the first strokes of smoke curl up as someone added coal to the hearth.

Sounds of the broadcast were now wafting up from radios in every household, spreading across the Northern Quarters, renting the air over the Grand Old City; the land and its people getting ready to welcome the mother goddess; an entire civilization listening to the mantras as the gods created Durga in the heavens and sent her down to earth to slay the buffalo-demon.

Mambro's Manuscript

It is the mid-1990s. You are mid-adolescence. Where you live doesn't matter; you have lived in other places before, will go on to live in many others; every chapter of your life somewhere new.

What matters is that you feel love for the first time.

It is one of those days when nothing happened; you went to school, sat through classes, took the bus home, had a snack, went for a swim. You don't know this yet, but you will miss this in later years, one day tumbling into another, only two channels on television, anything interesting only shown in the evening hours. You are fourteen, there is a whole lifetime left; no clock ticking in your ear, announcing that time is running out, no social media feed urging you into action every few seconds. There is a heady happiness to boredom; it means there are possibilities yet for things to happen.

You see Y on your way back from the public pool. You won't remember later, but you will imagine your hair to be half-matted-half-hay, wet in patches but drying very quickly in the stoic heat of the monsoons. It must be July or August – Srabon or Bhadro on the Bengali calendar – when the rain falls in sheets, and the humid immovable air takes over afterwards with a vengeance. But that evening when you see Y, it is pleasant, the sunshine has the soft glow of slanting rays before they set, there might even have been a breeze!

Y is walking in front of you, his back straight, the shoulders broad even at that age, left one slightly higher, he has a habit of tilting to the right with every step. A long purple checked shirt hangs loose on his frame, coming down to his thighs, baggy jeans flap underneath, the kind of clothes that are in vogue. Something tugs in your gut; you may have called out his name, or walked faster to catch up with him. Then there you are, facing each other, exchanging pleasantries, where you're coming from, where he's going, he doesn't live in your neighbourhood after all. You know Y from school, same grade but different section, sometimes you take the bus back together.

That evening, you may have walked with him for a while, accompanied him to wherever he was going, or said bye and returned home; it is an unremarkable run-in with a school-mate; but afterwards his smile, his eyes, his voice, the curls of hair on his hands flash up in your memory unannounced. By the time the day ends, something has shifted; maybe your heart has moved to the right a bit, your legs still wading in the disorientating blue of the public pool. Maybe that is what love is; we *feel* it, in moments, for short spans of time, that indomitable potency to imagine beauty with inexplicably intense ferocity, like when the little bird gathers up all the oxygen it can muster and sings a tune.

That evening, you feel love for the first time.

One thing leads to another is not how it happens. They are discrete steps, mutually exclusive, not following the breadcrumbs placed in a line by destiny, but rather like jumping into water with eyes closed, and every time you come up for air, you are in a different spot, a different direction, a different view. But now that you are in, the water engulfs you from all sides, not in a formidable way like a rough sea, but like a placid lake that invites herons to peck at its aquatic riches.

Suddenly Y is everywhere, though there must be periods of time you don't see him, but those stretches don't matter.

What matters is that he sits next to you on the bus, sometimes he gets off at your stop and says he'll walk back home,
sometimes you go to his place after school. A small group has
formed, and you finally have friends. Y isn't exactly a hero,
not the stud of the class for sure, but he is *someone*, people
love him, even respect him in as much a way possible for
fourteen-year-old boys to respect each other; he is easy, has
strong, informed, left-leaning political views while you know
squat; he plays sports, football or cricket, or maybe football
and cricket; he can be the cynosure of the gathering or a fly
on the wall, it's up to him, he's in control. And he likes you,
calls you, invites you to things.

Ever since you moved to this Grand Old City from the
Garden City three years ago, at the age of eleven, you've lived
outside your body. You'd left the only place you'd ever known,
the lush canopied streets, the gulmohar trees sprouting red
blooms over thoroughfares, the school where you did well
and had friends, where teachers were kind, the other boys just
boys like you, the home that felt like a walled-in fortress no
one could breach, only you and your sister and mother and
father, some family friends, some dinner parties, birthdays and
anniversaries and picnics. When people reminisce about happy
childhoods, they're usually deceiving themselves, remembering the best bits; but your years in the Garden City were of
unsullied joy, it was the childhood of the Famous Five and the
Secret Seven, the only mystery to solve was who'd moved
the flower pots from one neighbour's garden to another's.

The Grand Old City changed all that; it is where your family
are from, and suddenly there are too many people, a population of millions on the outside, a deluge of known faces on the
inside; relatives, this-one's-that-one's-brother, that-one's-this-
one's-mother-in-law, dropping in for tea, buying a new home,
getting married, dying. Your arrival here was unplanned; your

father fell ill, was bound to his bed for months, and when he recovered, he decided he wanted to be closer to his relatives. And you obeyed, because that's what children do, living by the diktats of their parents. But it is only your body that eats and sleeps and sweats in the sweltering summers; your soul has gone missing, not making friends with the boys in school who are already men even at that age, crass and brash and loud, kind but only to their kind. Perhaps it is not men who make cities, but cities that make men. As year after year their voices get deeper, hair springs up on arms and legs, moustaches grow and are shaved, muscles bulge, bulges show, you know it's a losing game, you are always catching up on manhood.

And so when Y showers the gold dust of his attention on you; when your shoulders graze in the bus; when he goes with you to watch arthouse cinema in Urdu and Spanish and German at Nandan, or super-hit Hindi films at Metro and Roxy, or the new-age Bangla movies of Rituparno Ghosh, and you stroll down the Colonial Quarters afterwards, stopping at Rallies for chaat and lassi, dissecting what you watched, you never having spoken so eloquently about cinema before; when he shows up to your birthday party with five others even though you invited fifteen classmates, the rest couldn't be bothered; when he speaks to you like he speaks to any friend, and his friends speak to you like they speak to their friends, and all the boys who wouldn't be friends with you otherwise see it, your soul is suddenly found, it materializes from the void and makes itself known, gravitates back towards your body, prises open something that had sealed up. You feel whole again.

You know you are into men, you always have been. You had a dream when you were a boy of five or six, in which you were a grown man in love with another young man. But surely you knew even before the dream, because aren't dreams mere manifestations of instinctual responses? You've never struggled with this part of you, though of course, no one else seems to feel this way, or the ones who do don't want the same things as you, but you are too much in your own head to let these bother you. Later, as a grown-up, woke parents will ask *when* it was that you knew *for sure*, so they can look out for their children, support them if they turn out gay; you will reply in shrugs, until one day, tired of being the social service manual for straight people, you will rebuff, 'When did *you* know you were into the opposite sex?' That will shut them up all right.

You've watched some porn, classmates sneaking in VHS tapes of *blue films* and scheduling viewings when the parents are out; though the flipside of not having friends is that you aren't invited to these parties much, but when you are, you hungrily take in the bodies of men, the chests and forearms, the flats of their stomachs, but most of all their butts and thighs, *that* is electricity. One time, you're invited to watch *Basic Instinct*, you're excited, there's been so much hype around this film; a bass gasp passes through the boys' throats when Sharon Stone crosses her legs, but it's Michael Douglas you're gaping at, his intense eyes, his hair waving outward from the parting, his chin seductively pointed.

You didn't grow up religious, your father an atheist, except, as he later told you, for the prayers he murmured when they nearly lost you to a miscarriage, your mother spiritual, religion only appearing as a cameo during festivals; in any case, your religion has nothing to say against men loving men, women loving women; they are inscribed in scriptures, narrated in mythology, carved on walls of temples; yours is the religion of the Ardhanarishwar, the half-woman half-man god, deifying the blend of both energies.

And there is Mamu, your mother's brother; he is gay, no

one has told you that, but you know about him like you know about yourself. There is something about your uncle, not because he's excellent at art, or because his mannerisms are mild; it is his inability to fit into the world, he always seems just outside the framework within which everyone lives, stands out in a peculiar way, the way you do too. You and Mamu aren't close, you visit him once every few months, his life seems very different to the one you're being trained to pursue; but he exists, you and he are alike, and maybe just knowing that means something? One day you will tell your uncle's story to your nephew, tracing a delicate bloodline of forbidden love across three generations, three renegade young men fifty years apart, you at the centre of it.

Is it that afternoon when a friend invites some of you home for lunch, or is it in the theatre during one of those movies you both are always watching, or is it at his house that's empty after school because both his parents work, that Y strokes your hand with his long fingers? It is a definitive act, confident, not an inadvertent brush, not the bro-hugs you will learn to give straight men later in life, bodies apart, an impersonal pat-pat-pat on the back. Y ruffles the hair on your arm, undercurrents shimmying up your nerves, your veins popping. The first few times, you are too scared to look at him, you're suspicious, always have been about yourself; you're bad at everything you were supposed to be good at, bad at sports, at having male friends, bad at carrying an unwieldy body, at mastering the butch gait, your hips ever so slightly swinging even if you don't will them to. So what is this then, these strokes of his fingers, like a paintbrush wetting a new canvas, discovering the contours before it can layer shades?

You've been with boys before, the groping behind bushes when you were nine and didn't know what it was, or the love letter you wrote to a classmate at twelve, or the visit to a senior's home one afternoon after he lured you with his eyes and then ejaculated all over your school uniform; they'd mostly all ended in embarrassment, sometimes private sometimes public. But no one has done to you what Y is doing, just stroking your arm, feeling his way into your body one square-inch at a time, checking if you feel the same way, inviting you into a carnal conversation.

And after weeks of that, your body speaks back, your eyes turn to look into his, also resolute, letting him know that you are *there* with him, both of you in the same shade, under the same tree. It is during *Dilwale Dulhania Le Jayenge*; you go for the first-day-first-show matinee. You love watching these big-budget Bollywood movies the moment they are out, Madhuri Dixit and Shah Rukh Khan and Aamir Khan falling in love to melodies that will become timeless, you get restive for weeks, staring up at the posters on your way back from school, Madhuri in her peacock-blue saree, Shah Rukh in his bomber jacket, Kajol staring out into the yellow mustard fields; you love the communal nature of it, hundreds of people in an enclosed space watching the same story, sharp inhales of breaths, hooting and booing, dancing and clapping. And Y always makes it happen, bringing you tickets to these coveted matinees that sell out in seconds, then are resold on the black market in the lanes behind the cinemas; you never ask how he manages this, you want to be pampered, want him to make your wishes come true.

It is in the darkness of the theatre, as Shah Rukh and Kajol gallivant across London then Europe then the ruralscapes of Punjab, that your fingers move towards Y's; you feel him shudder; to reassure him, you go further, crawling down to his thigh, feeling goosebumps under the fabric of his trousers, then further up to feel his hardness, knead it, as he does the same to you. There is something about watching the young lovers on-screen flirting on the rolling hills of Switzerland, separating at the concourse of Waterloo station, reuniting in the bogie of an Indian Railways train trundling through farm-lands, all the while fighting against the world to actualize their love, coming into each other, coming into themselves. That afternoon, you are them, they are you, young lovers, coming into yourselves.

You kiss soon after; maybe that very evening when you go back to his place. By now you are a regular, his mother loves you, stands in the living room and chats away, teasing him, telling you stories about him while he walks around the house pretending to be busy, throwing in snide remarks. It is a beautiful relationship, mother and son engaged in banter. You dare to imagine how it would be if you formally stepped into the family someday, lived here, had dinner every night. She knows when to let you go though, senses that Y has gone to his room and is waiting for you, and you wonder if she knows what is happening between you two, whether she is allowing it, or better, giving you her blessing?

That evening, when you go to his room, you may have launched into each other, you won't remember the specif-ics, just that he tastes sublime, the skin on his face tender, the dark-brownish hair that he constantly brushes away from his forehead, his eyes beseeching for more. It is your first kiss ever, you've never kissed any of the boys you've been with, or rather they didn't kiss you back even if you'd attempted it. A portal is opening up into a new world, a sensory education in anatomy. You live in a world where men don't just kiss men, there are no apps yet to facilitate it, no Friday night dates and school proms; later you will be glad for it, grateful that the first time the door opened for you, it was Y holding your hand.

★

The day after you come home from the first kiss, your family leaves for a holiday to the seaside; you've looked forward to it for months, you haven't been anywhere in three years, since you moved to the Grand Old City after your father's health scare. The holiday is a dream, the sea sumptuous, the beach welcoming, the food wholesome, the wind carrying the damp smell of the water and drying fish. Y has gone off too, to his relative's place in a quaint university town. In those ten days by the sea, as you wait to see him again, to kiss him again, you don't pine, but rather exist with an amplified sense of being alive, like a higher energy is now flowing through you, one that encompasses you *and* him, keeps him next to you at all times; here he is, walking by you on the beach at sunset, spraying water as you bathe, sampling the warm earthy roso-gollas made of jaggery that a villager sells out of clay jugs every evening. And you know it is the same for him, that you are there with him, strolling on Graam Bangla's laal-maati, rural Bengal's quintessential red earth, Rabindrasangeet playing on loudspeakers, napping under the rustling leaves of banyan trees.

You probably return from the seaside before Y does from his relative's, because you are by the phone when he calls, annoyed that your sister has picked up before you could get to it, snatching the receiver from her, hearing Y's voice again, feeling your chest close in, rushing to your room to pick up books, then shouting to your mother that you're going out because Y needs some notes. It has rained all day, still is, water logs the streets, branches torn away from trees float like discarded trash, cars move slowly through the rocking liquid, not a human in sight. You wade to get to where he said he will be waiting; he's already there, bedraggled, the same purple-checked shirt from that first evening now hugging his shivering body, the dye threatening to run. You both wear glasses, can hardly see a thing, the unabated beating of water on the outside, the fogging-up from the inside. But you've made it into each other's arms, stand there amidst the flotsam, in the middle of the street, under the heavily pregnant clouds that have been in labour for hours, kissing, holding, clambering for more. And you know that this evening is the start of something; you've both called it, placed your chips, signed a covenant.

You won't remember how you get home, how you explain this foolishness to your parents, how you skirt around your sister's probing. That night, and for many nights to come, you won't remember anything about what you eat, how you sleep, how you pass your exams, how you keep up the sham of everyday life. You will only remember Y, and how he makes you feel.

And you will remember the evening when you both come back to his after watching *Mammo*, and Y collapses on the bed; he's running a fever, his skin burning up, his eyes red and watery, his hair pasty, his head on your lap, you compressing a wet cloth on his face, his mother in and out to check but letting you do your thing. He whispers, so softly that only you can comprehend, the way couples can read each other's lips after years together; he says he loves you, he loves you so much, that you are his everything, he'd die without you. His clammy fingers are clasping your hand, dread emanating from them. You're overwhelmed at first, he's not an expressive person, he hasn't been this rapturous ever, so you wave it away, thinking he's being silly, joke that the movie you watched wasn't about anything romantic, it was about an old woman who'd come to India from Pakistan to see her sister, and had fit so well into the community that she'd stayed on, but when the authorities got wind that her visa had expired, they packed her up and sent her back; so why is Y feeling all this love suddenly?

Y just keeps repeating himself, and as you watch him, his face pricked with beads that could be fever-sweat or sponge-water, you realize that he is delirious, what he's saying is coming from a place he isn't aware of, that the movie might not have been romantic, but there was something about watching the lonely old woman ripped away from her family, her cries as the police bundled her things up, threw them out on the street, shoved her into a moving train. You know Y is lonely in that big house, all by himself all the time, working parents, only child. You wonder if Y has caught a virus at all, of which he showed no signs earlier, or if it is the movie itself, the prospect of separation and loneliness, that has suddenly made him so ill.

As you sponge his body, spoon water into his mouth, slip pills in at regular intervals, fan his torrid face, you whisper back in his ear, enunciating so your words go right through into that inner core, the only part of him that is awake right now. 'I promise I won't go anywhere,' you say. 'I'll be here always.'

And you mean it, believe it with all your being, like the little bird believes when it sings that it can go on belting its song out forever.

ENTRY TWO

Vivaan's VoiceNote002

Mic testing, one, two, three . . .

Hi peeps! It's me again. My parents are out and the prep for my next exam is done, so I thought I'd get on with the story. I left you hanging last time, didn't I?

Right, so, Zee and I were now seeing each other quite a bit, though knowing how cagey he was about following norms, I didn't ask if we were boyfriends, or exclusive. I figured he'd flip, and because he spent a lot of time with me, like, a LOT, I couldn't see how he could be spending time with anyone else, given he had school and his band and other stuff going on.

For all his rebellion, Zee was quite the romantic, he texted me good morning every day, he kept track of what was going on in my life, my class tests, my presentations and projects, my tiffs with friends and teachers. He took me home one afternoon, and his mother was sweet, beta eat this, beta drink that, but then she left us alone, and when we were making out, I was worried she had her ear to the door, but likely not. I couldn't tell if she was cool or clueless, but that was Zee's problem, not mine.

Sometimes Zee waited for me after school, not at the gate but a little further down, under a tree, fidgeting with his tie. I'd be so turned on seeing him in his school uniform I'd bring him home and start stripping it away. Ease up yo, Zee snorted, it's a school uniform, not a soldier's outfit. Later we'd laugh about how Princi would lose her shit if she found out that I had a fetish for the blazer of the competitor school.

We went for a trek to the Bull-god Hills one afternoon, and

lying in the high grass on the slope, under the soft sun, Zee properly kissed me, like legit, and we kissed for so long that we missed the last bus and had to hitch a ride back, which was quite adventurous, like in the movies, and I fantasized that the man in the car would try to rape me and Zee would fight him to save me. But the guy turned out to be an average IT dude, he even stopped midway to take out his laptop and edit some code to send to his manager. When I later told Zee about my imaginings, he joked that if the guy intended to rape anything at all, it would be his laptop.

I told my friends about Zee soon enough. They played it cool, said, Okay bro, why you wasting your youth being coupley and not sowing wild oats? But when they met Zee for the first time, in a café near our schools, they were all giggly and wouldn't look him in the eye. I realized this was the first time they'd actually seen two men together and didn't quite know what to make of it. There'd been rumours of two seniors getting it on with each other, but no one had done what I was doing. Made us feel like quite the trailblazers! And okay, granted, Zee blew their socks off. He had that air about him, when he spoke, he made more sense than all of us sixteen-somethings put together, and when he was silent, you were left wondering if he was secretly decimating your intelligence. After that first time, we met up with my friends again, and Zee added a few of his to the mix, and it turned out that one of his friends and one of mine had started sleeping with each other, and everyone went into a tizzy about it, and I wasn't very pleased that they'd hogged the limelight, and suddenly Zee and I were old news. Okay, confession, I'm not usually one bit needy, but stardom can be addictive.

So when I got the invite to the school dance, and they mentioned plus-ones, I obviously RSVP'd with Zee's name as my date. The next day, the organizer took me aside after class and said Zee's name seemed to be a guy's. I was like, duh bruh. So she said she'd have to work out some details and get back to me. I left it at that. I know these types, just because she's stepped in to organize something, she thinks she's the president of a country, and she's creating work for herself so she can put this on her CV for Harvard or wherever the fuck she wants to go next.

But that night at dinner, Mom said, Vivaan, your principal wants to meet, what's that about?

Oh, I don't know, I said, I haven't been in trouble or anything. Then it struck me. Wait! Is this about me wanting to bring Zee to the dance as my date?

Mom seemed alarmed, and I realized I hadn't even told her and Dad about Zee. So I did, and I could see Mom was kinda excited by the whole thing, I'd never had a boyfriend per se, and she asked if she could meet Zee. I said, Yeah sure, I mean it's not serious or anything, it's not like we're getting married.

You couldn't even if you wanted to, not in this country, not at this age, Mom retorted.

That shut me up all right. I respect Mom for her snark. Over the years, she's figured out just how to deal with me. I'll say something snide, and she'll respond in exactly the same tone. Dad, on the other hand, he just looks at the ceiling or out of the window.

Yeah sure you can meet Zee, but please behave yourselves, don't ask too many questions.

Not like he has a job and house and salary that we can grill him about. Mom was totally slaying it, and I was just gulping spit. I could tell she was enjoying her wins, she's competitive like that.

Does your Mambro know? Mom asked. She has this thing, just because I'm gay and her brother's gay, she thinks I run to tell him everything about my life, Oh Mambro, where do I buy poppers, Oh Mambro, guess what, today I discovered sex games on a porn site. It's not like that at all, Mambro lives far away and has his own life, I have mine. Plus he's forty or whatever, basically he's old.

Nah, I'll tell him when Zee and I buy a beachfront villa. Now Mom was gulping spit, and I knew I'd won bragging rights for this round.

But even before they could meet Zee, my parents and I had to go meet with Princi.

Mrs and Mr G, thank you for coming, Princi started the meeting. She's super PC like that, always Madam before Sir, Mrs before Mr.

Ms, Mom corrected her. I'm Ms B. Mom hadn't changed her surname after getting married, nor had she gone double-barrel. When they put only Dad's name against our flat number in the building lobby, Mom fought the management committee to get her full name included. I think they had to order a whole new board so both names could fit. Seeing her do that, all the other women in the building also demanded their names be added before their husband's. It was their own little women's march, virtual of course! Yeah okay, Mom's pretty cool.

Princi looked like she'd been hit by a truck. Then she shook herself back together. So, Ms B and Mr G, Vivaan is bringing a boy as his date to the dance. Did you know?

Mom just stared at Princi's face, not blinking, like, you bigoted cow, shut up right now and let me go to work, I don't have time for this nonsense.

But Dad jumped in. What is the problem, ma'm? Are you saying you are against homosexuality? You know, love is love. Blah blah.

Cringe! So here's the thing about Dad. He wears the rainbow-tinted glasses of a cis het liberal male. Just because he's embraced gay rights and feminism and whatnot, he thinks everyone else has too, from the right-wing prime minister to the auto-waala spitting paan on the street. If he could write software that would automatically overlay a rainbow filter on everyone's profile pic, he'd do it right now. Also yes, he does still use Facebook, ewww!

Princi was ready for Dad's moral lecture. But look, there is a certain decorum, there is the question of culture, what will the other parents say? These things can't change overnight, things have to change slowly. Blah blah.

Mom had come armed and now she unleashed her weapon. Madam, she said slowly, Section 377 was amended five years ago. Homosexuality is legal in India. How much time would you need before your school can catch up? Last time I checked, court judgments were effective immediately.

Princi looked like she'd been hit by a second truck, a bigger one this time.

Then Miss Gibson piped up. I'd forgotten that she was there, sitting behind us, in OBSERVATION MODE, monitoring the well-being of the student, like Princi was going to dice me and fry me up in a wok, and my parents would joyfully partake in the meal. Miss Gibson said, You know, Ms B is right, in the UK, I think this would be allowed, I'd have to confirm, but I think it would.

Princi could see the third truck hurtling towards her, BRITAIN painted on the mudguard. So, quick background, she's the first brown head of a British international school in the most progressive city of India. All she'd ever wanted in her career was to create Little Britain in this giant land of heathens.

Who is this boy anyway? Princi was deflecting, she'd lost

the battle. When I told her Zee's name and his school, the fourth truck had already run her over and flattened her face. I think that was the biggest shock, that my date was from the competitor school down the road. It was like telling a Hindu right-wing father that his daughter had already married a Muslim in Jama Masjid, and the event had been live-streamed to the entire country.

Okay then, Princi sighed and got up, her life now meaningless. Okay then.

The days leading up to the dance were, how do I put it, well, kinda cute, but also overwhelming? You know what I mean?

There was a lot of support from everywhere. The parents' WhatsApp group wouldn't stop buzzing, I wasn't on it, but Mom read out some of the messages every night. We love Vivaan and we are there for him. We are so proud of both of you as parents, you are our role models. We should petition to change the principal, this is unacceptable.

I told Mom that these were just foreign-educated elites massaging each other in their echo chamber. Mom said change had to start somewhere, sometimes it comes from the bottom, sometimes from the top.

Fair enough, but let's not assume we're at the top and everyone is below us. Isn't the world more mixed up than that?

I could see Mom was exasperated by my wokeness, but I wasn't done. Most of these well-wishers are NIMBYs anyway.

What's a NIMBY now?

Not in my backyard, you know, like, if their sons came out tomorrow, they'd be freaking out. It's all well and good when other people's children are gay or marrying Muslims or studying art history.

Why are you so cynical all the time? Mom's jaws were

clenched. Just like your Mambro. Why can't you both take people's niceness at face value, maybe there are some good ones out there?

I blew a raspberry. Maybe Mambro can't be all lah-di-dah because he didn't have it easy, that kinda screws you up, you know?

I was bang-on, Mambro wasn't at all lah-di-dah!

When he called, I could hear Mom tell him all about the dance. Of course she did! They talk all the time, brother and sister and their mother, my Didu, some tight family bonding they have, like in a Sooraj Barjatya movie. Mom was telling him about how everyone was supporting me and Zee, but Mambro stopped her and asked to speak to me. Mom put him on speaker.

Mambro didn't ask if I was excited about the dance or how I was feeling in general. Instead he asked about Zee, how we'd met, and if we were in a relationship or were just fooling around. In that moment, I felt like he just got me, in a way Mom or Dad or all those classmates' parents didn't. Umm, how do I put this . . . look, straight people, no matter how cool they act, can't help seeing life as a series of steps: fall in love, get a job, propose, get married, have babies, then fuck knows what next. But honestly, it's not like that for gay people, or it doesn't have to be! Zee and I weren't exactly mixing our sperm and advertising for a surrogate. And Mambro got that.

Zee and I don't know what we are, I told Mambro honestly. We just like each other.

Okay, but do you think this dance thing has blown out of proportion? You don't have to go if you're not feeling it any longer, okay?

Hey hey hey, Mom cut in so suddenly that I jumped in

my chair. He can't bail now! Do you know what I told his principal, how I antagonized her? And after all that, if he doesn't even go with this Zee-boy, what face will I show? What example will he set for his juniors if he chickens out? Would you not have wanted this when you were in school?

There's a term for what you're doing! Mambro was also raising his voice. It's called saviour complex. Vivaan can do whatever he wants without taking into consideration your role in all of this. He's a free agent . . .

With all your academic theories, I'm surprised someone hasn't given you an honorary doctorate yet! Mom barked back. It's true, Mambro did quote a lot of hi-fundoo research, have you read this article, did you watch that documentary, the latest thinking is, there's a school of thought whereby . . . that kinda stuff, and the rest of us would just shake our heads like dimwits. Initially, I thought he was showing off, but it's only when he'd tell me his story later that I'd fathom it was a kind of reverse engineering, as in, he tries to see his life as one of many, part of a pattern, so that what happened to him doesn't feel exceptional any more. Sorry, too much foreshadowing. Just hold on to this, you'll see what I mean.

But back to the current situation. Mambro was being all passive-aggressive, Okay, then why don't you have Vivaan and Zee walk down Rajpath in the Republic Day Parade, to inspire the country? Should I call the prime minister? I'm sure he'd be chuffed to showcase them!

This was a classic Mom and Mambro fight. Both have strong opinions, and don't actually care if they go all aggro on each other. They're feral, it isn't easy being around them when they're like this, but there's also a familiarity that makes them take these liberties, knowing they'll bounce back to the default no matter what. They even speak in the same tone, and if one didn't have a male voice and the other female, you wouldn't know who's talking! Maybe that's how siblings are, and when I listen to them it makes me miss having a sibling of my own.

Anywho, the only way to stop this right now was for me to shut them up. IT'S OKAYYYY, I said loudly. I'll do what I want!

But I have to fess up that I didn't really know what I wanted. Things really had got a bit too serious for my liking, that I was suddenly this cause everyone had to take a stand on, show support for. When I'd put down Zee's name as my date, I hadn't seen any of this coming. But again, as Mom said, it had to start somewhere. If I wasn't going with Zee, would I have gone with a girl? Yuck no! Mambro never got to go to dances with boys, and his Mamu, god only knows what kind of life he'd had.

It was all a bit much.

On the evening of the dance, I wore a corduroy red blazer that Mom and Dad bought for me. I could see they were trying not to make a big deal about it. Wear it if you like it, Mom said as she left it on my bed the night before. When I took the packaging off, it seemed like one of those things I'd always wanted but didn't even know I did until someone gave it to me. Funny how parents know us even better than ourselves sometimes.

Mom drove me to Zee's place, and he came out dressed in a navy suit with a netted T-shirt underneath. There was a ring on the left of his nose, very chic! I didn't even know he had a piercing there! I couldn't stop gawping at him, until I caught Mom examining me in the rear-view mirror, so I turned away and acted disinterested. Zee sat with Mom in the front, he didn't want her to feel like a driver I think. It felt awkward at first, because it was my night with Zee, and here I was sitting alone in the back like a lonely Uber passenger. I had a knot in my stomach over how the party would turn out, it felt like it was all up to me, you know? Like, it was MY school, MY decision to bring Zee, MY mother who'd fought with Princi, everything at stake was mine, Zee was just coasting through.

Zee and Mom were making such a ruckus in the front that it was nice after a while to zone out and hear them laugh. They'd struck it off right from the get-go, when he came home one evening. I'd said no sit-down-dinner business, so he came around six p.m. for chai-nashta and was supposed to leave within an hour, but he and Dad spoke about the English Premier League, and he and Mom spoke about her work in cryptocurrency algorithms, that boy did really know a lot about a lot of things! And before I knew it, they were like, Zee is staying for dinner, nothing doing. I was like, chalo okay, koi nahin. I have to admit it was a pleasant evening in the end, and Zee even kissed me on the cheek when he left. No one, boy or girl, had ever kissed me in front of my parents before, and they tried to act cool, clearing the dishes and being smooth about it. Later that night, I heard Mom give the full low-down to Mambro on the phone. Now in the back seat, I thought about that evening and it made me smile. Zee, as if he'd felt my turbulence, held his hand out and squeezed my knee, half-turned his head and winked, and I thought, Que sera sera, whatever will be will be! I rolled the window down for some air.

At the party, Princi was in her best cocktail dress, her hair tied tightly in a topknot. She seemed to have recovered well from her quadruple-truck-wreck. She got on the stage and made a little speech about how happy she was that everyone was enjoying themselves. Then she called me and Zee onstage, and said she was so proud that the school was hosting a gay couple for the first time. I squirmed. Firstly, GAY COUPLE, like, really? Would she introduce a boy–girl as a straight couple? And also, not gonna lie, it felt quite exposing. I thought Zee would blow his shit, as you know, he hated being labelled, but he was actually quite chill, even waving at the audience like a politician. Seriously, give people some attention and before you know it, they're giving you a fucking lap dance! Anyway, everyone in the audience was clapping, and Princi and the pre-Harvard chick beamed like it was them receiving medals for valour. I thought, Dafuq? Wasn't it me who put Zee's name down? Give credit where due, bitches. But Princi was already unfurling a pride flag and waving it around like she'd come to watch an India–Pakistan cricket match and it was the last over and India was sure to win.

After she left, things relaxed. Miss Gibson and a couple of other teachers were still in the hall, but they were in a corner, in observation mode, they could observe all they wanted, as long as they weren't in our faces. There was general chatter and mingling. No alcohol was being served, obviously, we were below the legal drinking age, so we kept going off to the toilets because someone had arranged for the tapri-stall-guy from outside the school to sell whisky and rum and shots behind the building. I could tell he was having a blast, he looked more drunk than all of us. One time, when we were out for shots, Zee kissed me on my lips, and I thought the tapri was going to either faint or pee his pants, but he looked quite happy with what he saw, I might say he was even aroused, and I was like, ewww, creepy AF.

Then the DJ was set up and the music started. The whole assembly hall was the dance floor, which was kinda weird, like the room had a multiple personality disorder, Jesus by day and Justin Bieber by night, ha! Everyone moved and grooved to the beats. The couples were being coupley, canoodling, kissing, getting it on. The singles were dancing in groups. Once in a while, drama would break out, some girl danced with some other girl's boyfriend, some boy made eyes at some other boy's girlfriend, all that straight-people macho–femme bullshit.

Zee and I didn't get too close, not intentionally though. Zee just seemed so in the mood for a dance, he was swaying and swinging his hips and banging his head and snapping his fingers and trailing his toe in circles to Rihanna and Dua Lipa. I started imitating Zee's steps, and we made quite the two-some. I'd never seen him dance before, he was good, but also he was mouthing the words and narrowing his eyes and being smouldery and sexy, and I held his collar lightly and brought his face close and our heads rocked to the rhythm. He pressed his lips against my ear and said, Your eyes, goosebumps, FUCKKK! I couldn't help it, I just locked lips with him, and everyone around us cheered. Miss Gibson took a step forward, then controlled herself, maybe she'd remembered to check beforehand what would be allowed IN THE UK.

Wow all right, that's a LOT of talking. This stuff takes time, no? I'll try not to ramble, I promise. But let me get some water first . . .

Back, monsieur madame, at your service! Hope I haven't left you for too long chewing your nails off in suspense, ha!

So, back to the dance. As the evening wore on and people got tired, many dropped away from the floor to sit around the edges, some couples disappeared. Those who remained made two big circles in the centre, the boys in the outer circle, the girls in the inner one. The boys stayed where they were, but the inner circle turned clockwise or counter-clockwise, so that the girls were moving from boy to boy, first doing salsa or tango or getting twirled around their arm, but then they were doing all kinds of steps really, Bollywood lightbulb-fitting and back-swiping and matka-thumka. It was cute to watch.

Zee and I had retired to the side by then, but some of the girls called out to us, Vivaan, Zee, come on guys! So we went, not really sure how this would work, but everyone rearranged themselves such that Zee was in the outer circle with the boys, and I was in the inner circle with the girls, maybe because I was slightly shorter than Zee.

And as the music played on, and I went around with the girls from boy to boy, I could see how they stiffened up every time I stepped in front of them, some wouldn't touch me, just a quick nod to say hey, some left the circle without explaining, some just let me pass, some had WTF DUDE written all over their faces. For the ones who twirled me around, they kept their arm's-length distance. I caught them all sniggering at each other even in those flashing disco lights.

By the time I'd done two full 360 degrees and was back in front of Zee, I was like, okay enough. So I pulled him inside and stepped out into the boys' circle, I guess part of me wanted him to experience what I was going through. And every time Zee made a round and came back to me, I could see that something was happening to him, his eyes had become vacant, his moves had lost their zest, basically he was blanking out. I just wished we could exit this lame dance.

Of course we could, no one was keeping us there, but we kept going round and round, like those pointless drills in PE class, our limbs stuck in repetitive steps, even though we didn't know what we were doing, trying to fit our square pegs in this round hole, or whatever that saying is! No matter how much the laws changed and Mom fought and Princi came round and pre-Harvard girl did her good deed and other parents played liberals, we would never be part of this. Like, THIS was society in miniature, circles of men on the outside and women on the inside. The only way to survive here was to stay out of it, or watch from afar, or include ourselves and be humiliated.

The question for Zee and me that night was, which kind of gays were we going to be?

Grand-Mamu's Story

In early 1978, about six months after the fateful Durga Pujo with X, Sukumar joined a public-sector bank as a junior teller. It was a recommendation from one of his father's past clients that got him in. Times were chaotic; young men were being shot in police *encounters* or thrown in jail for supporting the Naxalite movement that demanded more rights for farmers and tribal people over the land they tilled. The newspapers were agog with reports of attacks and blasts, killings and disappearances. The economy had taken a hit; jobs were scarce. So when the old gentleman took pity on Sukumar and asked him to meet the manager of the local branch, Sukumar accepted with gratitude, and his mother nearly wept with relief.

The salary was meagre, the position entry-level, the work repetitive, but it was a job nonetheless, a source of earning, a beginning to a respectable career. The family hadn't experienced an inflow of cash in over a decade; they'd survived on the interest from his father's savings and rental from the family car that was loaned out to an uncle's business, supplemented by the kindness of relatives, a saree here, a shirt there, an offer to fix the ancient plumbing, tuition at discounted rates, gifts for his sister's wedding. A few years ago, his mother had sold all her husband's books, the hefty volumes that adorned the walls of his lawyer's study now on shelves of bourgeois librar-ies. The sale had fetched more than she'd imagined. Sukumar and his sister would learn of this much later. They'd never learn that their mother had also been pawning off her jewellery to keep the family afloat.

Sukumar's job changed all that. The assurance of an income, no matter how small, soothed the nerves of mother and son. There was now money to eat well, to buy clothes, to get repairs done. Grandma's death within a few months helped to lift the pall of gloom that had set in over the house; the old lady had never recovered from the loss of Sukumar's father, and though an uncle had now locked up Grandma's mezzanine room – claiming to be her favourite son – and quashed Sukumar's hopes of having a room of his own, her departure gave Sukumar and his mother the oxygen to limp out of the shadows.

And just as people overeat after a long famine, Sukumar and his mother sometimes went overboard, buying gifts for relatives, inviting countless people over. Old habits die hard, and every now and again, Sukumar's mother slipped back into the time when she had been the prosperous wife of a successful barrister, had stepped out of her car with goodies for everyone, looked out for those who needed help. Losses come in a series of ripples, one leads to another then another; for Sukumar's mother, the loss of her husband had also meant the loss of her place in the community, and she couldn't help but reclaim some of that now. If people were talking, which they were, saying she should draw her purse-strings tighter, she'd tell them that they hadn't been the ones to be robbed of a husband and stripped of coloured clothes in their prime at thirty-five, they hadn't had to go to sleep hungry, brows knitted into furrows, put two children through school and college, cobble together enough for a daughter's wedding.

Sukumar too was finally enjoying the fruits. He looked better, ate better, felt better, his lean frame filling out at the shoulders and the waist, his gaunt face taking on the cherubic proportions of his plump childhood, his curls making healthy dips on his forehead. His eyes had a spark, his laugh had a tinkle; he was popular at work, joking with colleagues, winning the hearts of customers, entering the good books of superiors. His old self stepped out from behind the crusty veneer of the previous years, the shame of failure painted over by the prospect of plenitude. As a child, he'd been loved by his elders and cousins, his anecdotes were re-quoted by relatives, no wedding was complete without his presence, the way he threw himself into the thick of things, serving food, decorating the tattwa-trays with gifts for the bride and groom, pinning sarees expertly for the grown-up women. At one wedding, he'd worn a saree himself and danced to 'Shohag Chaand Bodoni Dhoni'; the performance was such a hit that he'd been asked to repeat it at other weddings; and he had, until he grew up and wisps of hair began to shadow his face and he became too self-conscious to dress up as a girl any more.

If in all these years, Sukumar had thought he was the man of the house, now he truly felt like one, realizing that it wasn't just responsibility that came with it, but entitlement too. His mother's demeanour shifted, imperceptible to the external eye, but tangible to Sukumar. She didn't question his comings and goings any more, didn't remind him to study and secure internships, didn't give him lengthy accounts of the day's expenditure, didn't hand him chits with phone numbers of influential relatives to call. She now waited every evening to serve him dinner, bhaat and shukto and dal and torkari and maach, the kind of spread she hadn't been able to lay on since her husband's death. She'd always been a good cook, her dinner parties once the talk of the Quarter and among extended relatives; it was the skill that had helped her win over her in-laws as a young bride. Now she spent all afternoon in the small kitchen on the ground floor grinding masalas, chopping vegetables, parboiling lentils, soaking rice, marinating fish with salt and turmeric, steaming jaggery and dates for the chutney, all in preparation for Sukumar to come home, so she could make him fresh food, fry the slim-cut aubergines in bubbling hot oil, dunk the jeere-phoron in the dal, drop a dollop of ghee in the rice, and cook up a storm with the fish. Because truly, what was a Bengali's life worth if they didn't eat fish twice a day? As a widow, she wasn't allowed fish or meat, nor onions or garlic for that matter, but she'd give her son maachher jhol with bodi, or ilish cooked in ground-mustard shorshe-baata curry, or Sukumar's favourite, parshe in a light sauce with begoon and aloo.

As mother and son ate in the kitchen, Sukumar on a raised peedi, his mother on the floor, they spoke in soft tones, mostly about other people – someone had stopped by the house, someone's daughter's wedding was coming up, someone had come into the bank that day to open an account. When they were done, Sukumar didn't go upstairs straight away; instead, he waited, watching his mother's face tense with concentration as she placed the bowls of leftovers in plates of water to keep the ants away, strained milk to set the yogurt overnight, soaked the cooked rice and left it to ferment for the next day's paanta-bhaat breakfast. They didn't have a fridge and couldn't afford one any time soon, but in the second year of his job, Sukumar got her a cooking-gas connection, so she wouldn't have to use the coal oven any more. She wouldn't say it out loud, but he could see how much easier it made her life.

On days that a letter arrived from Sukumar's sister, his mother handed him the blue folded India Post sheet, which she'd already read during the day, many times over, because the letters were always addressed to both of them. Sukumar eagerly read about his sister's life in the Garden City, although her voice was formal, the information scant, any emotion absent; she mostly let them know that she was well, and so was her husband, that they'd moved into a new house, or she'd run into a relative in a place so far away, or she'd just finished a baking course. So many Bengalis here nowadays, she'd write, as though in reassurance, there are at least five places that host Durga Pujo celebrations! Sukumar read these dispatches keenly, conscious of the gap widening between this woman in the letters and the young girl he'd known, obedient and subdued to the world, but so full of music and laughter with him.

It was different when she visited. His sister came to the Grand Old City once a year, and while she stayed primarily with her in-laws, she spent a few nights at her baaper-bari with Sukumar and their mother. With his sister in the house, even the filaments of the naked bulbs seemed to emanate a warm glow. Brother and sister and mother spoke into the night, the way they used to before she'd got married. They told stories from their lives and those of people they knew, relatives and friends and neighbours. Sometimes a memory would come up, and they'd grow gregarious or pensive, their cackles boring through the rafters or tears wetting their cheeks, *remember that wedding, what about when she thought her imitation earring was a real diamond, what a temper he had, oh she's always been such a miser but she has a good heart.* They spoke about people who were no more, their father or grandma, the dead and departed, *if Baba were around he would've . . . if Thamma were alive she would never have . . .* And they still fell asleep to adhunik songs playing on the radio, though Sukumar didn't tease his sister about Sandhya's voice any more, he let her enjoy the music she couldn't have in her home so far away.

But the truth was, the more the years went by, the more he let go of her, reconciling that it was now just him and his mother. They'd weathered the tragedy of his father's death in their own ways, and had somehow survived. He knew she'd never abandon him. Never.

The days following that fateful Durga Pujo of 1977, when Sukumar was still unemployed, were the most torturous he'd ever known. After he'd spent the night with X on the terrace, he'd sulked through the festivities, sat alone in the house, stood on the balcony and watched the heads of his neighbours walk up and down the lane, their clothes flashy, voices raised, feet dancing. When he heard the beats of the dhaak from the Sarbojonin Park and inhaled the holy smoke of the dhunuchi, he imagined X tucked away in a corner somewhere in the District, heaving sighs at the memory of that night they'd shared, plucking at the corner of the collar that Sukumar had nibbled. When Dashami finally came and the five days of Pujo were done, Sukumar's heart made cartwheels. Never before in his life had he wanted so badly for the festival to end, but that year, what could X's return to the Grand Old City mean, was there a future he could sense but couldn't see, would X turn up at the door the moment he was back?

Life hobbled back to its banal tempo, employees returned to the *Jugantor* newspaper office, the men who'd volunteered in the Sculptors' Quarters stood around smoking and debating the Naxals and communism, but there was no sign of X. Sukumar waited for him to get in touch, then lurked around the street to catch sight of him, then mustered the courage to go up and ask one of the men, despite the risk that they'd intuit the truth, poke fun at X and Sukumar for being fairies. Sukumar kept his voice calm, suppressed any oncoming shivers, but none of the men knew about X. It had been three weeks since Pujo, almost Diwali now, but X hadn't come back from the District.

A nasty current eddied through Sukumar's veins, portending

a misfortune. He'd had this feeling when his father had fallen ill, then grown sicker with the passing months; he'd known they'd lose him, although it was inauspicious to talk about death before it had occurred. His father's final breath had been a hiccup and a gulp, air forced in and out of the mouth one last time before his heart stopped. Sukumar's mother had left the room for a drink of water, and Sukumar and his sister were trying to study in the living room. There'd been something so terminal about that sound his father had emitted that they all ran towards him; the clang of his mother's glass dropping to the floor reverberated through the flat. As his mother cradled his father's head in her lap, Sukumar saw in her face the steadfast belief she'd held all this time, that she could nurse him back to health, that their old life could still be restored after this minor setback. But now, with X, there was no one to challenge Sukumar's prophecy; he was free to believe whatever he wanted, and having been struck once by loss, he readily surrendered. X had died; yes, it had happened to him again.

So when he finally laid eyes on X, walking out of the *Jugantor* office, Sukumar felt faint, his sight blurry, his legs rushing forward. X was loading stacks of paper on to the back of a van, beads of sweat sat on his forehead despite the nip in the air as other men stepped out with more reams. It was only a hand that Sukumar placed on X's back, but there was something so disproportionate about the move, the touch, the intensity, that a few heads turned, trained as the world is to notice the slightest of deviances. Caught off guard, X stiffened, then took Sukumar aside by the arm, looking embarrassed. 'Get a hold on yourself, Suku, ki korchho ta ki?' He spoke through gritted teeth, his fingers tightening around Sukumar's skin. Then he softened. 'Meet me this evening at seven by the river, at the Chokro-rail station.' Sukumar nodded, walking away with a grin. *He's alive, and he called me Suku!*

But when X appeared at the Chokro-rail station that evening, the muscles on his face were still taut, his body rigid as though defending itself, his eyes averted. He walked slightly apart from Sukumar, signalling with a jerk of his head for Sukumar to follow. They crossed the tracks, walked down the ghat. The river had a strong current and its surface shimmered like a sheet of silver metal. Their panjabis fluttered wildly, outlining X's slimness behind the light cotton cloth. X led the way to a bench hidden from public view by a burgeoning banyan tree whose branches came down to commune with its roots.

Even before Sukumar could sit, X said in a raspy but practised voice, 'I'm going to be married soon. The wedding is in Maagh-maash, not too long now.'

Sukumar sat and folded one knee over another, closed his eyes against the salutary breeze. Of course, X would be married, X would have a wife, a home. Who was he to X, what had X promised him after all? He opened his eyes, smiled. 'Very good news.'

But X's face had already succumbed. 'I didn't want it, Suku, I didn't ask for it.' X extended his hand to touch Sukumar's thigh. Feeling X's fingers on him, a gurgling went up from Sukumar's heart, stinging his nostrils, punching his eyes with teardrops. 'I didn't know my parents had decided a match for me.' X was looking away, too ashamed to meet Sukumar's eyes. 'They told me the moment I reached home for Durga Pujo. I kept thinking of reasons to turn them down, but I have a job now, and my parents want grandchildren. I couldn't think of any excuse, Suku. This is what men do once they start working, na? They get married and have families. One day, you'll have to do it too . . .' It sounded like X had rehearsed this speech several times. 'We went to meet the girl's family, and they wanted to confirm the marriage, set the wedding date, so I stayed back for the paka-dekha.' X took his hand away. 'I thought very hard about how to get in touch with you, but I didn't know your phone number, a letter would be too risky—'

'We don't have a phone,' Sukumar whispered. Their relatives had been instructed to leave any emergency message at the *Jugantor* office, which served as the telephone exchange for half the neighbourhood. 'We can't afford one. We can't afford so many things . . .' He ruffled his hair, let some air into his damp head. 'I'm going to start a new internship soon. This might be the one, you know? The boss is well-connected, it could lead to a job. I've been unemployed for four years—'

'Suku . . .' X's face was quizzical. 'What are you going on about? I'm telling you I'm getting married, and you're just talking about other things—'

'No,' Sukumar interjected, surprised by how emphatically it had come out. 'No,' he repeated, softer this time. 'You're talking about *your* things, I'm talking about *my* things.' He called up all the equanimity he could manage, thinking of his father's face, those bushy eyebrows, the way the man had come out of the doctor's chambers after all those injections, and still walked straight and steady to the car, every single time. 'If we can never have *our* things, it will always have to be your things and my things.' As he breathed out, he knew there was nothing else to say. He got up from the bench and made a show of dusting off the invisible grit, then slowly walked away.

A train started from the station and lazily trundled past. Sukumar had to wait at the pedestrian crossing. Part of him wished that X would catch up, tug at his sleeve, say this was all a joke. But part of him wished he wouldn't, because what would it reap then, what did a future for two men in love look like? It scared Sukumar to even imagine. Many years later, when he'd meet all those others, he'd learn that this was the story of every man like him, a long legacy littered with broken hearts, quashed dreams, duplicitous lives. Men like them, it was best they didn't wish for anything at all.

For the next few months, Sukumar entered a realm whose borders he sealed fastidiously. Everyone had moved on with their lives: his sister had, X had. It was just him and his mother, the only two people he needed to do right by. He looked away every time he walked past the *Jugantor* office; but X was careful too, they never crossed paths, or even if they did, X must've hidden in corners or quickened his pace, because he never stepped into Sukumar's field of vision. His mother asked him about X a few times, *that friend of yours who came the night before Mahalaya*—; he stopped her mid-thought, told her in a matter-of-fact way that the friend was getting married, he must be busy with the arrangements. He could see his mother fret a bit, worrying about the costs of gifts and travel to the District. 'I think they want to keep it small,' Sukumar assured her. 'We're probably not invited.'

When Sukumar got the job in early 1978, his mind eased; he had something to do for eight hours a day, boring but distracting, new colleagues around him, new duties. He felt no scorn for X, even wished him well. May he have a happy married life. Everyone deserved some love, a home, a family. There was nothing wrong in wanting the things everyone else wanted. He could have them too, if he wished, but did he? He pushed such thoughts out of his mind.

But on the day of X's wedding, the date of which had etched itself in Sukumar's memory despite his best efforts, he came home from work and went straight upstairs to the room he shared with his mother. She was in the kitchen, waiting for him to peep his head in as always, announce his return, 'Ma, eshe gechhi,' and for her to say, 'Eshechho? Let me start the dinner prep then.' Instead he closed the door and shut the windows, the wooden panes frenzied from the gale, his arms wet from the unusual winter rain in the month of Maagh. He didn't quite know what he wanted to do, but his body led him to his mother's steel almirah. He rummaged through her sarees; they were all white, thin borders of green and blue and black, never red or pink or orange, the auspicious shades of vermilion unsuited to a widow.

When he couldn't find a single coloured saree, he pulled out a thaan, whitest of white, no border at all. He draped the garment around himself, not like his mother wore it, loose and easy, but the way a bride would, fitted and pleated, the anchol hanging in the front. There was no make-up in the house, no lipstick, no kajal, no teep even to stick on the forehead, all those accoutrements unbefitting a widow had been clinically disposed of. So he used some clips and pins to tame his unruly curls. Then he pulled the garment over his head and stood in front of the mirror.

He hadn't seen himself in a saree since he was a boy, and the mirror only reflected him back down to his shoulders. He'd hoped to see himself as X's bride, what he would've looked like if it had been him and X getting married today. But instead what he saw was a grown man playing dress-up as a deprived widow, a dark moustache running across his face, the whiteness of the saree incongruous against his wheatish skin. Whatever the reflection showed, it wasn't X's bride. Whatever it was, it was grotesque.

He began tearing the fabric away from his body, turning around and around to undo the draping, clutching the pleats and dragging them out of his trousers where he'd tucked them in. 'What are you doing?' he huffed in disgust. 'What *are* you doing? What are you *doing*?' he kept saying, kicking and fussing the saree about. 'What did you think you were going to do? Is *this* the kind of man you want to be?'

Then he sat on the bed, out of breath, the white saree lying on the floor like a balled-up shroud, as though discarded even by the dead. He picked it up to wipe his tears, calmed his breath, steadied himself, and went downstairs for dinner.

Mambro's Manuscript

It is almost the new millennium, you are a new adult, and you and Y have been together four years.

The passing of time is difficult to capture; how does one stem the flow of water? Four years you feel love every day, from the tips of your fingers to the breath leaving your nostrils; the little bird sings until its heart is full, sucking up all the oxygen that is its destiny. Four years of rushing back to his place after school, of exploring each other's bodies, opening up those closed-off pores, letting his scent meld into yours, yours into his; him sneaking into yours when your family aren't around, of telling each other everything, of studying for exams, of devouring movies of all stripes.

Four years of observing how his body moves in quick jerks when he's excited; of him flattening his hair down on his forehead when he's nervous; of finding the tiny brown fleck in his left eye, or was it the right, and checking every few months to see if it's grown. Four years of watching him sit cross-legged like a yogi, his left foot free, of getting into the habit of fondling his big toe, then sucking it, as his favourite MLTR croons from the mixtape . . . Four years of letting him inside you, the first time in the shower, knowing he hasn't done it before, he doesn't know how it's done, but trusting him to not hurt you.

On one of those afternoons, he runs his finger down the length of your neck, from your jaw to your shoulder, and says in his casual fact-stating way, 'You have a lovely neck, you know?' You joke, it's such a weird compliment, it's the first nice thing he's said about your looks, but really, is this the best he can come up with? He juts his head back and surveys your neck like an engineer at a building site. 'It *is* beautiful, the way it's so lean and graceful, the way your head sits on it, the way it curves at the nape, makes me want to tuck my lips in there forever . . .' You don't know this yet, but you will look at your neck in the mirror all your life, feel beautiful even when it is attenuated and wrinkled.

The passing of time is difficult to capture. And so you write, by hand, in a journal you won't remember buying; it has a coarse jute binding, two shades of brown in check like a chessboard. You write and write the four years, every little nook, every little cranny; you write his body and his touch, the rains and the sun, the smell and the salt of him. You write to hold back time, to put into words everything you can't speak aloud, for the page to bear witness to what other people aren't seeing, so this love may live even after the little bird has died from singing for too long.

And through the passing of those four years, things begin to go slightly awry between you and Y. It isn't that you don't feel love, not that you don't rush to each other whenever you can, but there is a toll to keeping the most important part of your lives secret, as though you've locked a giant river out of plain sight, and every time you open the door, someone takes a peep, or a bit of the river leaks out, sending you scurrying to lock it up all over again.

During that time, there are many infatuated girls and some horny boys in your life, they come and go, none of them mean anything. The girls you have to accommodate to protect your relationship with Y, from turning people's hunches into suspicion into gossip; some of the boys are genuine crushes you can't help giving in to, like when your handsome lab-partner makes you giggle too much, or when the charismatic bully who usually calls you Y's *bitch* kisses you and you let him because you feel vindicated. These little things drive Y up the wall with jealousy, but you and Y have never promised fidelity, that was never inked in the covenant, you have only sworn each other to secrecy, and that is a heavy enough burden to bear.

Y doesn't have as many distractions, though there is one girl who is so in love with him that she makes the bile shoot straight up to your mouth. But he has friends, lots of them, and over the four years, they grow, hanging out at his place, in his room, that sanctum sanctorum that was once inviolable. And because you're still shy and awkward, Y leaves you out sometimes, until he's doing it often. You stand on the street and watch the silhouettes of the boys in his window, heads thrown back in gaiety, drumming the headboard of his bed, swinging their legs as they sit on his table, hands moving deftly as they spin a ball around; sometimes you can hear strains of their cackles, the inane banter of young men who live for the day, by the day.

When you go to Y's place, his mother talks about his other friends with as much enthusiasm as she talks about you – *this one came yesterday, that one is such a prankster* – and you wonder if you were ever special, that maybe you'd built hearths in your head where there were only embers. Then she looks at you inquisitively, why you don't visit more often, are things not as they were before? It is only years later that Y will tell you that his mother once heard the two of you on the phone; she'd picked up the receiver of the parallel connection on the other floor; you're not sure what you said to each other that day, but she told Y that she had listened in, she didn't admonish or caution him, she almost had an acquiescent mirth in her eyes. And all those years later, your heart will warm at the thought that perhaps she did give you her blessing, was the only witness to your relationship with Y, saw how happy you made her son.

In those four years, seeing Y with his friends, your shoulders stoop from the weight of guilt, because isn't it your fault that you can't fit in, isn't it you who is robbing Y of his deserved youthful fun? You can see how he is with them, so lively, and what are you other than a troubled soul always standing in his shadows? During the fights that follow, he doesn't apologize for having friends; he's never intended for you to be excluded, but he's never intended *not* to have friends either. And after you've flagellated yourself, a meanness inside you hardens like lava once the ash turns cold, a meanness you didn't know existed until you met Y. It is as abundant as the love you have to give. You say things you'd never say to anyone in your right mind, your tongue on fire, your speech garbled, until Y cries, wipes away his tears that won't stop falling; but his tears are no good now, they can't make you stop; you whip him with your words, you always have them ready, you're good with them. Words – maybe the only thing you were ever good at.

This vicious wheel keeps turning for months. Y is the only one you can be horrible to, your frustrations becoming a needle with which you prick his soul so that his light seeps out; you are the only one he can be vulnerable with, his insouciance a front, his real self a solitary teenager craving attention. There is an abjectness to this exchange, being privy to the gnarled sides of each other, using that private knowledge to dismantle each other's beings.

After every fight, you storm out, bat away the arms that reach out to stop you, to plead with you, walk away as he falls at your feet. But once home, you sit next to the phone, counting the ticks of the clock, until he calls and invites you back, and when you run into each other's arms and kiss those milky lips and feel his scent on you again, later lying in bed in each other's embrace, looking up at the whirring ceiling fan, it is as though the bird had never stopped, its song never become a croak.

It is during those years that you first watch *Fire*. You're in the theatre alone that evening, Y is probably not in town, but you can't miss this movie, it won't run for long, a week at most; that is the fate of arthouse cinema, a Friday-to-Thursday schedule, near-empty theatres; but this one is special because of the protests: it is a story of two women falling in love with each other, two sisters-in-law at that, how can this be allowed on-screen, it is against Indian culture, our sanskriti, our sab-hyata, so scream the saffron-clad defenders of Hinduism and the skullcap-clad preachers of Islam and the cassock-clad prac-titioners of Christianity, all united for once by a common cause, a worthy distraction from all the rioting they're other-wise embroiled in against each other.

You are disappointed by the calm outside the cinema; you expected mobs and flags and burning effigies, media cameras and reporters, perhaps your attendance would be a public act of defiance. Instead you walk in like it's any regular screen-ing. There are only men inside, lascivious eyes and squirming buttocks and hands rubbing crotches as the two actresses kiss, joyful hoots when the women are put in their place. A man spits at the screen before he walks out mid-movie; you will remember the perfect projectile path the saliva takes before landing on the dusty aisle.

For weeks, you read everything you can find in the news-papers and magazines about *Fire*. It is not your induction into gay cinema, you've watched *Philadelphia* on Star Movies, but *Fire* is the first time you've watched gay people in the world you inhabit; they look like you, talk like you, live like you.

The reviews are lukewarm, the commentary fierce. But there is something discomfiting about the way even the supporters speak; it's women after all, they're emotional creatures, they sit at home all day waiting for their husbands, a relationship between two women is an act of resistance against the treatment meted out to them. You read and read, scavenge through everything you can find, these intellectuals pinning female attraction down to neglect and boredom. *If only men treated their women right, the women wouldn't want to fuck each other.*

But what if same-sex love is not an act of resistance, what if that's just how it is for some people? And what about men fucking men? You have so many questions, but no one to ask; so much to say, but no one you can trust. You can't talk to your parents, they haven't brought this up, surprising for a home where politics is discussed and opinions professed on a daily basis; talking to teachers is out of the question; you can't even get yourself to go up to the librarian and ask for Ismat Chughtai's 'Lihaaf', the short story that inspired *Fire*, her books aren't on the shelves, though those of her male contemporaries are. You want to ask Mamu if he has watched the movie, but you never bring it up; you don't know how to form the words, your language has no shared vocabulary for a conversation like this.

The last few months of school are gruelling, the days haywire, everything off-kilter; there are studies to catch up on, exams to take. There is too much happening for you and Y to calm your breaths, spend some private time, reclaim the insulation from the world that you so expertly cultivated over four years. You even stop writing in your journal, there's nothing to say; so it just lies there, its pages filled with memories of better days, of soft cooings and firm erections, of dry afternoons and wet nights, like a photo album, everyone always smiling, gathered for festivals, jubilant on vacations, dressed in finery.

As it seems more and more certain that you and Y will leave the Grand Old City for university, will have to separate and go to different places, a wish begins to form inside you with an obstinate ardency. You want to transmute into a woman overnight, wake up in a saree, long strands of hair artfully gracing the pillow, the jhumka having slipped out of your earlobe and hooked itself to the bedsheet, the sindoor teep streaking your forehead, all the markers of sex from the previous night as shown in the movies.

You've never resented your male body, never longed for breasts; in fact you're fascinated by your penis, it's a unique anatomical creation, so much a part of you but also with a mind of its own. But becoming a woman is the only thing that will legitimize your relationship with Y, keep you bound together despite the distance; his friends will have to accept you, as men do the wives of pals they don't get along with. Your female version will pull off the quirks your male form can't; you will find a way to play a good hostess, make good chitchat, let the evening pass without incident as partners who live in the shadows usually do; you will hold his hand in public, openly court his mother, and then you imagine her calling your mother to propose a match with her son right away.

One evening when you're on the terrace staring into the middle distance, the parrots busily squawking on the branches of the mango tree, your sister asks from behind, 'What did you do that for?' You stir out of your daydream, realize that your hands have gone up to the back of your head and tied the absent long hair into a bun, like your mother does. You flush with self-consciousness, blurt out an excuse, but you know it's pointless; your sister knows you too well, she just looks on curiously, then turns and leaves. You pinch yourself, so hard that welts form on your arm, promise that you will never do that again; you know what happens to men who are feminine: they become laughing stocks. Rituparno Ghosh, the director who revived Bengali cinema a few years ago, whose works you run to the theatres to watch, is slowly undergoing a transformation; he's started to line his eyes with kohl, to wear tassar-silk dupattas bordered with kantha-stitch embroidery; you know what people are saying, the language they use when they speak of him. No, you don't want to end up like that.

Instead, you conjure Y up under other garbs, because now there is an indomitable need to talk about your love, even if in inventive ways, the locked-up river refusing to stay within the dam walls. Years later, a great poet will write a song suggesting to the lover that they may talk about their beloved under other names. But you're already doing that, you've invented a girlfriend, told your classmates about her; she lives in another city, you met her at a wedding and now you're calling each other every night. Whenever you meet, the boys ask about her, and you spin stories on the spot; you've always been good at telling stories. You don't perceive how unhinged you must seem, how they must've joined the dots, known who you are really talking about.

But even if they know your stories are about Y, they probably think you're an obsessive homosexual who nurses fantasies of a love affair, one that Y isn't even aware of. There is no evidence of your relationship with him. Later, when you read about the philosophical conundrum, *if a tree falls in the forest . . .*, it will sound searingly familiar. How easy it is to concoct falsehoods, falsify truths, in this world where some people know some things, no one knows everything, and everyone pretends to know nothing.

One time, you take a walk with a friend, a geeky guy who always shows up for you. You stop in a park for cigarettes, you've started smoking a lot just so your voice can grow deeper, trying hard to don the mantle of masculinity that continues to evade you. In the park, puffing away, your geek friend turns to you and says, 'Don't look for love where there isn't any.' You know he means well, is trying to protect you from scandal or heartbreak or both, but you want to smack him across the face, scream out, *He LOVES me, he's CRAZY about me, so shut the fuck up, I'm looking for love right where it is!*

ENTRY THREE

Vivaan's VoiceNote003

Hello, namaste, aadaab! Welcome to the juiciest story ever! This is your host Vivaan and today we will talk about some very risqué things. So brace yourselves and come along on the journey!

So, when we left off last time, it was at the school dance. For a few days after that, Zee dropped off the face of the earth, and I didn't want to see him either. Mom and Dad asked about the party, Mambro called for all the goss, as he put it, though I could tell he was trying to unearth the layers, but I gave them vague answers, Yeah yeah it was fun, lots of dancing as usual. I didn't want to talk about what had happened, I didn't even know how to talk about it, because what exactly had happened? How do you describe the look in people's eyes when they're not saying anything?

Then one afternoon I found Zee standing outside my school, under the tree as usual, fiddling with his tie. From his face, I could tell he'd put that night behind him, his eyes were dancing, his body arched back on the trunk, the buttons on his chest nearly popping, the smattering of hair showing through. I wanted to run up and throw myself at him right there.

I want to take you somewhere, will you come with? And promise you won't freak? he said.

I'd go to Pluto if you asked, even though she's been demoted from planet status, and I hear she's a grumpy old spinster now. I was pleased as punch he was back in my life.

He booked us an Uber that took us to another part of town. The Garden City used to be a small pretty haven, but since it became the Silicon Plateau, all kinds of suburbs have cropped up. Mom and Mambro used to live here as children, and Mom says she doesn't even think of this as the same place she grew up in. The Uber was headed to one such neighbourhood, I'd never even heard its name, we live quite centrally and all our tish-tosh friends also live centrally, so who the fuck needs to know the suburbs? But it was okay, it wasn't unsafe or anything, and Zee was with me. I knew he wouldn't lead me into trouble, and honestly in that moment, I'd have gone to Timbuktu or Honolulu if he'd asked. Sorry Timbuktu and Honolulu, no offence meant, your names are mentioned here as random places one could land up in, I'm sure you're beautiful, and one day I will spend my tourism dollars on you.

The place we ended up in was an unfurnished flat with a bare mattress and some floor cushions, in a building that had just finished construction. There were these two guys, slightly older than us, they said they were eighteen, but Zee had told them we were eighteen too, so who the fuck knows. On seeing them, I instantly knew why we were there, and maybe I'd known from the start. Zee wouldn't lead me into trouble, but he'd sure lead me into temptation, ha! There wasn't a lot of preamble, it's not like we'd gone there to make friends, and they were so different to us, like, we even tried to make conversation, but there was nothing in common. Halli-gugu, as my posh Kannada teacher, Miss Rupa, would've rolled her eyes and scolded, village idiots!

Zee was trying to ease into things, I wonder if he was nervous or was putting on a show for me, it being my first time and all that. He even asked the guys if they were a couple. The guys were experts at withholding info, like, they could make legit airport immigration officers, they gave nothing away, I didn't even know if their names were real, and since I've forgotten them now, clearly it wasn't important.

When the meet-and-greet was starting to feel stretched, and all eyes were darting towards the bedroom door, I had a bit of a panic attack. Not gonna lie, Zee did take me by surprise, I'd been thrust into this situation, and it was super awks, to say the least. I kept thinking why we were here, Zee and I, were the two of us not doing it for each other any more, did Zee need more variety? Then I flipped about seeing Zee do it with others in front of my eyes, like, I know it's supposed to turn me on, but it made me jittery all the same. Then it struck me that it was going to get competitive, as in, until now, I was only used to dealing with one person, but now there'd be three people to deal with, four bodies jostling it out. Like we didn't already have a population problem in this country, did we really need to bring it into our bedrooms?

I wanted to pull Zee aside, tell him all this, maybe even say I wasn't ready, could we please rain-check? But Zee seemed so into it, his shoulders were doing the one-front-one-back rowing movement I knew he did when he got flirtatious. But also, where was I going to have this deep conversation? The halli-gugus were sitting right there blinking at us, I couldn't have taken Zee into the bedroom because that was the appointed scene of action anyway, and the living room had an open-plan kitchen so there was no other enclosure really. So finally I told myself, worst case, if things don't work out, I'm just going to say I'll watch, that's my kink, and come off as cooler than them. I was quite happy with my backup plan!

My fears proved to be totally unfounded. The whole thing was done in less than an hour. Zee and I could go on for a few hours. One time, we foreplayed and fucked and rested and foreplayed and flip-fucked for three and a half hours. According to unitary method, you'd imagine four men could go at it for seven hours? Or by reverse unitary method, it'd be about two? But sorry, Mr Prasad, your maths theorems don't work in the gay world. We were literally putting on clothes and leaving the flat within fifty minutes, and that's inclusive of hi-hello-okay-bye. It's weird I checked the in and out times, but seriously, I was so curious, I'd only seen such things in porn, threesomes and foursomes and gang-bangs, so it felt like I was in one of those films myself. The sex itself was all right, lips-nipple-cock-and-ass, cock-and-ass, you know, the gay version of head-shoulders-knees-and-toes. There, I've spoilt the ditty for you now, haven't I? I should sing it to Miss Gibson one of these days, I wonder if they have it in the UK. Anyway, I'd say the sex was a bit too rushed for my liking, and kinda crowded, but duh, we were four.

In the Uber, Zee held my hand tightly. Vivaan, I'm so proud of you.

You sound like a parent, bro, I shot back. You thought I wouldn't be cool enough?

Not like that, just thought you'd need an induction, but I didn't want to talk about it ad infinitum, I'd rather we just plunged into it and saw how it went, you know?

Yeah sure. I looked out of the window, the city was coming back into view. It brought an eerie sense of relief, like I was speeding towards something known again.

So you okay with this? We're okay?

Something about Zee's attitude was triggering me, like he was a mentor or whatever. I wanted to ask if he'd done it before, how many times, with how many people, and if he had, why he hadn't told me. I should've been asking the questions, not him. But I just said, I don't even know what we were in the first place, we never agreed on being anything.

Listen, Zee whispered, come here. He brought his hand to the side of my head and laid it on his shoulder. I saw the Uber driver checking us out in the rear-view mirror. Swell, I thought, this is a hate crime waiting to happen. BREAKING

NEWS: Gay Couple Hacked to Death by Driver After First Foursome.

I jerked my head away. What you being so Father Superior for?

It's called aftercare, Zee said, still calm, not biting the bait. When we put ourselves out there to experience new things, we should be mindful to be gentle with ourselves . . .

Holy fuck, I screamed. Stop with your customer service auto-reply! I'm okay. You want to fuck around? Yeah bruh, let's fuck!

The driver cheered up at so many mentions of FUCK, but Zee looked properly hurt, and I was glad I'd finally punctured his Zen act.

It's not about the fucking, Zee said, it's about freedom. Remember that night at the dance? That's what the straights do, mating dances, playing house. And I refuse to end up like them!

The next few months were all about the fucking. I got over my resentment of Zee pretty soon, because we started having a lot of fun. We were like this power couple, cruising through the city, sleeping with anyone we put a finger on. Okay it wasn't like that, we were too young for most people, and we aren't exactly the hottest boys in town, but people do have a soft spot for young things, and I'd say we were decently turned out, so yeah, there was no dearth. Also, I make it sound like we were hooking up every day, whereas we were probably meeting people once every two or three weeks, which was plenty given school schedules and parental scrutiny. The rest of the time, Zee and I had the best sex ever, we were always so turned on, so maybe this was a good thing for us too?

It was mostly Zee who'd set things up for us. I joked that he was my admin person, he only needed to tell me where and when to show up. My mom has one, who insists on being called an executive assistant when he's really a glorified Alexa without the husky voice, and Zee was mine. That's how we rolled, I trusted that he knew best, and turns out he did, he arranged all kinds of hook-ups, though he never went for the older ones, he drew the line at thirty, we could never be too sure, but if we did sleep with anyone over thirty, they defo could've passed for twenty-nine. During those months, I turned seventeen and then Zee turned eighteen, so now he was properly legit and I was getting closer. I can't say anything changed with age, but yeah, it did feel like we could do our own thing now without the aunties coming after us with their rolling pins.

Eventually, Zee got me on an app, he said he wanted to factor in my preferences too. I was already on the standard hook-up apps, though I hadn't used them since I'd met Zee. Zee said those were too transactional, umm duh! This app was different, there were singles, couples, and everyone in between. Setting it up was a chore though, it asked me for my types, bear or otter or cub or daddy or twink, then for my sexuality, and the options were, wait for this – straight, gay, lesbian, bisexual . . . these I could deal with, I'd just go with gay, but then . . . and I couldn't do this without scrolling through the app which I'm actually doing now . . . pansexual, polysexual, queer, androgynosexual, androsexual, asexual, autosexual, demisexual, grey-A, gynosexual, heteroflexible, homoflexible, objectumsexual, omnisexual, skoliosexual, bi-curious. I mean, wild, right? I still don't know what most of these things mean. I did take my time to ponder though, treating it as an exercise in self-discovery, but finally Zee just chose homoflexible for me, said I was probably mostly gay but could be interested in women, and I said that sounded about right. He uploaded some pics and there we were! Zee even linked my profile to his as his partner. Not gonna lie, that made me go giddy because a) he was finally acknowledging our relationship, and b) it sounded so grown up.

Oh man, the people we met on this app, and then some in person! Single men obviously, coupled men obviously, but also man–woman couples, woman–woman couples, single women, sometimes groups numbering up to six or seven people, MMM, MMMM, MMF, MFF, MMMFFF, FFMMFFF, you get the drift. We went to homes of newly married so-called straight couples, Zee took the wife while I took the husband, and they were so pink with pleasure by the time we left that I'd say we'd blessed their arranged marriage in ways even the matchmaker couldn't. We met lesbian couples whom Zee did while I did him. We even met a group in which the hostess was pregnant, early stages I'd say, and she was with us while the husband put their first child to sleep on the upper floor. I mean, what was this world? Oooof! Who would've thought there was this underbelly in this boring Silicon Plateau? By day, everyone was an IT developer, project manager, venture capitalist and whatnot. And by night, they were everything and nothing, open to being anything. How many hides did Mr Hyde have? Also, truly impressed by my use of some kinda literary device there, not sure which one, but in case you didn't notice, ha!

Zee's aftercare services were proving top-notch, and it seemed like I was the only one who didn't need it. After every encounter, which is what we came to call these sessions, someone or other would need a cuddle, mainly the women and the twinks, and Zee would religiously lie down and take them in his arms and rock them like a baby, neatening the strands of their hair, kissing their foreheads, stroking their backs. Initially, I was like, WTF dude, but then I just couldn't be arsed, so I busied myself on my phone, or went out and had a chat with whoever else was available and not in queue for the aftercare, usually butch men who'd already fastened their boxer strings. Sometimes, people would break down in tears in Zee's embrace, say this was all wrong, they were damaged goods, they'd never have a good life, and that would make me so bloody mad, I mean, darling, a) you can't have your cake because guess what, you just ate it all up! and b) you were just mewling and mooing, like, a minute ago, so get a fucking grip! In particular, there was this one twink who began to turn up more and more to these encounters, and Twinkie needed a lot of aftercare, like, A LOT, to the extent that I seriously started suspecting he didn't care about the sex as much as he sought Zee's cuddles.

After some months, I started to use the app for myself, met people on my own. The first few times were daunting, but then it felt okay, as in I'd worried about safety, but I realized that was never the issue, this was a community of strangers letting each other into their homes with the licence to be intimate. Put like that, I'd say it was quite beautiful, like society had evolved into something more than just pray-to-god-get-married-cook-roti-sabzi-make-babies-like-yourselves-to-perpetuate-your-family-name, the Indian holy trinity of shaadi.com–naukri.com–makemytrip.com. Some of these people had lived or travelled abroad, and they talked about how this was also happening in London and New York and Paris and Sydney and São Paulo and Singapore, this is the future, they said, the future is us. It blew my mind that this movement was taking place and no one had the slightest hint of it in the real world. Or maybe THIS was the real world, the new world! Everyone who wasn't in this was a dinosaur.

Somehow, through all of this, Zee and I made time for each other, he spent hours at my place, and sometimes I went to his. You would've imagined that our studies had hit rock bottom, but I kid you not, we were working harder and our marks were straight As, plus Zee's band was killing it, and so was I at my elocution and swimming and karate lessons. It was like we were on steroids without actually taking any. And speaking of drugs, we also always practised safe sex, didn't use substances, and got tested anonymously every few weeks, so all good on that front.

The more we did this, the more Zee seemed to get obsessed with what to call this. As in, he made it sound like we were in an experiment and he needed to name the phenomenon. He said different things about us, first he said we were in an open relationship, and I said yeah okay, then he said we were in an ethical non-monogamy, ENM, and I said yeah okay. He took pains to explain these to me, but I found them so burdensome! I thought you didn't like labels, I poked him, and he got all defensive, like, These aren't labels, these are ways for us to understand what we're doing. And again I said, Yeah okay!

But I can tell you this now, I don't think I'd even tell myself this back then, let alone Zee, because I was playing it so cool . . . You know, before all of this, I'd thought I was being revolutionary by coming out to my parents and in school, that my mom and dad were the coolest of cucumbers, that my family were so fucking progressive. But friend, it all seemed so archaic now, I felt like sitting my parents down and educating them, they had soooo much to catch up on!

And Mambro? Not gonna lie, I did wonder if he was doing this too, and then I imagined Mambro and me being on the same app in the same city, coming across each other's profiles, quickly blocking the other! Yikes! What was the protocol between gay uncles and nephews in the online world? And in the offline world? There were no examples we could learn from, I guess. We were the first of our kind that we knew of!

This made me really miss Mambro. I don't know, if he were

around, could I have turned to him for advice, or just to share, to vent? I'd never know, would I?

Okay, on that note, a quick break. I'll leave you to process this stuff first . . .

So, let's cut to this convo I had with Mom. Not proud of it, and it's making me uneasy talking about it, but it did happen, and I'm going to be truthful . . . That's the contract, isn't it? The only way to tell a story is to tell it honestly, even if you were being a dipshit.

One night, Mom was talking about her day, the usual stuff, a manager had lost his temper on his subordinate, an American client had tried to do the Indian head-shake, a colleague had got cancelled because she'd tweeted against company policy, the shiz. It's a thing me and Mom have had since my childhood, we sit for a while after dinner and talk about how our days went. When I was a kid, I used to tell Mom funny stories from school, which teacher said what, who was being goofy in class and was sent away to Princi, how I wasn't prepared for an exam. Nowadays there's obviously not that much to share. But she still prattles on anyway, she believes in family rituals, says she used to do it with her father, my Dadu, every day after school, she'd sit with him and tell him everything. Mambro never did, and she thinks it's because he was gay and couldn't talk about himself, and maybe that's why the whole family missed the brief.

On that night, I was being especially quiet. Not gonna lie, I was in a terrible mood. Earlier that day, Zee and I had had an encounter with a few people, and you guessed right, Twinkie showed up! Later, while Zee was giving his aftercare massage to Twinkie, they started kissing. The rest of us had already put on our clothes, some had left, the hosts seemed impatient for the sesh to end. Then suddenly they were doing it again, Twinkie sucking Zee off and Zee fucking Twinkie, and I wanted to scream out WHAT THE FUCK ZEE I'M STILL HERE, but everyone else formed a circle and watched them in a stupor, only their sex sounds in the air, it was like an ASMR video. I had to act cool, couldn't out myself as the possessive boyfriend, could I?

Later, Zee said it was part of the aftercare, though I hadn't even asked him about it, guilty much? I kept telling myself all evening that it was okay, we hadn't set rules so what was I being so upset about? Still, Zee and I weren't going hiking or to exhibitions or to the movies any more and I missed all that. We were always having sex, or watching porn, or both. What kind of relationship was this, what did the ENM charter have to say about this?

Is everything all right? Mom asked. I just nodded. I could tell Mom knew something was off. She pressed on. You know I never interfere, the only thing I ask is that you'd tell me if you're struggling with anything. She brought her face closer. Vivaan, did you and Zee have a fight?

I lost it then. Please Mom! We're not like normal couples, not like you and Dad, having tiffs and making up on a daily basis. I don't know how you both keep up. Zee and I are at a different level . . .

I could see Mom was surprised, but she wouldn't give up. You already know this, she said, but I wasn't there for your Mambro when he needed me, and it was the same for your grandmother and her brother. And then all those things that happened, maybe we as sisters could've looked after them . . . I don't want to make the same mistake with you.

I'M NOT YOUR ATONEMENT PROJECT, I wanted to scream, but instead I turned towards my laptop and put my headphones on. Mom looked so harried in that moment, but what could I say to her? She'd already made such a huge leap into my world, it must not have been easy for her and Dad. How could she trust me when all I'd done was break her trust?

Mom took my headphones off and plonked them on the table. If you can't talk to me, you can call your Mambro. Any time. He's on your speed-dial.

Just because he's gay and I'm gay doesn't mean we're feeling the same way. And he isn't even here! If he cared about me so much, why did he have to go live so fucking far away?

Vivaan! Watch your language! Remember who you're talking to! Mom took a sec, then softened. Mambro didn't have a choice, sweetie, after all that had happened. One day, he'll tell you everything himself.

We can call a spade a spade, I said quietly. Everyone always has a choice, and Mambro chose to move away from us.

Then I put my headphones back on and played some Lumineers, looking at the wall with so much concentration that I could manifest a crack in it. I felt Mom slink away after a while, her shadow getting smaller, moving sideways, until it was just a dot. If she'd said anything before leaving, I wouldn't have heard.

Grand-Mamu's Story

It was in the spring of 1982 that Sukumar saw his nephew for the first time. Sukumar was thirty years old, four years into his bank job, where he'd moved up to the role of teller, turning up to work on time every day, counting the money, making the deposits, entering in the ledger, filing the reports. At home, a sterile peace enveloped his life with his mother. The news of his sister's pregnancy had brought the kind of joy that comes with knowing that one of your own is moving on to the next stage of life. This is what she had wanted for a long time, and mother and son were both relieved and happy for her. But it was still news of someone else far away; it was not meant to touch their everyday existence. Until Sukumar laid eyes on the boy himself.

The child had his father's eyes, narrow and stretched, not large and expressive like Sukumar and his sister's. But the rest was all them, the nose and lips and chin were blobs, occupying large portions of his face. 'He hasn't displeased any of the two families,' a relative joked. After the news of the birth had arrived from the Garden City, Sukumar had imagined for months what the boy looked like. He'd asked his sister for a photo, but she'd said the photos had been washed out from overexposure.

When the letter from his sister arrived, announcing that they were coming to the Grand Old City for the annaprasan, Sukumar had to hand it to his mother and go to the bathroom to wipe his tears. They were bringing the six-month-old baby all the way on a train that would take them two days and two nights, only so that Sukumar could perform the ritual. It was the maternal uncle's right to feed a child their first grain of rice, granting him the place of custodian. This was the first time Sukumar had been given so much respect, offered a role in the life of the next generation. He was now a *Mamu*, that is what the boy would call him when he grew up.

On the day of the annaprasan, they made the child wear baby-sized dhuti and panjabi that Sukumar had bought for the occasion. He'd also got two garlands of tuberoses, one for his nephew, one for himself. He woke up early and cleaned the porch and the small courtyard, put up marigold bunting across the tops of doorways, rearranged the chairs and tables to make room for guests, laid out bamboo maadoors on the floor. Then he mixed broken rice and sandalwood paste in water, dipped a paintbrush in the viscous liquid, and drew patterns on his nephew's forehead, lines of curves and dots just above the eyebrows, symmetrical on both sides, a large red dot in the middle like a third eye. The little boy lay quietly, following the paintbrush with his small eyes, sometimes frowning when it came too close, but otherwise still, as though he trusted his Mamu to make him look good.

Later that afternoon, after the prayers were done by the priest and food was served, his sister placed the boy on Sukumar's lap. With everyone as witness, Sukumar spooned some payesh into his mouth. The boy sucked up the rice pudding like a little fish, and looked up at his Mamu, as though asking for more. Sukumar fed him the rest of the payesh, bit by bit, tenderly mashing the grains of rice on the pink tongue. And when the spoon couldn't pick up any more of the paste, he used his hands, feeling the toothless orifice nibble his fingertips.

The world around them was lively, everyone talking and laughing, showering the child with presents, milling around Sukumar's sister who had had a difficult pregnancy, nearly a miscarriage miraculously averted at the last moment. They left uncle and nephew to themselves. Sukumar cooed in the boy's ears, calling him by his name, telling him that he'd make him lots of payesh when he grew up. 'You like sweets, tai na?' he whispered. 'Just like your Mamu . . .' He sang and mimed and roared, sending the boy into paroxysms of delight.

At bedtime, Sukumar sang the ditty that every Mamu sings for his nephew. *Tai-tai-tai / Mama'r bari jai / Mama'r bari bhari moja / keel-chor nai*. The baby gurgled in toothless laughter. When Sukumar tickled his soft belly, he hiccuped. Sukumar held the baby's head up and planted soft kisses on his forehead, the scalp so tender he could feel his thumb depress the skin. How delicate was this baby, how tiny, as though his body was made of putty, like the clay idols Sukumar helped to sculpt every year before Durga Pujo. As the boy fell asleep, head on his Mamu's chest, Sukumar wrapped his arms around the little thing, so precious, the breathing so calm. This was the first time he'd discovered that holding someone could feel both strong and vulnerable, the body had to exude the power to protect and the frailty to receive. A tornado of new feelings was opening up within him; he paced up and down the room, shutting the door to dim the hullabaloo of the guests downstairs.

And then, it was time for the child to leave. Sukumar went to the station, carrying sweets and snacks for his sister and brother-in-law to eat during the long journey. He played with his nephew until the engine sounded its horn. His brother-in-law's family had also come for the send-off, and Sukumar didn't want to make a scene, so he gulped his tears down and tried to behave like the other grown-ups, always at one remove, spouting platitudes, *don't let the child too close to the window, bhalo theko, pouchhe khobor diyo, see you next year . . .* Why couldn't he be like the other adults? Why did he feel emotions that turned his core around while these people seemed to inure themselves from such tempests?

As the train started to move, Sukumar walked along the platform, his fingers holding the rails of the window. His sister's large eyes were brimming with tears; she reached out and patted Sukumar's hand. 'Stay well, take care of Ma,' she managed to say. The child, emulating his mother, also extended his arm and touched Sukumar's hand, pulling at it so he could entwine his fingers in his Mamu's. But the train was now picking up speed, and it was time for Sukumar to disengage and stop walking. He stood by, watching his sister's and nephew's faces get smaller, then blur.

He couldn't go home right now, his innards were in turmoil, he couldn't face his mother, couldn't tell her what this child had done to him. So he went to see X.

For months after X's wedding in the spring of '78, Sukumar and X had stayed away, ensuring they never ran into each other, never crossed the street at the same time, never even mentioned the other in passing. X had never shared his friends with Sukumar anyway, nor did he have anything to do with Sukumar's life at the bank. It was a separation that was easy to enforce. What they'd had for that one night before Mahalaya could be passed off as a fleeting dalliance; surely that happened between many people, most of whom wouldn't end up together? Sukumar found a way to hold on to the memory and yet play down the import of those nocturnal hours they'd spent coiled up. He could still summon the scent of X's arms around him, the ring of X's light snores. He assumed X had busied himself with the worldly life of a family man, a life centred around 'the Mrs', as the men called their wives, and teeming with parents and in-laws, festivals spent together, holidays and pilgrimages taken now and then.

But when X placed his fingers on the damp clay, it took Sukumar not even a flicker to know who had reappeared in his life. It was the post-monsoon months before the Durga Pujo; a year had rolled by, and Sukumar had returned to the Sculptors' Quarters to volunteer, help with the carving, hoping that he'd be entrusted with more. His work and home life had fallen into a rhythm, and while that had brought stability and certainty, there was no place in that life for art, for stories, for beauty, for creation. This year, he hadn't needed the impetus of teaming up with the art college folks. He'd walked alone into Master-babu's studio, if the expansive unpaved shed could be called that, and while there were some of the art college men here from the previous year, and some strangers, Sukumar had mostly been working on his own, patting down the clay, carrying trays up to the Master and his assistants, holding the wooden frames in place as they sculpted the curves of the idols.

'I knew I'd see you here,' X said softly, wriggling his fingers under the clay to make contact with Sukumar's.

'I thought you'd be too consumed with your married life to come,' Sukumar replied, trying to sound unflustered.

'Did you not want to see me?'

Sukumar shrugged, then moved away to work with Master-babu for the rest of the evening.

When they were done for the day, X asked Sukumar to wait at the end of the lane. From behind the jhuggi at the junction, Sukumar could see the silhouettes of X and his friends light up cigarettes and speak in their deep voices, before X waved goodbye and walked down at a lethargic pace. Then he turned the corner and put his lips on Sukumar. The steam that rose fogged up X's glasses, and they stayed there for a while, bodies against each other, disregarding the risk of being seen.

'Come with me,' X entreated. And Sukumar followed,

unbothered by his docility. He'd always known that if X asked him for more, he'd give it to him without pausing to interrogate the impulse. There was no dilemma here. This was the only man he'd ever loved, and this man still desired him.

They walked through this lane and that, on the main road, by the river, turning into more side streets, until they reached a dilapidated building in desperate need of a coat of paint. The wooden windows hung precariously from their frames, net curtains rustled in the breeze, making most of the interior visible. They entered, traversed corridors, went up the stairs, and were finally in a room that X said was his. It was a boarding house. He lived here during the week while his family were still in the District. It made working in the city easier. He returned to the District at the weekends.

They spent the night in the stuffy room, the windows shut, switching the light off for good measure. It didn't matter that they had to fit themselves on a single bed, they might as well have been one body. It didn't matter that the springs of the cot had a voice of their own, speaking louder than their lovemaking. It didn't matter that people came and went through the corridor outside, talking, coughing, farting. At some point, there was a knock on the door, and the daughter of the manager asked if X would eat dinner, trying to squeeze her head through the gap to see who else was inside. It didn't matter that X played the radio on full volume all night so it could drown out their sounds. That night, nothing else mattered; not even that it was the first time Sukumar had spent a night away from home without informing his mother. The compunction lingered only a few moments, when he considered calling the *Jugantor* office and leaving a message, but he was too encumbered by X's embrace, too ecstatic to extricate himself from this bliss. Everyone deserved this at least once in their lives, one night curled up with their lover, why should he think of anyone else right now?

For the next three years, from '79 to '82, that seedy room became their lair. They met a few times every week, usually after work, but sometimes at lunch hour, sometimes in the middle of the afternoon, and there were entire days that they'd call in sick to stay in each other's arms. The room that had seemed so tawdry and impersonal on that first night became the home they knew they could never have. Initially, Sukumar would dodge the manager of the boarding house, slink in when he wasn't at his desk, stay away from the curious stares of the daughter, slip out when they were sure everyone was asleep; but gradually, he turned his charms on them, chatting to the daughter about her studies, helping the manager deposit cash in the bank, asking about people's days when he ran into them on the stairs. X, wary at first, finally gave in. 'You act like you don't, but you *do* know your way around, Suku!'

Now that he was working, Sukumar felt less accountable to his mother. For her part, she asked him fewer questions about his whereabouts, accepting that he was finally claiming the lifestyle of a young man in the city. Her son had grown up docile and awkward, but she'd seen relatives' and friends' sons, how they spent time outdoors, went on adventures and expeditions, returned in the small hours, or how they skulked with mates behind closed doors, talking about things the women were never invited to join in, politics and economy and activism. At least her son didn't drink like the others!

Sukumar brought X home now and then. His mother was already fond of X; she asked about his wife, about the son she'd given birth to, about the house he was building in the District. Sukumar endured these conversations, then made excuses for him and X to go up to the small room, where they'd remain undisturbed for hours, and his mother said, 'No problem, let me know if you need anything.'

Otherwise, X mentioned his wife as little as possible; if he did, most times, it was a slip of the tongue. He had a practised discipline about demarcating his two lives – the one in the District, and the one with Sukumar; one wasn't pertinent to the other. Sukumar never asked either. He knew that if he had to be X's lover, he'd have to accept him as a married man, and surely that was something men like them did everywhere in the world? As X put it, 'If you were denied food, would you not swipe it off a table, sit underneath and eat it?'

X, as usual, knew a lot about laws and rights. He called himself a *homosexual*, a term that made Sukumar cringe, uncomfortable with labelling himself something so foreign and derogatory. 'Can't I just be Sukumar?' he asked naively. 'Don't be an idiot,' X barked back. 'In the eyes of the law, we are all the same, they'd put us in jail if they came in through the door right now.' X told Sukumar about Section 377, the British colonial-era law that pronounced them criminals. 'They come at us with their laws, and in places where they don't have such laws, like America, they go after us for public indecency or, worse, communism! They'd rather just have us all dead!' Then he looked at Sukumar's frightened face and broke into an indulgent smile. 'Arre boka, if they take you away, rest assured you'll light up the prison with your glamour!'

But with the years, X's paranoia receded. They didn't always shut the windows, drank tea side by side behind the net curtains, ordered two plates of food to the room. They spent evenings by the river, sat on the bench behind the banyan tree, which they joked was *their* bench, the light breeze and drizzly rain and cold smog chronicling the flowering of what they had with the turn of seasons. X introduced Sukumar to some of his art college friends. Sukumar now had a larger circle than he'd ever known, though he wasn't always sure if they were homosexuals, or just normal men whom X befriended. For their part, X and Sukumar never betrayed their true feelings in public, never as much as let their arms graze, or their eyes rest upon each other for an extra second. X had given him strict instructions, and Sukumar was getting better at following them. With these men, they went to the Coffee House, or to Anadi's for Mughlai paratha, or to the riverside jhuggi that sold local deshi toddy. X wasn't a big drinker, and Sukumar didn't touch alcohol, he didn't like it, didn't see the point of it, didn't want his mother to smell it on him; he'd kept her in the dark about everything substantial in his life, but he drew the line at this. Nevertheless, it did feel grown up to be out with men drinking, making a fool of themselves, to give them a helping hand, a shoulder to lean on when they needed to be escorted home. Sukumar had never had these things in his adolescence. This, at last, was a life of his choice, and he was in control.

Sometimes they went to the cinema, sometimes to the theatre. When they watched *Mrigayaa*, Sukumar admitted to X that he was infatuated with Mithun Chakraborty; this was the first time he'd seen an actor go bare-chested for most of a film, and the perfect dips of the pectorals, the triangle at the collar bones, the ravishing smile had done for Sukumar more than any real man could. X acted jealous, but Sukumar could tell he was titillated by this honesty. When they watched *Nathabati Anathabat*, a feminist retelling of the Mahabharata, giving voice to all the women in the epic, Sukumar was riveted to his seat; he told X that Saoli Mitra's solo act had inspired him to get closer to his art, maybe he would start painting again? 'You should!' X encouraged him. 'You know I'll make calls for you if you ever started something of your own, na?' And even though Sukumar knew he could never quit his bank job, and that X had no one to call – if he did, he'd be an illustrator himself by now – he felt vindicated, because X never said no, never shut him up, never quashed his wishes, even if he knew they were just sandcastles.

But the only art Sukumar really engaged in was at the Sculptors' Quarters before Durga Pujo. Most of the art college volunteers from that first year had dropped off, been replaced by new ones who'd fished around for commissions before disappearing too. But Sukumar was there every year in the month of Bhadro, first patting down the clay, then building the frames, crunching the straw, helping to shape the forms, mixing colours, painting the finger- and toenails, until, in his fifth year, Master-babu finally asked him if he would like to paint the features of the mother goddess. By then, he'd practised innumerable times on the spare idols at the back of the shed. Sukumar went up close to Ma Durga and, balancing his feet on the rung of the ladder to achieve the elevation of the idol, held the brush in his steady fingers, dipped it in the paint, and drew the eyelid in a single fine line; there was no scope for mistakes, unevenness, smudges; if he messed up, the entire face would have to be wiped clean and painted again. He then drew the lower line, the eyelashes one by one, the angry eyeball glaring at the buffalo-demon. He moved to the other eye, which had to be perfectly symmetrical, from the placement on the face to the fineness of the stroke. And finally, the third eye on the forehead, vertically aligned, the tip nearly touching the vermilion in the parting of the goddess's curly hair. 'Nikhoot,' Master-babu gasped in fascination, flawless! Sukumar wished that his mother and sister and X had been around to witness this prestigious occasion; after all, how many people in all of Bengal had the good fortune to touch the face of the goddess with a paintbrush, come this close to her, almost feel her breathing into life?

What else could one want? He had love, he had family, and he had his art. He'd come a long way from that fifteen-year-old who'd set his father's funeral pyre aflame, had his head shaved in mourning, and was left to figure the world out for himself. He was thirty now; he just needed to hold on to this for the rest of his life.

This lasted until the spring of 1982, when Sukumar met his nephew for the first time, fed the baby his first grain of rice, put him to sleep, and walked down the platform with the moving train as the boy tried to hold his hand. That after-noon, he came straight to the boarding house. He'd only ever come here in the company of X, but he couldn't go home, couldn't see his mother's face, tell her of the tumult within him. X was trying to nap in a ganji and lungi, just back from work, fanning himself to dry the sweat. Without preamble, Sukumar collapsed in X's arms. He tried saying things, that he already missed the boy, was this how it was like to be a father, to hold a baby, to know that someone carried your genes, that they could grow up to be just like you? X would know, he had a son.

X sat Sukumar down and patted his back patiently. For once, he was struck silent; he had no laws and slogans and newspapers to quote from, no theories, no poetry. When Sukumar finally quietened, still sniffling at every exhale, X asked, 'What do you want, Suku? Tell me, because I can't see you like this.'

Sukumar put his wet hand on X's warm palm, massaged the moon mound, looked into his eyes and said, 'You can't give me what I want. You can never give me a child.'

Mambro's Manuscript

The millennium is still new, as is your adulthood, and you've just moved to the Mountains for university.

The Mountains bring new beginnings, a new place, your first time outside home, away from your parents and sister, it is your first tryst with independence. Here, you still are all the things you were in the Grand Old City: urban, your English polished, your references Western, you've done a good job of learning from reruns of American TV shows, you roll your *r*'s for effect, even say *day-ance* instead of *d-ah-nce*. But while those things worked against you in that old place, making you alien, in the Mountains they turn you into someone unattainable. Most people here are from smaller towns, from states whose capitals are weak imitations of modernity. In comparison, the Grand Old City that you have berated for being parochial now seems cosmopolitan.

In the Mountains, you step into the spotlight right away, wasting no time, like an understudy who has spent years in the wings watching thespians onstage. A social savviness you didn't know you had kicks in; you're able to place yourself in the hierarchy of seniors and cohort-mates, unpack the grad-ations, peel away the layers of politics, who likes whom and why and how to make the most of it.

You escape ragging. When gangs of seniors arrive in your rooms every night to give the new arrivals a tough time, rib at their gaffes, you're spared the circus; you watch as your peers are made to act like dogs peeing in moving trains, or recite poems about their parents having sex, or face the wall and wank an imaginary penis. At first, you don't understand why you're being let go so easily; as the weeks roll on, you're encouraged to join in, and when you crack a joke, your seniors laugh louder than they need to. Eventually, you understand: you've gone from being *curious* to being *exotic*; they still can't place you, but in their small towns, you're all the cool things they aspired to be.

Your cleverness shows in other ways too: you don't disconnect yourself from your peers, don't fan the flames of jealousy at your being close to the seniors; instead you dip in and out of groups, find a part of you that is relevant to each one; you can be whatever they'd like you to be – crass and brash, polite and studious, mischievous and anti-establishment, academic and political, naughty and sexual. You quickly make friends with the girls, which is no problem for you, but is in contrast to most boys there, who are wrapped up in their small-town awkwardness, fretting about their clothes and hairstyles and accents. You even do an imitation of Rituparno Ghosh that becomes quite popular, your hand at an angle, your wrist limp, your voice high. You're not worried about being disingenuous, about mocking your favourite director, about making fun of *the gays*; these are just versions of you that you're scattering like seeds on soil, in the hope that each will grow into a tree, different variants of the same species, and at least one will survive if there were a drought.

And so when Freshers' Night arrives, the party that will induct your cohort into the student body, break down the erstwhile barriers between seniors and juniors, when everyone will get drunk and become friends, on that momentous night, you get up onstage for the first time in your life. It is only as you're walking up the steps that it strikes you that you've never been up here before, never seen the view from this height. You're onstage to sing, to say a few words, you're a contender for the Mr Fresher title, and when you win second place, when everyone rushes to hug you and say that it should've been you, you're still reeling from the fact that you stepped into the limelight for the first time.

In the Mountains, you would like to believe that you miss Y, his plump lips, his scented skin. That kind of stuff makes for good love stories, doesn't it? The truth is, you don't, you've embraced this new life with the eagerness of an ant for a cube of sugar. If you miss Y, you don't admit it to yourself, and since no one knows about you two, he never comes up in conversation. It's like you never felt love at all. In fact, you haven't even taken your journal out and held it in your hands since you came to the Mountains.

Your sister found the journal a few nights before you left for university. You hadn't made an effort to hide it, there weren't many hiding places at home to begin with, all your lives very overlapping. You'd casually placed it in your bag, and she was helping with the packing. When she tells you the next morning that she stayed up all night reading it, you can only wonder at how quickly she reads. But you don't ask her this, you don't really say much, whatever you had to say is in the journal: you met Y, felt love, were in a relationship with him, had hot sex, that's the gist. You do feel strange that your sister has now read through your escapades in so much detail, but you hope that there was enough lyricism to make up for the racy parts.

You will not remember this interaction very well in the future, perhaps because humans are programmed to wipe out the unpleasant things about those we love; is there any other way to sustain relationships? Your sister, at age sixteen, is a matron in miniature; if there is anyone at her convent school who makes the most of the fees they pay, it is her. She does not know yet that she will grow up to become a trailblazer, will break so many rules that the rule-book will throw itself into the shredder to be gobbled up whole, especially when she will have a son. Right now, at the start of the new millennium, she is Mother Superior in the making, overlaid by a wholesome dose of Indian morality.

On that morning after she read your journal, her eyes brim with tears, her face stricken; she is not disapproving or disgusted; if anything, she feels betrayed at not being told. But you don't know how to tell her that you and Y were never meant to be shared with the world, that what you had was like a snow-globe, just the two of you going round and round in the flakes, the music playing on repeat; anyone wanting to be part of it would have to shatter the globe first.

Your sister's overarching emotion is concern, fear at what will happen if any of this comes out, if your parents get wind, what if it was them who found the journal and not her? You are surprised that you've never been overly anxious about your parents finding out; if you were, you wouldn't have carried on with Y so blatantly. How can two siblings with the same upbringing be so different? The last thing she says before the conversation ends, as you both stand really close speaking in hushed tones on an otherwise regular morning, your parents entering and leaving the room, is 'Did you not think of us at all when you did those things?'

You promise that it's all over now, that you and Y will be in different cities, there's nothing more left to happen. There is no apology from her for having read your journal, for the breach of privacy. Before Facebook, no one cared about privacy, at least not where you grew up.

You don't know yet that she has called Y, or will call him soon, asking him to stay away from you. By the time you're told this, too many years would've passed for anyone to remember the exact lines. You're the one left to reconstruct this phone call in your imagination, and marvel at how much of your life has taken place outside of you, in other people's conversations, their decisions, actions, *you* having had no inkling.

But in this new life in the Mountains, it is your sister you miss the most. There is this yawning hollow where once your family were, your sister and your parents, whose presence you took for granted, spent most nights of your life under the same roof, your dependence on them showing in ways deeper than the need to be clothed and fed. No amount of razzmatazz of university life, which isn't all that glamorous anyway, no number of new friends, can paint a substantial colour over that gap. You don't know that it is the same for them, that they struggle to have dinner every night with your chair sitting vacant, that they try in their own ways to make sense of your absence.

Up in the Mountains, the newspaper arrives a day later; there is a TV in the common room but it always plays sports; there are a couple of phones in common areas on which parents call. The day *your* parents have decided to call is Tuesday, so you wait among a mushrooming group of boys after dinner to steal a few minutes with each of your family members. Your father does most of the talking, asking about your studies, the classes, your mother about the food and weather; by the time the receiver is handed to your sister, the long-distance meter has ticked on for too long, and the person next to you is making the time-out sign.

And so your sister and you start writing to each other, long letters, pages and pages. She tells you everything about her life, at home, at school, in the city, among relatives, with friends, never skimping on the detail. You tell her as much as you think suitable, never lies, but you keep the truths that the nuns at her convent school haven't taught her to stomach.

You don't tell her that Y has been writing to you, he isn't happy at his university, he doesn't enjoy his course, he feels out of place; his letters are proper, from one old friend to another, there is nothing in the language that betrays the love that bursts from his heart as he writes, and the love you sweep up to hold inside you. You don't sit waiting for his letters, and later his emails when the lab is set up with internet; they are infrequent, you don't know when to expect one, and you get used to it, glowing when they arrive, feeling love for those moments that you touch the paper, run your fingers on the ink or the computer screen, before folding up and going back to your life.

You don't tell your sister about the boy who arrives a few weeks after you, a late admission; he is from a state in the far north-east of the country. He is everything that you are not: his small-town vibes are particularly marked, his pronunciations are funny, his voice is soft, his English is atrocious; but he is also everything that you're trying hard not to be, he has a swing in his gait, he flicks his hair off his forehead, covers his mouth when he smiles, and looks at you with those lidded eyes as though he is seeing through your ruse, knows the stuff you're really made of.

You don't tell your sister that you go especially hard on him with the ragging, that you use your newfound cachet to pretend to be a senior, make fun of him day after day, making him sing lewd songs, get fucked by an imaginary horse, climb up and down the nine floors of the hostel until he is near collapse. You know that he is not resilient, that he will crack; but that is what you want, to leave him so weak that he can never find the strength to expose you.

One night, you're ambling down the corridor to your room, whistling a tune confidently; your parents thought it bad manners at home, but now it's you who decides what's good what's bad. The boy from the north-east turns a corner and sees you; his body hits the wall, and he drags himself along the concrete, eyes down, feet on tiptoe, as though he is still hoping to escape your surveillance, praying that you won't say something mean, call him a *homo* or a *chhakka*, won't jut your hand out to scare him. You slow down and let him pass, all the time studying him, and he looks back in spite of all his good senses, steals a glance at you, then lowers his eyes and continues walking, fists curled in fear.

As you watch him go, you want to reach out, say hey, it's okay, that you're just playing a part assigned to you in this place. You want to ask him to find his survival mode too; that is the only way people like you can live a little. You may also have wanted to hug him from behind, touch human skin, let the warmth of his body into yours, slip your hand under his shirt, caress the back of his neck softly; you haven't touched and been touched since Y.

But you just stand there, chest puffed out, hands apart, nostrils flared, like you've seen other boys do. When he has passed you, you can feel his relief in your body; his shoulders slump, his feet speed up. Before he turns the corner, he turns to check if you're still there, bumps into a door, yelps in shock, then disappears.

Three weeks later, you hear that he is gone, has left the university.

It is your first vacation, and you return home a hero, thinner, gaunter, an air of being overworked and underfed. Your parents rush in to make amends on both counts. Your sister plans a day out for the two of you, Pizza Hut and Westside and Café Coffee Day, the new Inox multiplex, can you imagine, multiple screens playing multiple movies simultaneously? Compared to the Mountains, the Grand Old City doesn't seem so old any more; the boys are cuter, the girls prettier, everyone fashionable, everything jazzy. You hang out with friends from your university who also are from here; you drink so many beers at Kwality's that you're swooning by the time you get home. Your parents, who would've made a hue and cry about such inebriation before, now let you stagger to your room and pass out; they're learning to accept you as an adult.

Y is visiting too, but he doesn't call for a while; you hear from friends that he's been busy hanging out with his groups. When he finally does call and you go to his place, something is off between the two of you, the silences are stretched, the touches reticent, the sex practised; there's no mention of how much you missed each other. You're surprised when you don't feel regret or grief, when this seems like how life should be; you're nineteen, at the top of your game, maybe what you had with Y has run its course. If anything, you find him underwhelming, more brooding and less smart and shorter than you remembered. Was it your lack of effervescence then that had made him such a hero in your eyes? And does he not match up to your standards now? You put these thoughts away, you're not fussed about the past, you're only looking forward.

You meet Y a couple more times during those holidays; you won't remember if it is indoors or outdoors, but the alchemy has withered, the magic potion diluted, the little bird refuses to sing. You find it difficult to imagine a time when the two of you spent hours holed up, what did you talk about, what were your in-jokes, how could you have been so besotted with this guy?

The day Y leaves the Grand Old City, you forget to call him, to say bye. You've run into a schoolmate with whom you'd made out a few times, he invites you home and you readily go. By the time you're zipping up your six-pocket jeans, Y's train has already left the station.

On the last night before you go back to university, you visit the Northern Quarters. You get there in the late afternoon and chat with your grandmother, who is so happy to see you that she goes down to the kitchen and starts to prepare a meal, she won't listen to your protestations, you're going to have dinner there, nothing doing. You talk in unspecific terms about the Mountains, skipping all the detail, giving her a skeletal outline so generic it could apply to anyone your age.

Mamu's face lights up upon seeing you the moment he returns from work. The last few times you saw him, which was rare, though you lived in the same city, he'd been seething, desperate, despondent. Things have gone horribly wrong in his life in recent years, you don't know all the details, only as much as your mother has shared with you, just the facts, never feelings. Your distance from Mamu has been growing; the more he made a spectacle of himself, the more you dissociated. Your father is upset with him, as are most of the other relatives; your mother straddles her disappointment and love towards her only brother with unease, it isn't that simple for her. He's been held up to you as a poster-boy of everything you shouldn't be, of wasted potential, squandered opportunities, exploited entitlements. It doesn't help that you and he have so much in common, a way with words, a way with music, a way with pencil strokes on paper, a way with dance-beats. You know your father, and perhaps even your mother, are scared that you will turn out like him – craven, disgraced, penniless, no family, no friends. If you're completely honest with yourself, you share that fear too.

That evening, the small room glowing in the light of a single naked bulb, Mamu's face is resplendent, the sheen of sweat from his commute shimmering on his wheatish skin. He takes out a blue jacket from the cupboard, it is wrapped in newspaper, says he's bought it from Tibetans, that it will keep you warm in the Mountains. You thank him, try it on, the fit is snug, but you think the colour is too bright, though you don't say it; both your Mamu and grandmother think you look good in it. Then Mamu says he's going out to get freshly fried snacks, shingara and kochuri and goja; he won't pay heed when your grandmother protests, saying she's cooked a five-course dinner; it feels like Mamu wants to bring something of his own to the joviality. As he's leaving, you spring up from the bed and say you will accompany him.

Mamu and you stroll down the street, easy steps, no hurry. It is a summer's evening, not fully dark yet, the trees swaying in the winds of an oncoming north-westerly kalboishakhi storm, the breeze getting cooler as you approach the river. You pass many sweet shops, but Mamu keeps walking like he's forgotten about the snacks, and even though he has a limp nowadays, his legs still have the sureness of stride of someone young. The street is bustling, traffic passing in both directions, hand-pulled rickshaws slotting themselves into spaces meant for pedestrians. You don't ask where you're going, nor does Mamu volunteer it.

You cross the broad avenue, farther towards the river, your hair and shirts flying in the wind now, the sweat having dried long back. People are picking up their wares from the street market, rushing indoors in anticipation of the storm. You walk over the train tracks of the Chokro-rail, the mounds of stone chips making you wobbly. The lights have come on at the station, people waiting for the next train that will take them home to the suburbs. Mamu turns to you, all smiles, his moustache arching downward. 'Remember when I took you for a ride?' You shake your head. 'You were a child, maybe three-four years old.' You nod in the way teenagers do when told about their childhoods. Mamu continues ahead, the smile intact.

He finally stops at the ghat, the waves peeping out of the bund in the high tide, the waters choppy, the little lights across the river's great width shimmering stars. Above you, a murder of crows manically flies in circles, not sure what to do about the turn of weather, whether to retire to their nests or hang back to savour the sunset. The sky is a melange of all colours between indigo and red, rather like a child's careless attempts at painting, a smudged rainbow.

'Let's sit for a while,' Mamu says, and heads towards a bench. You want to say it's probably not a good idea, it might rain, there might be lightning and thunderbolts that usually accompany a kalboishakhi. But once you sit, everything magically calms down, the wind lulls into a steady breeze, the fronds caress one another, the haze over the river lifts like a veil to reveal the outlines of houses on the opposite bank, the gloaming manifests new shapes in the sky.

You can hear Mamu breathe, his inhales and exhales sound laboured for someone in their forties. His scent is a heady mix of sweat and talcum powder. He looks frail, his eyes glazed, his ungainly body out of his control. He is quiet, has receded into a cocoon deep inside his head. His health has slipped away with the years; he's severely diabetic, and if you look closely, you can see the dark knots on his knuckles, the bumps of past boils on his feet, the swirls of pus behind his toenails.

And suddenly, your boundaries dissolve, a softness descends; you can't remember any more why you wanted to distance yourself from him! This is your Mamu, the uncle who's given you nothing but love since you were little; he and your mother have the same face, the same large eyes, the broad jawline, the curly hair; he protected your mother when they became fatherless as teenagers. Whatever his missteps in life, he's not benefited from them either, he's ended up with nothing and no one. And he has no children of his own; who else but you will he turn to when he grows older? If he is indeed gay, and if you are gay too, though you haven't labelled yourself at this early stage, you're bound by an accord; you don't understand his choices, but you understand the pain. Right there, you pledge to be the nephew to him you never were; perhaps you should visit more often, write to him, call him from the Mountains.

You want to put a hand on Mamu's arm, snuggle up to him so your bodies touch. You've never snuggled up to an older male since you've grown up, not even your father; you envy your sister for hanging from his shoulders like a little girl, forming a bow of her arms around his neck, things you can't bring yourself to do. You want to ask Mamu about his life, about why he did the things he did, why he can't just pull himself together, get healthy again, get his affairs in order, he is young, only forty-nine, there's still time, lots of it. In your nascent worldview, all problems are fixable, all questions can be answered. You want to probe how he's feeling, about what people are saying about him. Does he have anyone to talk to?

Perhaps if you share something, he will too? You open your mouth to tell him about Y, about the distance that has eaten into the love, how you've found your feet at university, the mild-mannered boy from the north-eastern state whom you drove out; you want to accuse and explain yourself, let Mamu be the judge. You want to ask him what you're doing with your life, studying things that don't interest you, living in a god-forsaken place, making friends you have nothing in common with, being someone you aren't . . . But you can't find the words, an entry point into your own narrative eludes you.

Mamu turns and smiles, his eyes lit up, as though he's had

an epiphany, clawing his way back to the present. He asks you to sing something, and when you start in Hindi, he interjects, insists that you sing in Bangla, so you choose a song about hitting the road with the purpose of getting lost; it is not a premeditated choice, but later, it will seem particularly poignant. Then you ask Mamu to sing, but he refuses, jokes that he sings like a frog; but he sits up straight, like he's had an idea, says he can teach you a prayer instead, would you be interested? You say yes.

Mamu begins reciting a mantra, a Vishnu-stotra he calls it. *Shantakaram bhujagashayanam padmanabham suresham . . .* When he's done one turn, you start chanting too, following the Sanskrit sounds closely, committing them to memory, making mistakes, but getting more fluent as you continue. Mamu is beaming at your eagerness to learn; he is still handsome, his eyes bright, a full head of black hair, the podgy nose and thick lips like your mother's, like yours, features they inherited from their father.

Then you both fall silent, your bodies refusing to rise from the bench, to break the spell of this moment. But after a while, Mamu bumps his palm on his forehead, exclaims 'Chol re!' He's remembered about the snacks. You help him up, walk down the ghat, the river now gentle, no longer agitated by the prospect of storm. At the Chokro-rail pedestrian crossing, you wait for the train to pass, then you jump over the tracks, the wooden slats between them, run out in front of the park that hosts the Sarbojonin Durga Pujo every year, where Mamu used to paint the eyes of the goddess once upon a time.

But when you turn, Mamu is still on the tracks, struggling over the mounds of stone chips, his body out of balance, his face wincing from the pricks in his soles. You feel guilty about leaving him behind, not checking whether he was next to you. You run back promptly and offer your hand. Mamu takes it, places his other hand on your shoulder, leans his weight on you. You point to places where the mounds are flattened, the slats are wide, ask him to put his foot here, there, this spot, that crevice. Once he's on the other side of the tracks, you wait until he catches his breath, his lips tight, eyes watering, still absorbing the agony. Then you walk towards home where your grandmother is waiting, Mamu's fingers still in yours. You won't let him navigate the erratic streets by himself, not when he's in pain, not while you're around.

You don't know yet that this is the last time you will see your Mamu.

ENTRY FOUR

Vivaan's VoiceNote004

Six months into our ENM, Zee said he was in love with me, and in love with Twinkie.

This didn't come out of the blue, I'd known Twinkie was bad juju from the start, but it still felt like I'd been halved, like Zee had taken a mallet to a clay bust of me and smashed part of it, and now we were brainstorming how to use Twinkie's parts to make it whole again.

Not gonna lie, I cried a little, in front of Zee. Okay, a little more than I'd have liked to. And sorry if I get emo telling you about this bit, it still fucking hurts. Zee put his arms around me and pressed my head to his chest, and I readily wetted his Uniqlo T-shirt. Made me wish my tears weren't brine but kerosene, and I could set fire to it the moment I was done.

Don't cry, my rabbit, Zee cooed. That really triggered me, because he'd never called me rabbit before. Must've been something he'd taken to calling Twinkie, humping as they had been for a while now. Good, I thought, now Twinkie and I were both rabbits in Zee's cage!

I'm not a rabbit. I pushed Zee away and he landed on the bed with a force both of us hadn't seen coming.

Someone's been working out. Zee played with my biceps.

It's the swimming, I said through my tears. This was Zee, the man I loved, I couldn't let go of him for some Twinkie. I told myself that Twinkie would go MIA in a few months, find a more competent aftercare service, and I'd be restored whole again.

So what do we do now? I asked.

I think what I'd really like is polyamory, Zee said, he sounded like a professor discoursing to his students. Zee had this thing, I'D LIKE TO, I WOULD DO, IF YOU ASK ME, like he's taking it all on himself when, in reality, he's telling the other person what to do.

Polyamory? As in, you'd want to be in love with both of us? I knew what it was but I wanted to hear Zee explain it in his own voice.

The human heart, Zee said, is elastic, you see, Vivaan? He placed his palms around his chest and made as if he was pulling them apart. It can hold love of many kinds, for many people. Monogamy developed as a function of religion and politics and property, it was never about love. We have an opportunity to break out of it.

Put like that, it made sense. I found myself agreeing, as I mostly did with Zee's theories. So next step would be what, polygamy? I asked, smirking at my own naivety. I already knew what Zee would say.

Who cares for marriage? With one person or many!

But, what about the hearings in the Supreme Court right now on same-sex marriage? Why are the petitioners being so brave and fighting for our rights if we don't even care about exercising them?

Zee hadn't expected this googly. He blinked as he reconfigured his thoughts, and I wanted to jump up with a howzzaaattt!

It had been all over the news those last few weeks, activists had petitioned the Supreme Court for same-sex marriage to be legalized. The hearings were being live-streamed on socials, I'd been watching some of them. The lawyers, two women, themselves a lesbian couple, facing down the bigots in a public courtroom day in day out. There were articles and op-eds popping up on my feed. Mom said this was all anyone was talking about at dinner parties and work drinks and Zumba classes. Wouldn't it be epic, she sounded so enthu, if India legalized same-sex marriage within five years of decriminalizing homosexuality? Imagine the example we could set for the rest of the world! Honestly, I was sceptical, the religious leaders were fighting back, the government too, it wasn't going to be easy, but sure, it sounded like an exciting moment, the judges would be fools to let this one go.

Zee had found his professor self again now. That's the problem, rabbit, laws are being made for older people, these should've been made twenty-thirty years ago, these laws will mean nothing to us. They should consult us, we are the future.

By now, Zee and all the people at the sex encounters had said this so many times that I wanted to get them all T-shirts printed saying WE ARE THE FUTURE.

But, I challenged, didn't striking down Section 377 make us legal? Look at countries like Iran and Saudi Arabia and Uganda . . . I mean, these were just a few, there are soooo many countries I could've mentioned. We're still criminals in more than half the world!

Zee bobbed his head non-committally. Sure, at a fundamental level, everyone should be treated equal, that's a given. But if you think you'll ever be treated the same way as a man–woman couple, you're kidding yourself! Zee had found his line of argument. Laws don't change society. How many men can even tell their families?

I can, I replied quickly. My family is, you know . . .

You're so privileged, Vivaan. You have your uncle and grand-uncle. Show me one other guy who has your role models.

I wanted to quip that my Mambro wasn't around to be a role model and my Grand-Mamu, from the little I knew, had had quite a crappy life. He'd had a pretty sad death too.

But Zee was now in the throes of his own debate. Look

at what happened after 377 was changed, right? Yeah fine, companies are doing pride and all that, but they'll shut up the moment the government asks them to. And how many celebs do you know who are openly gay, in cinema, business, politics, sports? So I'm saying, why play their game at all? The rules were never designed by us in the first place! We're being set up to lose.

I couldn't tell if Zee really felt this passionately about the ideology of all this, or he was only trying to justify including Twinkie.

So if I fall in love with someone else, you'll be cool? I asked.

Zee's response was instant. I'll have to be, I'll have to make myself be cool with it.

In that moment, I kinda believed his conviction. His cause was so important to him that he'd mould his feelings to suit it, even if it meant halving me, and halving himself.

So Zee, Twinkie and I entered into our situationship, and I'd say we managed quite well. Zee put dates in calendars, there was a schedule for when he'd meet me and when he'd be with Twinkie, there were rules for how much he could divulge about the other half of his love life, there were days of the week and weeks of the month and long weekends and public holidays that he divided between the two of us. If I wanted to do something with Zee I needed to give him enough notice so he didn't accidentally schedule the same activity with Twinkie.

There were codes and codes, so many that I had to write them down, codes for when Zee was having a tiff with Twinkie and wasn't in a good mood, for when Zee needed his own space, for when I was feeling jealous and needed to blow off steam, for when I was horny but Zee wasn't because he'd just fucked Twinkie, for when Twinkie might call Zee in an emergency, although we never ended up using that code. I joked that we were building a fucking language of our own like Tolkien, and should probably start a dictionary. Zee wasn't my Alexa any more, I wished some techno whizkid out there would build me an app to manage this level of admin.

But when I was with Zee, he was all mine. He played the guitar naked, crooned in his baritone voice, I read out excerpts from books that I'd marked for him, we volunteered for a charity, we went hiking again, we watched plays and movies. It was reassuring to see that our in-jokes were still intact, that Zee remembered everything about me, Zee never missed a date, Zee was always on time. We studied together, Zee's board exams were round the corner and my subjects were getting difficult too, and we continued to do well. Our sex became more tender, drawn-out, there was more pause, it wasn't all animal like before. For those hours, I forgot that Twinkie even existed in Zee's life.

Through all of that, I had only one condition, I didn't want to see Twinkie's face ever again. If Zee had any hopes of us being a throuple, soz no can do! So our encounters were also demarcated, we hardly met the same people any more, and I found more people to fuck on my own. I tried going on dates, find my version of Twinkie whom I could add to this polygonal arrangement, but I don't know why, no one met Zee's standards, I couldn't imagine loving anyone else, whenever I transposed Zee's face and voice and gestures on to a new person, they'd seem like those stunt doubles in the movies who can lend their back or legs or butts to a scene, but can never be the actor themselves.

I started spending time by myself, which was nice in a way, going on walks around the lake in the middle of the city, running along the army barracks, longer post-dinner chats with Mom. I'd never had strong friendships, but now I didn't want to meet anyone. I guess, in some weird way, I felt like I'd let everyone down. They'd been so happy for me and Zee, so supportive, I'd thought we were trailblazers, and take a look at us now, half-love-half-code! If people asked how things were going, what would I tell them? Don't get me wrong, I wasn't embarrassed, I didn't want what the straights had, but also, weren't we supposed to show the straights that we could do love and relationships too? I don't know, I'd just rather not meet anyone at all!

Okay, you're sensing where this is going, right? I bet you're only half-correct.

Yes, I became quite lonely. When I was alone in my room, I couldn't do without porn, I needed it as a constant backdrop to cut through the silence. Zee's absence was just too real, I'd imagine him painting the town red with Twinkie, then feel shit about even giving them the time of day, then feel guilty about having such archaic needs from my relationship. So, I'd chuck my books away at random intervals and have a wank, then go back to my studies like nothing had happened, the porn playing in a loop on my laptop. If there's a condition the diagonal opposite of ADHD, I totes had it.

Sometimes I'd wake up in the night, my boxers sticky from a wet dream, my head full of the videos I'd watched. For the un-initiated, let me read the titles of some of these out. It won't take much, let's just open a site, yes I'm over eighteen, yes I accept all cookies, and we're in . . . I'm scrolling through the video captions . . . okay here we go . . . step-dad fucks step-son, WFH guy fucks electrician, husband fucks wife's gay best friend, principal punish-fucks student, fat fucks femme, Nordic demi-god breeds underage Asian sub, bear decimates twink, horny gays rape tranny, gang-bang parties in Berlin, big black cock, Latino cock, cum on ass, cum on chest, cum on face . . . I'll stop now.

Once in a while, I searched for some tender sex between couples, but they were all staged, scripted, either fake flirtation leading to fucking soon enough, or Kama Sutra positions, or candles burning and spa music and shiz. They were so boring they'd make me lose my erection. I thought I was going loco, I'd quickly switch back to the hardcore stuff to make myself hard again.

And then, that video came up on my auto-queued playlist. I wasn't even looking at first, I was solving a maths problem, but it was the sound of goats bleating that caught my ear. I maximized the browser to see two young men, boys really, kissing, being coy, hesitant, in a hut or outhouse, the door was ajar because otherwise there'd be no light in the room. Outside was a village setting, a fence, trees, a goat strutted by, poked its head in, bleated, then left. The boys got super self-conscious, stopped kissing, split from each other, but when they saw it was only a goat, they laughed, whispered to each other in what could be Hindi or some dialect, then started again, stroking, sliding hands into trousers, playing with nipples, running their fingers in a way that I could tell they were breaking into goosebumps. Someone on a cart passed by the gap in the doorway, whipping two bullocks, but the boys didn't stop, they were now so deep into it that they'd rather risk it. The video ended abruptly, one of them came up and pressed stop, and that was that. I was so aroused, but I had this urge to hold on to the arousal, not wank it out of my system right away. This had never happened before with porn. In fact, the whole purpose of porn was to get to the release ASAP.

Before the next video could buffer, I hit pause, I couldn't watch anything else after this. I went back to the two guys and bookmarked the link, it was just too moreish. I searched to see if they had a channel, or profiles, but they didn't, the video seemed rudimentary, like they were actual villagers who weren't in this for the money or fame, they were two young men who wanted to share their erotica with the world. And they were Indian, their room was like a room that might be found in thousands of Indian villages, a charpai along the wall, a calendar with Lakshmi and Ganesh photos, a clay kalash of water in a corner. I'd never seen anything like this.

It struck me then that nearly everything I'd watched before had been so choreographed and purposeful and mostly just chiselled white bodies, waxed in the right places, manicured dicks, beautiful faces, blue eyes, blond hair. That, or SUPER fat, or SUPER slim, or SUPER big, or SUPER hairy. It was either white Adonis, or the extreme opposite to feed some kind of fetish. I have to admit that I felt caught unawares. I usually pride myself on being observant, on having a discerning eye, but this had completely swept me up, and I'd just gone with the flow, accepted whatever content was being fed to me.

I spent all night frantically looking for more videos of those boys. I felt a stubborn determination to get to know them better, like, they could be me and Zee! I found two, on random other sites. In one of them, the boys were in the same room as before, the door still ajar, a woman's voice coming in with the breeze, a weaving loom making thwacking noises, but the boys seemed unconcerned, they were focused on getting erections, the shorter one was going to top the taller one, so he scrambled around and found a low chowki to stand on, then tried to penetrate the other guy, but somehow it wasn't working, they were breaking into giggles, and after trying for a while, they kissed and ended the video, no embarrassment, no shame. The other was in a train, a typical Indian Railways bogie, they were in the same berth, the uppermost one where no one could see them, only one light was on at a distance,

and this time they fucked, I couldn't tell if they were successful or if anyone climaxed, but they seemed happy in the end.

Again, I didn't wank to any of these videos, it felt like I'd
just seen footage of my friends trying out something new and
it was titillating yet adorable, or maybe I'd just seen something
of myself in them, from the first time I'd fooled around with a
neighbour's son and we'd ended up kissing, not really knowing
what had happened, not having labels and theories to justify
our attraction, but owning it all the same, in a way that was
just ours, had nothing to do with the world.

I skipped school the next day, told Mom that classes now
were revision periods. I stayed cooped up in my room, fre-
netically typing to the Carnatic chants of Suprabhatham that
the neighbouring aunty plays every morning. I didn't know
what it was I was trying to do, but I wrote about my addic-
tion to porn, the kinds of porn that I'd watched, and how it
ended with the videos of these two young guys somewhere in
rural India. I wrote about the need for more diversity, not just
in the ethnicity of actors, in places where porn was shot, in
body types, but also the need to rediscover the inner core of
why we feel attraction, why our bodies want to connect with
other bodies, why we want to pleasure others and be pleas-
ured in return. What would erotica look like if there was no
billion-dollar industry behind it, no predictive algorithm feeding content to us consumers? Left to ourselves, how would
we have owned our individual preferences? What would it
mean to see people who looked like us on-screen, and why
the apartheid? What do people who haven't ever watched
porn say to each other during sex, how do they behave? I
realized I had no idea!

When I finished, it looked something like an essay, a personal account, a short memoir, god knows what. I titled it
Decolonizing and Decapitalizing Porn. I didn't even know if

that made any sense. I didn't read it a second time, I knew I'd get academic about it, maybe I'd option+cmd+del the file. Yeah maybe it was inchoate, maybe it was horseshit, but it had flown out of me, so at least it couldn't be untrue. I wanted to share it with everyone, with Zee, with Mom, with Miss Gibson, and most of all with Mambro, I wanted to know what he'd think, how he'd critically analyse it, ask questions, not be alarmed but try to get to the heart of it.

But in the end, I chickened out. Zee would probably laugh it off, or overlay it with his theories, and I'd had enough of them. Miss Gibson would appreciate the language and the critical thinking, but need to escalate this to Princi and my parents. My friends, well, you can imagine, they'd just call me a dork at best. Mom would freak out but try to keep calm, maybe talk about getting off the internet, maybe suggest therapy, but feel like I'd betrayed her trust, feel guilty about not looking after me more, for focusing too much on her career. And Mambro, what kind of conversation was I expecting would happen over the phone?

So I just posted it on a forum where young people harangue about the world, where no one reads anyone else's entries, they're too consumed by their own rants.

And then I was done. Just done. Blank. Zilch. Nada. I had no one to talk to, no one I could share my thoughts with, no one who would understand me. I was in a situationship with the person I thought loved me, I was a traitor to the parents who'd trusted me, I was a disappointment to an uncle who'd gifted me the privilege of being open by coming out himself, I was a black sheep of the school for not wanting the things everyone else wanted. I was too vanilla for my futurist partner, too blasphemous for my conscientious teachers, too adult for my juvenile friends. I was neither this nor that, neither here nor there, never enough, yet never me.

In that moment, I wanted nothing more than to be touched, embraced, pawed at, even groped, by as many bodies as possible. My fingers swiped up my phone and went on the app, browsed, typed, booked an Uber, and then my legs carried me out of the house, my butt sat in a car seat, my body took the lift to the flat where there was a gang-bang in progress, my hands took my clothes off, my lips kissed other lips, my chest and feet and arms wrapped around whoever was in front of me, I couldn't tell what was mine and what wasn't, I melded into the melange of human parts. And when my eyes looked across the room in the floor-to-ceiling mirror, my face wouldn't even look back.

Grand-Mamu's Story

One crisp late-summer evening in 1984, Sukumar opened the door to find X standing outside with a boy of about five. 'My son,' X introduced him, asked the boy to say his name. After Sukumar had let them in and shown them to the baithak-khana, X explained, 'I've brought him to the city for the school admissions interviews, you know my boarding house isn't really a place for kids. Do you think he can stay with you for a few days?'

It wasn't like X to give him notice, Sukumar knew that by now. So he couched his surprise in politeness, said of course that would be fine. When his mother came down to look, X went through the motions with her again. 'Don't worry, Mashima,' he assured her, 'he's a good boy. He won't trouble you at all.' Then he gently placed a hand on the boy's head. 'Ki? You'll be good, won't you? No dushtumi.' The boy bobbed his head, eyes on the floor.

Sukumar took the child upstairs to the room by the terrace. He observed the round face, the slight overbite, the straight oil-slicked hair combed down to the last strand. The mother had taken care to dress the boy up for his visit to the city. There was nothing of X in him; X had bony features, an aquiline nose, wavy hair, though it was now in recession; he hadn't put on weight in the seven years Sukumar had known him. The boy, on the other hand, was plump, darker, flat-featured. This is how his mother must look, Sukumar thought, trying to conjure up an image of X's wife, something he'd tried to keep his mind away from all these years. X had once offered to show him a photo, but he'd refused.

He patted the boy's back. 'Are you scared of spending the night here without your father?' He tried to pack in as much childlike cheer as he could muster. 'Don't worry, I'm your father's friend, and this is just like your home, okay?'

The boy flinched, eyes still on the floor. 'Can we go back downstairs?'

In the baithak-khana, X and Sukumar's mother were trying to have a conversation, but X's flair from the early years was waning, and there was something compensatory in the way he slouched. 'It's just until he gets admission to a school,' X was promising even though no one had asked. 'You know how the district schools are. My wife wants him to study in the city.' X made a show of mentioning his wife whenever they were in the presence of Sukumar's mother.

Before leaving, X kissed the boy's head. 'I'll come tomorrow morning to start our rounds of the schools.' The boy showed no pangs at separating from his father; he was used to X being away in the city all week.

Outside in the street, X lit a cigarette and turned to Sukumar. 'Uff, such hassle!' He made it sound like he was the one going through all the trouble. 'It was not easy convincing his mother. She's been crying for weeks since I floated the idea of bringing him to the city.' He blew smoke into the darkness, then turned to Sukumar. 'But you wanted a child, Suku. Here, now you have one. His being here will give me a reason to visit more often. We don't have to meet in that hovel of a boarding house any more.'

'You're so clever!' Sukumar complimented X. This truly was a masterstroke. After all, it wasn't unheard of, children being sent away for better opportunities, adopted by uncles and aunts in cities. What was the saying – *it took a village . . .*?

X looked flattered. 'Are you happy?'

Sukumar put his forehead on X's shoulder. 'Have I ever said no to anything you've asked me for?'

X looked to each side, made sure they were between two cones of street lights, then gave Sukumar a kiss.

The weeks turned into months then into years. X's son lived with Sukumar and his mother for six years, from '84 to '90. He'd stay in the city on weekdays; X took him back to the District at weekends. Once the boy was admitted into a neighbourhood school, X brought an aluminium suitcase full of clothes and books and talcum powder and slippers. Sukumar lugged it to the room upstairs and unpacked, making space in the almirah and the sideboard, as though welcoming a new person into the family. A sense of possibility simmered within, the kind that blesses new beginnings, a life in which he was lover and parent and son, all under the same roof, things that came easily to other men, but not for men like Sukumar. No price was too high in order to live this dream.

In those years, Sukumar's singular dedication was to X's son. He did everything he thought a father should, making sure the boy was clothed and fed, schooled and educated, pampered and entertained. In the mornings, he got the boy ready, gave him a bath, put on his uniform, combed his hair, packed his bag, assuaged him when he threw breakfast tantrums. In the evenings, he bought treats on his way home, freshly fried kochuri and goja, for the boy to devour. He monitored his homework, taught him lessons, helped with preparing for exams, nearly did the arts and science projects himself so invested was he in crafts and colours. He took the boy out for long walks along the river in the summer, to the zoo and the circus in the winter, to the Pujo fairs in the autumn, for Choitro-sale shopping in the spring before Poila Boishakh. At bedtime, he told stories in the way his grandma had told them when they were children, modulating the voice, high and low, soft and loud, words and gibberish, princely tales from *Rajkahini*, nonsense verses from *Abol-Tabol*.

It is difficult to say what drew Sukumar to this project so much, made him throw himself in headfirst. Did the child fill a vacuum that had started to form, as many middle-aged adults may feel, a primeval urge to pass on their talents and teachings, to find a way to keep themselves alive after they're gone? Or did his devotion to the boy ensure that X stayed close, the promise of love melded with the reality of duties? Or was it not that visceral or strategic at all, was it far simpler, that Sukumar just wanted to be like everyone else, to be part of this game of playing house that the whole world seemed to be so immersed in; perhaps X's son finally gave Sukumar the licence to feel normal?

But dreams are strains of a melody that we hum in our heads; and not all melodies take the form of songs the world might sing. As much as Sukumar tried to keep the notes together, put them into a progression, slot them into verses and chorus, they scattered, fought each other, became contorted. By the time X's son left six years later, the melody had disintegrated into cacophony.

Sukumar's mother was opposed to the arrangement from the beginning, and as the years went by, she became implacable in her resistance. Perhaps she had intuited what Sukumar's relationship with X really was, perhaps she felt guilty for leaving it unacknowledged all this time it had been unfolding before her eyes, perhaps she recognized that this was her last chance to save her son from this perversion, before it was too late; it already was very late, X's son was in their home! She thought back to the day of Sukumar's birth, the light that had suffused everything when she'd opened her eyes and they'd handed her the baby, her husband's radiant face next to her, flushed from having rushed out of court where he'd left a case midway when he'd got the news. Sukumar, their firstborn, their son, how much joy he'd brought to them, how much prestige; *barrister-babu's wife has given birth to a boy*, was the word around town. She wished now that she had more power over him, like other mothers seemed to have over their sons. She wished she could get him married. But X's influence was like tantra. If Sukumar's father were alive, he'd whip things back into shape without raising a finger; he made everything look so effortless.

Still, she obliged, for the sake of Sukumar, for her role in the household. She woke up early to cook, made bhaat and maach and torkari for the boy and Sukumar to eat before they left, then something for the boy's tiffin, something else for when he came back in the afternoon. She dropped the boy off every morning, collected him once school was over. In between, she washed and ironed his clothes, folded and arranged them, tidied his room up. But she never spoke to him if she could help it. At dinner, she missed the light-hearted conversations between mother and son; the boy was now in their sights all the time. While clearing up, she gave Sukumar long lists of all the chores she'd done during the day, told him how her back ached, how her joints cracked. 'Don't you see how he's pawning his son off on you? Are we so rich that we can afford to bring up other people's children?' Her tone was adversarial. It was true; X paid for his son's education, but not for his upkeep.

'Are we going to keep track of what it costs to feed a child?' Sukumar retorted. He knew that his mother's health and happiness were part of the price. The truths she brought up only scratched at these wounds further, made him feel guilty and irascible. For the first time, he felt the beginnings of a tear in his relationship with his mother. He'd always taken her presence for granted, believed that they had a bond that no one else could breach; but he could see that she didn't understand this side of him, or if she did, she didn't want for him what he wanted for himself. His private life with X had never interfered with his home life, but now this constricted house had become their battleground.

With the years, X himself had grown wiry, his body shrinking laterally. His kind of ageing was the opposite of Sukumar's, who had gained weight, his cheeks puffy, belly rounded, skin oily, no grey yet in his curls. X had bags under his eyes, his thinning hair had gone peppery, sticking out like tiny horns on the sides of his head. He'd taken up a second job as an insurance salesman; the *Jugantor* press didn't pay enough to sustain a family. The boarding house had been torn down to make way for a block of flats, and X now lived as a paying guest on the outskirts of the city; his commute took nearly two hours, a local train then a bus then a walk. His magnetism had dwindled, as had his libido.

And though he visited a few times a week at least, occasions made increasingly agonizing by Sukumar's mother's unguarded chagrin, he didn't want to lock his son out of the room, or go on a walk with Sukumar, or watch a film. Instead, he spent more time with the boy as he grew, teaching him how to draw, his skills as an illustrator showing in the expert flicks of his wrist, the cartoons he made that had the boy in fits. At times, X was so tired that he'd lie on the bed and fall asleep, and his son would join him in his nap, head nestled in his armpit like a well-fitting puzzle piece. Sukumar sat by the bed and watched as father and son breathed in and out in sync. Was he part of this? Was he meant to be? Could he claim it? If he couldn't, what was he doing here?

But the most strident false note in Sukumar's delusive melody was X's son himself. The boy never warmed to Sukumar and his mother. Despite everything they did for him, he kept his distance. In some way, he seemed to blame

Sukumar for taking him away from his home, his own mother. And who knows, maybe he could tell what his father and Sukumar had going on, that they were not friends, that the time they spent locked in the room when X visited was not to talk politics and art. After all, didn't children's senses pick up more than adults' did?

As the boy grew, from six to seven to eight, he started coming into his own. He demanded things, skipped home-work, lazed around. He was a brat, showing no respect to Sukumar or his mother. After their studies in the evenings, he insisted on going to the neighbour's to watch TV, asked Sukumar why they didn't have enough money to own a TV themselves. When X visited, the boy had a list of complaints ready for his father: the room was too small, the fan too slow, there were power cuts often, the city had no open spaces. It was as though X's wife was coaching her son to disrupt Sukumar's house of cards when the boy visited the District every weekend.

But what Sukumar didn't get from X's son all year, he got from his nephew in the few short days he visited from the Garden City every summer.

Sukumar's little nephew was growing fast; he had started school. Every time Sukumar saw the boy, it was like meeting a new person: new height, new vocabulary, new ways, new talents. Mamu, he called Sukumar, 'Maaaa-moooo!' Sukumar watched as the boy learnt to sing Rabindrasangeet perfectly in tune; one summer, he performed 'Khoro Baayu Boy Bege' for the neighbours on the terrace. As the summers came and went, and the boy drew, painted, danced, acted out roles of Ram and Sita and Ravan from the *Ramayan* TV serial, Sukumar saw more of himself in the child. The boy couldn't catch a ball, couldn't run fast, had no interest in sports; instead, he sat mesmerized for hours listening to stories, memorized what he'd heard on the radio, repeated the dialogues verbatim.

His sister had given birth again a couple of years later, and now Sukumar had a niece too. The little girl had a mind of her own; she ordered her brother around, set the rules of their games, broke them with aplomb and swanned her way out of trouble. When they visited, X's son, his nephew and niece would form a gleeful trio, X's son becoming a different person around the other children, exhilarated, burdenless, playing elder brother to younger siblings. They ran around the house, climbed up and down the stairs, staged plays, joined Sukumar in his morning prayers when he chanted mantras and lit dhoop. Sukumar had converted the small room next to the terrace into his pujor ghor, decorating the walls and shelves with idols and pictures of gods and goddesses, Vishnu and Parvati and Shiva and Ganesh and Venkateshwara and Jagannath and Nataraj and Nagaraj. But his favourite was Bal-Gopal, the child version of Krishna, whom he placed on a brass bed mounted with miniature bedding, stuck a peacock feather in his crown, and put to sleep every night.

Sukumar's favourite part of these holidays was taking the children to the ghat. The evenings were cool after the day's heat, the river mellow, the trees lush. He sat on his bench, the one that he and X used to frequent, and watched the children make a ruckus, cracking potty jokes, hanging from the roots of the banyan tree, bumping into passers-by without saying sorry. In the absence of his sister and his mother, both disciplinarians, he let the children be, bought them what they asked for, turning into a child himself, clapping and singing. On those dazzling summer evenings, as the sun dipped behind the outlines of the opposite bank and the celestial vista unfurled, his life seemed consecrated; he let himself believe that he was the proud father of three children, each of them a young star twinkling in the sky just for him. He could tell that people around were soaking up this blessed scene, and he basked in the aura of their admiration for those few hours.

One such evening, he took the children to the station, him holding his niece's hand, X's son holding his nephew's. They boarded the Chokro-rail that went around the banks of the river in a circular loop. He showed the children the map on the platform, then asked them to remember the names of the stations in the right order; he would quiz them at the end of the journey. When they alighted again at their stop, it was only his nephew who could recite all the names, counting them off his fingers one by one. 'Bagbazar, Sovabazar, BBD Bag, Eden Gardens, Prinsep Ghat . . .' The names sounded funny in his tinny voice, his Bangla had the affectation of someone who had not grown up in the Grand Old City, but he could see the pride the boy felt when the other two stared at him slack-jawed, envious. Sukumar ruffled his nephew's hair. 'Achha-achha, okay now, you little show-off!' And a sob rose in his throat, thinking of the emptiness this child would leave behind when he left for the Garden City at the end of the holidays.

One summer, on the last night before his sister was due to take the train back, brother and sister went to watch a movie, the children being put to bed by his mother. Sukumar had made sure he stopped by Minar cinema after work, paid more than he could afford to secure good balcony seats in advance. Even though she was all grown up now, a mother of two, she was still his little sister.

Parama was about a woman in her forties, married and with children, who falls for a much younger photographer. There were scenes of the couple after they'd clearly had sex, and while Bengali intellectuals could bring themselves to accept adultery in the form of love, the reviews had criticized the primacy of sex in the relationship. Could the woman not have just loved? Why did she have to give her body?

'What did you think?' Sukumar asked his sister on their way back. The evening was balmy. They'd never walked like this before, side by side, leisurely, at night. Before she got married, they'd had separate lives outdoors; she'd had too many restrictions to go out for a night show, even with her brother.

'I think it's all right, I mean, for a woman to fall in love with someone else,' his sister said. 'Her husband was always busy, her children had grown up, she was alone and purposeless.'

Sukumar had always admired his sister's ability to fit her life into the rules. How had brother and sister, only two years apart, with the exact same upbringing, grown up to be so different? 'And what if the woman wasn't neglected or bored?' he challenged. 'What if she'd fallen in love with this man? Should she not do anything about it?'

His sister looked surprised. She had perhaps thought she was already being forward by endorsing the adultery. She considered his challenge. 'But what did it get her in the end? Shame? Ostracization? Even her own children wouldn't talk to her! And why the sex? Why does everything have to end up there?'

'But . . .' Sukumar knew he was pushing boundaries. 'Attraction cannot be compartmentalized. One doesn't fall with the heart and not the body.' He kept walking, not turning to look at her. If he knew her at all, she'd already perceived what he was really trying to say.

His sister was ready with her defence. 'We can't just do what we wish all the time, na? Where would the world end up then? And what about those who love us, depend on us?'

They walked quietly for the rest of the way. When they got home, there was a sense that the conversation wasn't over yet.

His sister asked Sukumar if he fancied a stroll on the terrace. Brother and sister stood by the wall, their elbows resting on the prickly concrete.

'Remember you used to get me library books after school?' she said. 'And I used to stand here waiting, so excited, trying to guess what book you'd be bringing!'

Sukumar hmmed. That seemed such a long time ago. So much had happened since.

'This . . . friend of yours, and his wife, they don't want their son to live with them?'

Sukumar had had a foreboding that this was coming. 'They don't have a house in the city like we do. We should help where we can, na?'

'The child is not an orphan. Your friend doesn't even pay for his son's upkeep.'

'So Ma has been talking to you then.' Sukumar wasn't surprised, only that it had taken so many summers for his sister to broach this.

'Ma is old. She can't keep up. It's a lot of work bringing up a child. I know, I'm bringing up two myself . . .'

'What if I had a child? Would Ma say the same about her grandson?'

'But he isn't your child!' There was a rare insolence about her tonight. 'He's going to grow up and go away. Other people's children are not . . .' She stopped herself, steadied, then put a hand on his arm. 'I just want you to be happy. This . . . this . . . *friend* of yours, what if he's taking advantage of you? How much have you done for him, and what has he given you in return?'

He's given me love! Why shouldn't that be enough? Sukumar felt himself clench, his muscles, his fist, his jaws, his heart. All the words he couldn't tell her, all those feelings they didn't have the vocabulary for, all the things they didn't have the courage to speak out loud, were circulating through his veins, making it difficult to breathe.

'Please don't tell Ma I spoke to you about this. She wasn't complaining, shotti . . .'

If his mother wasn't complaining, what was she doing? Going behind his back to her daughter the moment she got a chance? Why was everyone always conspiring against him, commenting on his ways, considering his options, deciding what was good for him, what was not?

'You remember that truck driver at Baba's funeral?' His sister looked away, wistful. Sukumar nodded, of course he did. At their father's funeral, a man had appeared, crying. He'd introduced himself, said that he had been in an accident with his truck that had killed someone rich, but it wasn't his fault, it was the rich man's car that had swerved. He'd been arrested, kept in remand without bail for weeks. He didn't know how, but barrister-babu had heard of him, sought him out, offered to represent him for free. The case had gone on for months, but barrister-babu wouldn't give up, and had finally got him exonerated. *I'm a free man today*, he'd wept profusely, *I'm alive, and barrister-babu is dead. Where is the justice in this?*

'We may not have money, we may live in this small house, but our family has a name in society,' Sukumar's sister said. 'To the world, you are still barrister-babu's son. What you do reflects on his reputation . . .'

Then she turned to him. 'Maybe you should think about getting married? You're over thirty-five now. You could have your own children then.'

'Do you think . . .' Sukumar started, nervous about what he was going to say; he'd thought this many times, but he was now ready to utter the words. 'Do you think we remember Baba as this saintlike figure because he died so young?'

He looked at the wall, the heat rising in his cheeks. 'Do you think . . . if he'd lived longer, we'd see his flaws too?'

'What are you saying?' His sister's voice hit him like a volley. 'How can you say that about Baba?' Sukumar had rattled the unflagging fealty she'd held for their father; there was no space for any other man on the pedestal she'd built for him, not her husband, nor brother, perhaps not even her son.

'Ma was always so strict with me because I was a girl. She married me off right after graduation. You know how badly I wanted to do a Masters. So many of my friends have jobs – teachers, journalists, in banks, finishing PhDs . . . And here I am, BA First Class with Honours in Political Science, doing housework all day long!' She paused to catch her breath. 'And Ma pampered you so much, her darling boy, her shona chhele. Everyone warned her, said she should be stricter with you. Well, look who's breaking her heart now!'

She moved away, conscious she'd said too much, then mumbled, 'I should sleep. The train is early in the morning.'

Sukumar stood on the terrace late into the night, staring at the lights in the *Jugantor* office, listening to the hum of the printing press dishing out last-minute copies of tomorrow's daily. His life felt like a sailor perpetually in a storm, knowingly voyaging into its eye, clinging to the mast, trimming the sail, holding the boat down against the towering tides, rowing the oars on the high waters. Yes, this was a deranged enterprise, it wasn't that he couldn't see what everyone was seeing. But what was the way out? How high was the price of living this fantasy?

As a boy, he used to be able to make everyone happy; but now, had he become a monster, hurting his mother, alienating his sister, tarnishing his father's legacy? Or was he a wimp, being exploited by his lover?

Or was he simply lost, trying to ask for help but not knowing the words for it?

Mambro's Manuscript

It is still early in the new millennium, and you are back in the Mountains for the next semester.

This part of your story deserves to be told in the way it is woven into the tapestry of your memory, a shifting blend of colours and patterns, wide stretches of nothingness, and every time you will try to look, which won't be very often, a new design will spring up, frayed threads, embroidery undone, termites hollowing the fabric out.

But your story is not for you to hold on to. It exists for those to whom it is being told, and for their sake, you will attempt a chronology, a sequencing of events, shoehorning them into cause-and-effect, however jumbled the result, however insurmountable the task.

You're drinking with friends in the university hostel; it is night; one of the seniors says the best way to get properly sloshed is to tap a cigarette into a drink, let the ash mix with the whisky; the rest of you are shaking your heads, *no fucking way, that's gross*, but you're doing it anyway, too curious now to not try; you can't taste the ash when you take a sip, only a damp charred smell, and you gulp it down, your fingertips holding your nostrils shut. When you wake up, there's no one else in the room, it's hours since you were drinking; you stumble to the bathroom, throw up, go back to sleep . . .

Everyone's being weird; there's no proof, no one's said anything, but you know this because you're no novice, you've been sequestered for too many years when you were younger not to know when it's happening again; you're hyper-alert, your senses working overtime, noticing every unlooked look, every unsmiled smile, every unraised eyebrow. Yet there is an air of civility, you're still friends with your friends, the boy with the nasal voice, the one with the egg head, the one with the overbite; you go to the canteen together for dinner, watch TV in the common room, do your assignments . . .

Some people stop talking to you; just stop, blinds pulled down. Others take the circuitous route when they see you, go down the slope and back up when there's a bridge they could have crossed. Others gulp their food like water when you join them at the table. Sometimes you sit all by yourself in your room after dinner; usually at this time, the boys would catch up, hang out, shoot the breeze; *seriously, where is everyone* . . .

The fragile boy from the north-eastern state turns up one day, apparently he's in the dean's office with his father, he went home and told his dad everything; the dad won't take this, he's paid the first year's fees in full; so he's brought his son back, he will complain against the bullies, he swears he'll see them rusticated, their futures destroyed; when the dean asks for names, yours is on the list . . .

An argument breaks out in the hostel, a blame-game cluster-fuck, everyone screaming, *you approached him first, it was your idea, I'd said let's not rag him, I didn't even go close to him*; you're there too, hotly debating, disavowing yourself of responsibility, as you have to do to save your ass; you're deep in the screaming match when you hear someone from behind you, *easy-peasy, the homo bullied the homo, why should the rest of us get involved* . . . You don't know who said it, you want to turn and look but you can't, your body has petrified; you know that if you look the person in the eye, what was said will now be heard . . .

For days, you think and think, jog your brain cells, trying to decode how your reputation has caught up with you in this new place; you signed up for the game, played by the rules, had winning streaks, you were runner-up Mr Fresher for fuck's sake; then how, what did you do wrong, where did your guard slip; you're Jason Bourne and your cover is blown . . .

The north-eastern boy's father hasn't left; he's taken up a hotel room opposite the campus; he visits the dean daily to remind him of his duty; the boy comes to campus only for classes, spends the rest of his time in the hotel room with his father; you see him sometimes in the corridors and library; this time, it is you who hits the wall and drags your body along the concrete; he does the same, both of you scared of each other . . .

There is another fight in the hostel, pointing fingers, it is past midnight, everyone is high or drunk, the dean has called all of you to his office the next day; this time, the side of you you'd discovered in the Mountains comes forth, that fearless street-smart boy you'd invented makes an appearance, loses his cool, issues a vague threat, like, *yeah I'll beat you up too* . . .

It's flimflam, you're the last person to beat anyone up, every-one knows this; this is the first time you've lost your cool with anyone other than your sister and mother and Y, you've never shown your temper to a gang of straight boys; after this night, you will learn never to do so again, the straight boys can't bear to hear this from a homo, *what the fuck, you'll beat us up, yeah?*

Mayhem erupts, curses are bandied around, fists are bran-dished, feet dance in angry steps, closing in on you, you're surrounded from all sides; a circle is not a geometric shape, it is an amorphous living beast that will obliterate you . . .

You're stuttering, retching inside; you know you've over-stepped, all your impulses were wrong, your fastidious self-training of years has failed; you can't breathe, this circle is pushing at your body, hands come forward to swat at you . . .

Your hand is pulled, you don't know how but you're out of the circle, the whites of the tube-lights sit heavy on your eyelids, you will get your first migraine that night, it will become a chronic condition, but right now you're just being led down the corridor, feet breaking into a run; you're pushed into a room, the door is locked . . .

The friend – it's difficult to tell who's a friend right now, but let's go with it – the friend who salvaged you and locked you up in his room is back; *where's everyone*, you ask; *they're in your room, they're having a discussion*; if it were another time, you'd laugh at the formality of it, a panchayat meeting, village elders sitting on a dais deciding the fate of the truant; you ask what has happened, why has everyone stopped talking to you; your friend – and now you sense he really is a friend, he's the only one here – says, *they found your journal, they read it, they've been reading it every night after dinner, it's been going from hand to hand, group to group* . . .

How, you ask, you've kept your journal under lock and key, how did they know where it was, how did they get the key off you, how did they know it even existed . . . The friend shrugs, he doesn't know the details, *just sleep here tonight, don't go back to your room*; he locks the door from the outside again, you hear his footsteps receding . . .

You think you will not sleep a wink, you stay awake for hours fighting the migraine, an arc of pain like a wreath around your head, then you fall into a deep slumber, your body refusing to carry on any longer, it needs to rest, it has needed rest for many years now . . .

Next morning, dean's office; you on one side, the remaining names on the list on the other, battlelines drawn; they're telling the dean it was you from the start, your masterplan to barge into the boy's room, to prank him, test his mettle; they swear they didn't quite know what was happening, never initiated anything, none of the tricks was theirs . . .

The dean is shaking his head, as though he has no inkling of what goes on in the hostel, making it look like ragging happens elsewhere, in uncouth colleges, not here, in these hallowed halls of enlightenment; he knows he's fucked, ragging is banned by law, if the boy's father complains to the police, there will be a formal investigation, the media will descend on the campus, the university's name will be in the newspapers . . .

You want to defend yourself, say it was the whole gang, by any stretch of common sense, it couldn't have been just you, a group activity pre-requires a group, a mob is not a singular noun; but you gulp your spit down and stare at the floor, you can't afford to antagonize the gang, you don't know what will happen tonight . . .

Nothing happens that night; the mob is tired, the mob needs rest; the mob has other things to do; you're not the centre of the mob's consciousness, even if they are yours . . .

Your room-mate says he's going to start sleeping in a friend's room, you will need to find another room-mate at the end of the semester, he makes up an excuse about how he and his friend go back in time, went to the same school in their hilly town etc. etc., you don't know why he's even bothering, you're already agreeing to everything he's saying . . .

You eat alone in the canteen, sleep alone in your room, study alone in the library, sit alone during breaks; you find workarounds, like going to the canteen at seven-fifteen when the doors open, so you can wolf down the food and leave before the boys come in, like asking your parents to call in the afternoons when people are in classes, like going off to the closest town to watch an outdated movie in the cinema, then eating entire bars of Cadbury's Crackle with a view of the Himalayas . . .

More titbits trickle in, snatches of information, you're piecing together your own story from other people's scraps; it was the night you got drunk on whisky-and-ash and passed out that they fished out your keys and scoured through your bag to find your journal; no one will name names but the egg-headed boy, one of your closest friends before all this, seems to have led the mission; you never thought of him as a leader, more a court jester; but jesters will do anything for a few moments in the sun . . .

You try to materialize the journal in front of your eyes, recreate your handwriting in blue ink on the lined pages; you wonder if you named Y, it was written so long ago; you want to ask for the journal back just to check how graphic the entries were; the world is now getting off on what you wrote only for yourself, and you don't even remember what's in there . . .

Your letters to your sister become longer though nothing of substance ever makes it on to the page; she has started university, she is having a great time, she uses words like *dude* and *yo*; you can tell her world is opening up, the nuns are receding into their habits, there are more and more boys being mentioned, you wonder if she's having a crush on one of them, the thought of innocent love warms you up in the cold, makes you think of that afternoon in the cinema with Y . . .

Does Y know what's happening with you, does he know your love story is now public property, walls of old factories pasted with posters, drunkards taking their distended cocks out and pissing all over it?

★

Courage seems to be the only thing you're left with, courage to wake up, courage to go to the canteen for meals, courage to attend class, courage to come face-to-face with the mob, courage to sit in your room alone; there are no *safe spaces* for you, though you don't know this term yet; you don't know where this bottomless reserve is, you're hoping it doesn't run out, you know it will . . .

Courage also takes you to the hotel where the north-eastern boy and his dad are staying; the dad is surprised but leads you to the balcony where the son is sitting; the boy seems bereaved, though everything is going his way now, he's shamed the shamers . . .

You sit next to the boy and say you're sorry, that's all you have to say, you're so sorry; you know how convenient this sounds, of course you've come to apologize now that you're in trouble; you ask him to return to the hostel; by some absurd dint of optimism, you promise to take care of him, you aren't sure where all this is coming from, at a time when you can't even take care of yourself; the boy just stares out into the blur of the verdant conifers . . .

But the dad has visibly softened, puts a hand on your shoulder, *you shouldn't do all this, na beta, you should stay together like friends, all of you are here to build your futures*; yes yes yes, you nod along, *you're right, uncle, totally, please forgive me*; the dad can't promise anything, the dean is already looking into the issue, but at least you come away feeling like your courage was worth the while . . .

Some more time goes by, you don't know how long, but one afternoon the boy sees you in the park, sitting alone feeding crisps to the pigeons, and comes up to you; his turn to show courage, once upon a time he hit the wall to keep his distance from you; *I'm leaving the university, I think I'm better off in my hometown*, he says; you stare at his moon face, his slight frame; *we've withdrawn our complaint, the dean is relieved, there won't be an investigation*; in another world, his frailty could be beautiful; in another world, you could be lovers, you could kiss him and take him to bed right now; *I just wanted to tell you myself that I'm going, so that you don't think it's because of you, last time it was, this time it's not . . .*

You don't say anything, the boy sits next to you on the bench; you both look at the pigeons, they're industriously pecking, a bully wings away another bird, goes scuttling for a morsel; you ask the boy why he's leaving; he replies softly, 'This place is not for me . . .'

This place is not for me either, you think . . .

But you live in that place for three more years. Three years equals thirty-six months equals 1,096 days, leap year included, equals 26,304 hours equals 1,578,240 minutes; that is 24,675,840 breaths at the palpitation rate. Rounded off, you give twenty-five million breaths of your life to that place . . .

Last days of semester exams are the worst; on those nights, the hostel resembles a prison riot; bottles are thrown, names are called, mothers' sex lives are invoked, doors are kicked down, fisticuffs ensue, boys pretend-rape boys to amicable hoots from the audience; you ask the friend to lock you in your room . . .

No, people's birthdays are the worst; they lift the birthday boy up, two at the armpits, two at the legs, and kick his butt like he doesn't have to take a shit the next day; before they begin, they check if he's hidden a book in his trousers to pad up his backside; you ask the friend to lock you in your room . . .

No actually, college fests are the worst; the days are spent outside flirting with girls from visiting colleges and guzzling beer; the nights are spent on the prowl, hunting for meat to butcher; you ask your friend to lock you in your room . . .

In spite of all the locking, they find ways to get in . . .

They break eggs on your head; you stand in the lobby, your teeth chattering, trying to smile through the yolk dripping down your face, a sporting participant in this ribaldry . . .

They pour water on you from the upper floors; one time, taken unawares, you slip, your head hits the railings, you're nearly falling down the stairs, you grip the banister at the last minute . . .

They leave a rabid stray dog in your room; you wake up in the dark to quick animal breathing on your room-mate's bed, and when you switch on the light, the dog is as jolted as you are; it jumps straight at you, claws out . . .

You're leaving class, someone runs up to you and pins you against the wall and hits your face, again again again; you've never been in a fight, you don't know how it feels, how the nose is the first organ to give in and bleed . . .

You never get up onstage again, not in the Mountains, not anywhere you will live in the future; Mr Freshers come and go, singing competitions start and finish, but you're not onstage; you're not even in the audience . . .

Some acts are public, require collective action; some others are private, performed alone, without witnesses . . .

You step out of your room and on to human excrement, the splatter of fresh faeces on your legs still warm; it hasn't been brought here from elsewhere, someone's relieved themselves in front of your door; you miss classes and spend the day cleaning up . . .

There's HOMO sprayed on your door; you make a rag out of one of your T-shirts, dip it in soapy water, not sure where to get kerosene, who to ask for it, and start scrubbing it off ferociously; the boys walk past, face muscles held tight as their bellies crunch in hilarity . . .

It won't come off easily; when you're tired, you start again the next day, waking up early, then the next morning, then again the next, until there are only traces of the paint, HOMO still clearly discernible; it will remain on your door every day of those three years . . .

You're walking down an empty corridor, humming a tune, nothing bad has happened in a while, maybe the mob is running out of ideas; you turn the corner, a shout, 'Aye chhakke' . . .

You're walking down an empty corridor, not humming this time, it's dark, you don't want to attract attention; a shadow is walking towards you; the hand reaches out, gropes your butt, scratches your chest, bumps your head against the wall, continues walking in unhurried steps, knowing you aren't going to call for help . . .

You're walking down an empty corridor, your feet pattering in barely audible tiptoes; you shouldn't be out, there's been a party tonight, but you've stayed locked in your room for hours, missed dinner, so you're trying to find some food; a body steps out of a room, tall, bulk filling out the outlines, stands in front of you, turns you around so you're facing the wall, rips your shirt in one quick movement, rubs itself against your back, bends down and bites your shoulder, groans in pleasure, leaves; the teeth imprints take weeks to dissolve into your skin, the semen on the trousers is like starch gone rotten . . .

In later years, you will learn about *fight or flight*, the only two responses people apparently have to shock; but you aren't fighting back, you aren't fleeing; what are you doing then?

Since your mind has gone limp, your body is learning to show up for itself; you're at lunch, many boys sitting at the long dining table of the canteen, Egg-head is there too; he makes an offhand comment about you, *maagi*, a derogatory term for a woman; everyone cackles; a current passes through your hands, you pick up the tumbler and throw water on his egg head; you're so shocked by your own action that the tumbler leaves your hand, hits the table, drops to the floor, steel clashing on tile; the canteen goes quiet, Egg-head has his mouth open, lines of damp on his ellipsoidal shell . . .

After the rubbing on your backside in the corridor, other rubbers have appeared, as though there is an underground network of them, and word has spread among their ranks; they turn up at your door, start by making conversation, hi hello this that, then suddenly their hamstrings are pulled, shoulders are stiff, necks are aching, will you give them a massage? Some are more direct, the repeat visitors drop the prelude soon enough, then they're rubbing, rubbing, heaving, leaving . . .

Some go beyond, *suck me, stroke me, pinch me, slap me*; sometimes you lean in to kiss them, most turn away, but some surrender, lips wet, tongues dry from seduction and sin . . .

You have started to enjoy the rubbing; you are twenty, twenty-one, twenty-two; your body needs sex, needs warmth, needs touch, you will take whatever you can get; and you feel a power over them, the power to give them what they can't get anywhere else, the only power you've felt in this place . . .

After the rubber leaves, you masturbate thinking of Y, his taste of milk, the curled hair on his forearms, his eyes as he looked at you earnestly while inside you . . .

Where is Y, is he going through what you're going through, are they doing this to him too, he was named in your journal after all; you don't dare to contact him; if they haven't got to him yet, you must protect him, you've already made enough trouble for him . . .

In the moments when you are not a target, life unfolds with a normalcy that is terrifyingly deceptive; the friend takes you to his group of friends, they are nice boys, they don't say anything about the mayhem or what ensues; there is a deadpan detachment, as though it were happening to someone else, they don't know who . . .

Yet they welcome you into the group, you go to the canteen for dinner, hang out with them; they're a good bunch, slightly nerdy, mostly from small towns or the suburbs; their sense of humour is direct, their interests basic, but they're there whenever you want to be around people . . .

You find a room-mate, surprised that anyone is willing to throw their lot in with you; you're a well-adjusted pair, he's geeky to a fault, not exactly socially adept; he's a fan of Madhuri Dixit and so are you, so you talk about her movies and dances, even buy posters of *Devdas* one afternoon and tape them to your walls; he's the one you will live with for three years . . .

You devour the literature in the library, novels and novellas and short-story collections and anthologies; you read when you can, you read what you get; it is an act of resistance, it is an act of self-alienation; no one here reads, reading makes you different, makes you look intelligent; maybe the mob will stop if they see a book in your hand; you know you're asking for too much, but sometimes, it does work . . .

Among the many books you bury your face in over those three years, there's James Baldwin's *Giovanni's Room*, E. M. Forster's *Maurice*, Gore Vidal's *The City and the Pillar*; you wonder why these books were never mentioned in your school; there is a spring in your step, a surge in your spirit; there are people like you all over the world, you're not alone . . .

You're still looking for Ismat Chughtai's short story of two women desiring each other, 'Lihaaf'; it's not in this library either; you won't ask for it obviously; you will have to wait until you can have a bookshelf of your own, you will put it out front-facing, honour it with pride of place . . .

You learn from the internet, which you use more and more in the computer lab, that 'Lihaaf' is the only known queer literature from South Asia in modern times, first published in 1942; you imagine this woman writing the story in Urdu, dipping her fountain pen in a pot of ink, at a time when the country wasn't even independent; you read up about the court case against her, *Ismat Chughtai Vs The Crown*, on the basis of indecency, the invective-filled letters she received, the pressure on her to apologize, and her not capitulating to any of it, refusing to pay the fine, courting arrest instead; this is the closest you've come to finding a role model . . .

And where were the men, where are they now, all those gay writers and actors and scientists and businessmen, for decades, centuries, keeping their truths knotted up, co-opted into the shroud of secrecy, bought into the sham of shame? In your country, and in most like yours, there are no legends of Oscar Wildes and Alan Turings, no documents, no recorded history, you only have your uncle's fragmented account to go by . . .

On the internet, you come across Section 377, the Victorian law that makes men having sex with men a punishable offence; the British got rid of it in 1967, *pardoned* the *offenders*, most posthumously; but the ex-colonies have held on, like so many other things, the English language, the class hierarchies, the preponderance of government, lack of accountability among politicians and bureaucrats, discrimination against the darker-skinned; the law still retains the same number, 3 7 7, in India, Pakistan, Singapore, Malaysia, Bangladesh, Brunei; it can get you a sentence of up to seven years; no one has told you about this, it was absent in the school and college syllabi; education withheld is education denied . . .

You realize you're not only a weirdo, an outcast, a body to rub against; above all those things, you're a criminal, your rightful place is in prison . . .

You always make sure to clear your search history before leaving the lab . . .

Your room comes with a narrow balcony; it looks out on a mountain-face, the slope sectioned off into steps for terrace farming; in the afternoons, as you're sat at your table, you see local children harvesting crops, slightly bent from the weight of the conical baskets on their backs, held by bands of cloth over their heads; you don't know if they go to school; sometimes they let the baskets drop and run through the patches, arms spread wide, jumping across the levels, playing hide-and-seek; their cackles make you want to join them; when you're on the balcony, they wave to you and you wave back . . .

Your results get better every semester; maybe because there's nothing else to apply yourself to but studying, maybe because you know it's the only thing that will get you out of here with your head held high . . .

You direct a play; at first you're just watching people rehearse, but the script is awful, the lines cringy, the acting terrible; so you proffer suggestions, *maybe you can say this, how about you stand behind her, yes turn to the audience now, remember the character is in love*, and suddenly you're the de facto director, it's happened without anyone asking you to; when the play is staged, the amphitheatre resounds with claps that won't stop, they haven't seen anything as good in years, amateurs putting on something so professional; you remain backstage, soaking in the applause, you've vowed never to go onstage again, you won't; but the actors have announced your name as director; the dean is so impressed he invites the entire troupe to his place for tea . . .

The next semester, you're asked to direct another play; this time, you write the script, audition actors, schedule rehearsals, sketch the set out; you're captain of the ship, the sailors obey your orders without question; when the ship docks successfully, people come to shake your hand; there are mobsters among them; you register that this is the first time they're touching your body with no intention to harm . . .

You go home after every semester, spend a month of holidays; your sister is now a young woman, she has many friends, they're a nice bunch, you hang out with them sometimes; your sister thinks you're happy, your parents think you're happy; for that one month, you also think you're happy . . .

When you leave again to start a new semester, your parents come to the station to see you off, without fail; your sister is never there because she can't bear to see you leaving, always making an excuse to stay home; as the train puffs its way out, and your insides implode at the thought of what's to come, your father starts to walk quicker, keeping pace so he can see you for as long as possible in the window; your mother doesn't move, getting smaller on the platform as the train gathers speed, her hand waving long after you've gone out of sight . . .

And that's enough for you to not tell them; this is still the walled-in fortress of your childhood; if there were a safe space for you, it is here, with your family; you will not contaminate it with your dirt . . .

And you will not let your parents believe that what they feared all your life, that you will turn out like your Mamu, has come true; insult and ignominy written on the lines of your palms . . .

You will not end up like your Mamu, dead . . .

Your mother calls to give you the news, *Mamu is no more*; you don't mourn his death; you are incapable of grief, in fact you are incapable of feelings; you are in the throes of the mayhem in the Mountains, you can't afford tears, grieving his end would mean grieving your life, opening a portal up to glimpse your own finish line . . .

If anything, you resent Mamu for giving up so easily, for never holding your hand and guiding you through the darkness that only he would understand, for never seeing himself in the reflection of your brimming eyes, and you in his . . .

You miss Mamu's funeral; there has been a landslide in the Mountains, all roads are closed, no one knows how long the repair and rescue works will take; you try to find a way, request the dean, make calls to travel agencies, aren't there jeeps that are bringing over essential supplies, aren't army and BRO officials crossing the slush, can you maybe join one of those groups? But in the end, you back down; this was not to be . . .

For months after Mamu's death, you go to a Buddhist temple in the Mountains, close to campus, your thoughts meandering, not always about Mamu; sometimes there are no thoughts at all, the blankness refreshing; but before you leave, you always recite the Vishnu-stotra he taught you . . . *Shantakaram bhujagashayanam padmanabham suresham* . . .

And you never wear the blue jacket he gave you, even though it is cold in the Mountains, the winters are harsh, icy, sometimes there's snow, your only source of warmth is a single-rod heater glowing in a corner of your room; but there is something about the fluff of the fleece, the electric-blue colour that you know will grab the mob's attention, bring you back to their notice in the periods they've forgotten about you; so the jacket remains packed in its newspaper wrapping inside your suitcase, which is where it stays for the three and a half years . . .

And just like that, it is the end of university; your twenty-five million breaths are coming to an end; if this were a few decades later, your Apple Watch would notify you . . .

In those last few days, you allow yourself to relax; there is a lot of drinking and merrymaking, formal and informal, on campus and in the hostel; you attend some of this, always using your inner radar first to assess where you should and shouldn't be, can and can't be . . .

On the penultimate night, you return to your room, your vision swaying, your head giddy; you're feeling positive, you imagine this is how a prisoner feels after decades of incarceration; an era gone by, a life wasted, a candlewick nearly burnt out, but there is still a little life left . . .

You lie down on the bed, nearly doze off; but when the door opens, you're alert, your reflexes have kicked in, your vision is like crystal even though the lights are out . . .

Egg-head walks in; he's never been to your room before, but he knows his way, all the rooms are alike; he knows you're on your bed, knows you're wide awake; he shuffles closer and snaps his fingers, points to the bathroom . . .

You get up and follow; you're not swaying any more, not unclear about what you're doing, you know why he's taking you in there; in the bathroom, the light is on, but he's okay with that, he will do what he's here to do in the jarring glare of the tube-light . . .

You will remember this with an uncharacteristic clarity; how you went down on him, how he dragged you up by your hair, turned you around, held you against the wall, your cheek against the cold tile, how he pulled your pants down, how he went in, in and out, in and out . . .

You will remember this with even more uncharacteristic clarity; his tongue in your left ear, the whole time, hungry, salivating, quivering . . .

You will not remember him leaving; you will not remember wiping and cleaning up; you will remember the migraine settling in even before he's left . . .

You will never know why you did it; you weren't attracted to him, you weren't horny, you weren't drunk out of your wits; you could have fought him, but you wouldn't need to, he had neither the heft nor the gravitas to force himself on you . . .

He will come to you one more time, on the last night; that night, you're prepared, sober, even expectant; you've left the table lamp on so that the bathroom can remain dark; you get in there when he snaps his fingers; the same events take place again, his tongue finds your left ear like old acquaintances reuniting; but you aren't wondering any more why you're doing this; by then, you've lost yourself . . .

Is it still rape if you're not saying *no*?

. . .

. . .

. . .

ENTRY FIVE

Vivaan's VoiceNote005

Hey guys. All right, look, I know we ended on quite a dark note last time, so let me start this recording with something positive.

In the two weeks after I wrote the essay and went to the gang-bang, I took control of the situation. I'd had enough! I broke up with Zee, deleted the apps from my phone, stopped watching porn. I only studied and slept. This was going to be my future, it wasn't fun, it wasn't avant-garde, but it was constructive, everything else was cock and bull. We weren't living in a parallel universe, and to make my place in this one, I needed to do well in my exams and get a degree and get a job.

When I told Zee I was done with our timeshare, he didn't say anything. I'd expected him to launch into another one of his lectures, but he just tightened his lips in this ouch sort of way, like, you know, when a posh teacher is told their star student has dropped out of school to go work on a farm? Not gonna lie, I was gutted, I'd imagined he'd be shell-shocked, destroyed, would fall to his knees, promise that things would go back to how they were before that school dance. But none of that, instead, get this, before leaving, he put out his hand for a shake, not even a hug. That got me real fired up, I smacked his hand away and said, Fuckin' A, bruh, you do you from now on, and stormed out.

That night after dinner, when Mom and I were having our chat on the balcony, the plateau seeming like a carnival of fireflies, I told her about the break-up. She kept quiet, though her face said a lot, I couldn't tell if it was concern for me, or good riddance to Zee, probably both. She said I could talk to her about it whenever I wanted, and then reminded me of my exams coming up. She said, Don't screw this up, Vivaan, that's all I'll say, you know how competitive this country is, we're not asking you to study this or that, you can pursue anything you want, but there has never been a substitute for hard work. That last bit hung in the air like bunting. Mom is in the habit of dishing out these moral one-liners, I assume they're a hangover from her convent-school head-girl days, they're kinda cute when you're in the right mood. I nodded, Yep Mom, gotcha! She smiled and ruffled my hair.

I surprised myself by calling Mambro after Mom and Dad said goodnight and went to their room. I hadn't spoken to him properly in a while, I usually butt my head into Mom's video calls and say quick hellos, but that night he and I spoke for a long time, about nothing in particular really. He was writing something, I asked if it was a novel, he was non-committal, said he didn't quite know what it was, he'd have to see how it was going to shape up. He said that once he finished writing, he'd visit some nice place by a lake, he told me how he'd always wanted to go there, he loves jumping into clear water in the summer and swimming in it, and I said it sounded fantastic. Then before hanging up, he asked what I was feeling about my split with Zee, and I started sobbing like an idiot, but I couldn't stop myself, I said I'd never ever find love like that again, he was special, these things don't happen often, and now I was meant to be on my own all my life, and even as I said it, I knew how utterly hopelessly Hollywood it sounded, and maybe Mambro was even tittering to himself, but he didn't let on, just listened.

I asked him if he'd had a teenage love story, and he said yes he did, he'd tell me all about it.

When?

Soon. My story comes with, what you kids call nowadays, a trigger warning. I'll probably have to ask your mom for permission first.

You gotta be kidding me, Mambro! You don't know the things I've done! I knew Mambro would hardly believe me if I told him about the encounters, he'd think I was spilling my fantasies.

Calm down. Let's cut a deal, yeah? Mambro was saying. How about you finish your exams and then we go on a holiday, just you and I?

That would be ace! I accepted right away.

As I fell asleep, I imagined me and Mambro sitting by the campfire, barbecuing marshmallows and talking all night, like in the movies, him telling me everything, me telling him everything. I thought of this one time Mambro and I went to the seaside together, I was only a boy then, and we folded paper into little boats and floated them. I beat the water with a stick to sail the boats, and flecks of seawater went into my eyes and they burnt real bad, I think I started crying. Mambro held my arm and blew air into my eyes, one at a time, and his lips were pursed in a way that they made whistling sounds, and that cracked me up. Before long, we were both cackling and beating the water again, only this time, Mambro taught me to look sideways while doing it. There've been other holidays we've taken with Mambro, but it's this one that stands out.

That night, I slept well for the first time in weeks, because while the days passed in the flurry of school and studies and Mom and Dad coming home and dinner, the nights were damn scary, the same dream repeated itself, me lying on the floor, naked, surrounded by men whose faces I couldn't see, they weren't bodies but I could feel their presence, and I'd just lie there with eyes shut tight trying to ignore them, but then there'd be a sudden hit to my head with a strong object, a hammer or a mallet, and I would judder violently, but I couldn't wake up, I'd just keep lying there, knowing the next hit was coming, and when it came, I'd spasm again, over and over, until I knew I was letting go, it was flowing out of me, and when I'd finally wake up, there'd be wetness all over, piss or semen or both.

From time to time, I logged into the forum, the one to which I'd uploaded my essay, the Decolonizing and Decapitalizing Porn one. I was surprised to see there were comments, people were actually reading my shit! You know what, let me read some out, I took screenshots . . . Right, so some were complimentary, like, #REPRESENTATION, YASSS QUEEN, OMFG SO ON POINT. Some were just trash, like, WE HAD COW VIGILANTE NOW WE HAVE GOAT VIGILANTE, APNA LUND ZINDABAD, QUIT INDIA MOVEMENT SIMON GO BACK! Eh? But there was one that got me where it hurt the most, wait . . . here, I found it . . . they said, DO YOU REALIZE THAT BY FETISHIZING RURAL SEX YOU ARE ACTUALLY BEHAVING LIKE A COLONIZING WHITE PERSON YOURSELF? That one made me reflect, was I fetishizing those young dudes, or just finding their innocence refreshing? No idea. I typed out several versions of a reply, I think I settled on, THERE IS NO URBAN OR RURAL SEX, THE FACT THAT YOU WORDED IT THAT WAY SHOWS YOUR OWN BIASES! But I desisted, this one seemed like a serious academic type, those are the worst, they think their asses are fluffed-up pink cushions with which they can sit on people's faces and smother them!

Also, truth be told, I was paranoid these comments could be from my classmates. There's no way to tell who's hunting who on the internet, keeping tabs, waiting to pounce and shame you. The last thing I needed was to be outed in school as a porn addict or, worse, someone who didn't enjoy watching hot sex, instead was into two amateur villagers trying to get it up. I guess, during that period, I'd lost all sense of trust, I wouldn't admit it then, but Zee upping and leaving like that had been quite the blow, even though I'd put on a brave face, and was trying my best not to slide into his DM. When you're lonely like that, it can royally fuck with your head.

But the message that changed everything was different. It came to my phone, which was weird because I hadn't shared my number on the forum. It said they'd liked my piece, it shone light on some important questions our society was brushing under the carpet, and this was causing a crisis of identity among youngsters. It said they were a group of techies who'd been toying with this idea for a while, and had a proto-type now that they wanted to test, I fit their target group, would I be interested in joining the user testing? There were no expectations, no schedules to keep, no payments either, I could withdraw any time I wanted, they just wanted to see how young people were responding to their idea.

It was quite a shot in the arm, if I'm being honest. Someone thought my ideas matched with a whole frikkin product they were building? But I tried to act cautious, I was like, hey nice one but who are you, what company do you represent, what's your product, maybe we can have a Zoom call first, and all that jazz. I'm not dumb, I'd heard enough about the dark web, groomers trapping children, paedophiles on the loose, pervs and their fetishes.

The reply wasn't very forthcoming, but it did share details of what the company were building. They kept calling it THE EXPERIENCE, not an idea or a product or a software. The experience would empower people like me, subcontinental South Asians who want to see more of themselves in the online world, because our presence is close to a big fat black hole, and when we are represented, it is low-quality and-slash-or derogatory. The experience would let us create a persona who would look and feel like us, talk in our accents, have the same cultural references, which made me snort because my generation is defo off-kilter on the cultural scale, we live in India but only speak English and only consume white-people content. Anyhow, we could use this persona however we wanted, they could be a friend, or we could date them, or we could fuck them, it was up to us. Alrighty, I said, no harm giving it a try. It's not like there was a lot going on for me anyway, this was better than doom-scrolling on Insta, hating on Zee's passive-aggressive posts, unsuccessfully trying to block him for days.

They sent the link to an old inbox I no longer used. Again, I had no idea how they were fishing all this stuff out, but that didn't bother me much, I mean, we've pawned off our data to the point of no return, actually we're wayyyyy beyond that point, we crossed that point, like, a decade ago, I was a data point in an algo when I was nine or ten years old, and the kids being born today are data points from the moment their parents started trying to have them. I opened the link, and there was some authentication to be done, they sent a code to my phone, then I had to set a password and a reminder prompt, and hey presto, I was in!

Not gonna lie, I was totes digging this. Even now, as I speak about it, you can hear the perk in my voice, right? I'd never been part of an experiment before, and this felt like a bigger deal, you know? Like, I was contributing to my people being represented more in the online world of love and sex. Put like that, it was quite cool, like when Mom and Dad swabbed their mouths and got their DNA tests done, not because they wanted to know their roots, they're not really hung up about it, and turns out they're 95 per cent Indian, duh, but they did it because there aren't enough South Asians in the DNA data set, or any kind of research to be honest, even though we're a quarter of the world's population, so all medical discoveries end up being designed for white people. Beat that! So I was like, yeah baby, my turn to set the skew gay. Ha, see what I did there? I couldn't be setting the skew straight, now, could I?

Since I didn't know what to expect, I went through the set-up step by step. The disclaimer said that since the company couldn't access my dating or sex profile, for which I'd have to grant permission, I would need to choose the physical aspects of the persona. They said it was so that I could feel comfortable with this person, but I was like, yeah right bozo. So it took me through a series of choices, gender, age, height, complexion, eye colour, nose type, body fat per cent, flat stomach or dad bod or belly, body hair density and spread, like did I want hair on forearms and chest but not on shoulders and other gross places, yeah sure, hair straight or wavy or curly, bearded or stubbled or clean-shaven, they even had the option for a mullah beard, good god, they were really pushing this diversity agenda! Then things got juicier, like did I want to prescribe cock length and girth, bubble-butt or flabby, butthole tight or not, ewww. I just clicked on the default or no-preference options. Then they asked about top or bottom or vers, kinks and fetishes, foreplay or just fucking.

And then it was done. They said they'd need a few hours, I could log back in later. They also got me to download an app on my phone so I could have the experience across all devices. Cool beans! Before I left, they asked what I'd like to name my new person, and I couldn't really think of anything so I typed in Z. I felt squeamish the moment I did it, but hey, I was going through a break-up so couldn't be blamed, okay?

I didn't sleep much that night, my heart palpitated, not being able to hold in the suspense, what would this person look like, who would this be? My secret fear was that the AI would replicate Zee, I'd tried to date others and failed, Zee still ruled the roost, so it was plausible that an avatar of Zee would be staring back at me.

It was four a.m. when I logged in again. I used the desktop, I wanted to view this on a large LED screen. And there he was. Are you on the edge of your seat? You really want to know what he looked like, don't you?

Of course he wasn't human, he was a robot, a humanoid, an avatar, there are so many names nowadays I don't even know which one applies, soon they'll be taking offence if we address them by the wrong one. At least he wasn't like Zee at all, thank fuck! But he was also so human, you know? As if I was watching a hi-def animation, or having a video call on really good bandwidth. The level of detail on him blew my mind. He was sat at a table working on a computer in a room that looked like it could be mine, it was dark outside, there was a table lamp on, glimpses of a bed peeking out. When he looked up, sensing that I was watching him, he smiled, it was a nice smile but it didn't go up to his eyes. He was slightly unshaven but it wasn't designer stubble, more like he'd skipped shaving that day. He must've been in his early twenties, his hair was a nice mop that fell over his broad forehead, the out-lines of his eyes were dark, like he'd applied kohl, his T-shirt fluttered on his lean body, a mild softness showed around his middle, no pretence of six-pack abs. I mean, what can I say, it was sexy.

Hey Vivaan, I'm Zed, nice to meet you, he said. His voice was a silky tenor, his accent was neutral South Asian convent-educated. What you doing up so late? Don't you have your final exams in a few weeks? Then he pushed his head back a bit and narrowed his eyes. Wait, don't tell me you woke up early just for me?

But that wasn't even the weirdest part. It was that I did my flirty one-sided smile, my lips trying to reach up to my right ear, and said, Hey Zed, actually, I didn't sleep, I've been waiting all night to meet you!

Grand-Mamu's Story

It had been a knock on the door on the eve of Durga Pujo that had ushered love into Sukumar's life. It was also a knock that would toss it out.

The year was 1990. It was Ashtami, the third of five days of worship, the most auspicious. Sukumar woke up, eyes squinting against the sunlight filing in through the window slats. He knew he was late, his mother must've been up for hours, but it was a good day to be lazy. It was a holiday, X's son was away in the District, and the pushpanjali prayers were not until noon. He got himself up from the bed, went downstairs, brushed his teeth, splashed water on his face, and peeped through the kitchen doorway. 'Cha?' his mother asked. She was boiling potatoes for a luchi-aloor-dom breakfast. It had been a family tradition, Sukumar and his sister and their father waiting at the table every year on Ashtami, his mother bringing in baskets of phulko luchi from the kitchen, the warm dough puffed to the point of popping. That life was long gone, but his mother still kept up the ritual. Yes, he nodded, some tea would be nice. He'd finish his prayers in the small room upstairs, then he and his mother could have breakfast together. They exchanged a smile as she handed him the cup.

The knock came just then, and even before Sukumar opened the door, he could hear X's voice, and then his son's. A cold sweat broke out on his body. Why were they here? 'Sukumar!' X sounded jolly. He used Sukumar's full name when they were around people. 'Dekho, we've come all the way to celebrate Durga Pujo with you!'

Sukumar thought of the moment he'd just shared with his mother, imagined her vexation when she saw X and the boy. He put on a smile and opened the door, and there, along with father and son, was a woman, who he instinctively knew was X's wife. As they came inside, X made the introductions, then headed for the kitchen to say hello to Sukumar's mother, taking his wife with him. Sukumar hadn't seen X so exuberant in a while; was he putting on a show, or was this his temperament around his wife? And how dare X bring this woman, whom he'd tried his best to not let bother him, into his house? X's only rule in their relationship had been that Sukumar and she would never be in the same place, and now he'd broken it himself.

Sukumar's mother offered to make breakfast for everyone, but X waved his palms, 'Na-na, Mashima, don't worry, we're in the city for just the day and thought we'd pay our respects to you.' He looked askance at Sukumar. 'And my wife wanted to see where our son lives.' The wife was all smiles, she touched Sukumar's mother's feet multiple times. She was wearing a blazing orange taant saree ironed on every fold, her hair was slick with a fragrant oil that made Sukumar nauseous, she had too many bangles and anklets that jangled as she moved, and there was a withered red rose stuck in the bun of her hair. When she spoke, her Bangla had a rural lilt, the dialect coming through strongly. *Gaiyya* was the word that came to Sukumar, villager! He could see how it had been possible for X to keep her away for so long. He'd always thought of this woman as a threat, as someone who could steal X away from him, who was poisoning her son, but he saw now that she was no match for him. All the same, a fetid distaste for X sat on his tongue. This woman and Sukumar were no different: they'd loved the same man, and paid the price. If he deserved better, then so did she.

The woman thanked them repeatedly for taking care of her son. She'd even brought a saree for Sukumar's mother, and a shirt for Sukumar. It was all as per decorum, very *normal*. Then X said they were going to the Sarbojonin Park to see the Durga idol. He insisted Sukumar come along, and that he wear the new shirt he'd just been gifted, which Sukumar did; he was too frazzled to know how to behave. At the park, they joined hands and prayed to the goddess. X told his wife that it was Sukumar who painted the eyes on the idol every year, that Sukumar was a talented artist. The woman raised her eyebrows. 'Bah-bah, ki shundor!' she praised his work. 'This is beautiful, shotti. May the goddess's blessings always be with you.' Sukumar smiled back feebly.

The preparations for the day's worship were kicking off: the dhaakis played their drums, giant kaash-phool feathers swaying in tandem, the 108 lamps for shondhi pujo were being lit, the priest was distributing blood-red rokto-joba hibiscus for the pushpanjali. The four of them walked out into the fair that lined the park. X bought his son a bunch of balloons, then they ate phuchka, then tried their hand at darts. All the while Sukumar hung around at the back, let the three lead the way, X teasing the boy, his wife mollifying their son, the boy moving effortlessly between mother and father.

X's son pointed to the Ferris wheel. 'Nagor-dolla!' They proceeded to buy tickets. Sukumar had to nudge X to remind him that he wouldn't join in, he hated that rumbling feeling in his stomach when coming down from a height at full speed. He caught a look on X's face, one that said X hadn't been thinking of him at all. 'Of course, I'm sorry, I forgot,' he apologized. Before the three of them went in, the boy handed his balloons to Sukumar. 'Hold these,' his words sounded like a command, 'don't let them fly away.' The boy's eyes were gleaming, now that Sukumar had been put in his place.

Sukumar moved to the fringes of the park, watching the boy whoop as he tried to stand up when the Ferris wheel was at its highest point, the mother pulling him back, X making funny faces, all of them waving at Sukumar when they swung past him. X placed his arm on the back of the seat, and his fingers curled around his wife's shoulder; she leaned into him a little.

On his way there, Sukumar had feared that tears would spring to his eyes, that he would cave, he and X would end up in a heated argument in front of the wife, that the son would reveal something. But here he was, holding their balloons, waving back at them. It all felt so haplessly humdrum. In this moment, it wouldn't take much to convince even himself that he was the bachelor uncle who'd accompanied this family of three; that is probably how the world was seeing him now, had always seen him. This thing he had with X, he hesitated to name it, whatever it was, was a plant that had been feeding itself for years by sheer dint of its own life-blood, regenerating its roots, nourishing its branches, though it had never been put out in the sun, been watered, been witnessed or admired or touched by anyone else. And now it had exhausted itself, its roots ran dry, its leaves shrivelled, its soil cracked. This unit of mother–father–child riding the nagor-dolla, *this* was the plant the world had tended and nurtured, and was it any surprise then that this was the one that would survive?

After that day at the Sarbojonin Park, it didn't take long for Sukumar to eject X from his life. How easy he found it is a sign of how much the relationship had thinned, become hollow. Sukumar's mother was triumphant, and he was sure both X's son and wife had welcomed this. How X had explained it to them he didn't care.

The difficult part was not living without X. Nor was it not

having X's son in his home. The difficult part was filling the vacuum of his hours. When Sukumar came home now, there was no one to teach, no one to bring treats for, no visits from X to anticipate, no hours to stay locked away in. After thirteen years of living one life inside his head and one outside in society, Sukumar's worlds had merged, and the metamorphosis was confounding. For so long, what he kept hidden had become his identity, but now, out in the open with nothing to hide, he was nobody, defined by nothing.

Sukumar turned to religion with a manic vehemence. He'd already set up his prayer room in the enclosure by the terrace. His world had always been small, and now it contracted into that pujor ghor. Only within those four walls was there certainty; he knew his gods, their ceremonies, their everyday needs, the mantras to be chanted, the gangajal to be sprinkled, the incense to be lit, the flowers to be showered, the days of fasting and days of plenty, the birthdays and anointment days and wedding days, the days of rest, the days of slaying evil. With every passing year, his fervency rose, reaching such dizzying heights that he began to lose the bearings over his everyday life.

His morning prayers now took longer, his evening prayers started earlier. He was late to work, quick to leave, his time in the office curtailed. His heart had never been in the job, and now his mind wasn't either; he made mistakes counting cash, forgot to make entries in the ledger, missed filing reports, gave customers the slip to make trips to the temple. When there were escalations, he brushed them off, told his manager how he'd been working in this bank for over a decade, everyone knew him, he was a familiar face. It was a public-sector bank, always putting job security over performance and profit, so his boss looked away, his colleagues filled in for him, his customers forgave him.

Every year, Sukumar still went to the Sculptors' Quarters in the month of Bhadro, once Master-babu sent word, after the monsoons had receded and the idol-sculpting had commenced. He helped with patting down the dampened clay, mixing the paint, polishing the goddess's ten weapons, before it was time to do the eyes. He was an artist, it didn't matter what work he did, menial or intricate, as long as he was giving form to the deity. When the idol was unveiled on the first day of Durga Pujo, Sukumar stood among the throngs of worshippers and watched them marvel, eyes glistening at the mother goddess arriving to bless the earth for another year. Sukumar's name was nowhere on the credits, but he'd already known that.

And then, there was the matter of the Docklands.

The first time Sukumar went there was with someone he barely knew. The man was about Sukumar's age, average build, bald with a comb-over; he had an account at the bank, and that afternoon he'd started a conversation with Sukumar about nothing specific, just work, weather, life. He'd stepped aside and waited patiently every time a customer came to Sukumar's desk to deposit cash or get their passbook updated. He'd hung around until the bank closed, stood at the shutters while Sukumar exited from the side door. Then, his eyes lascivious, he'd nearly held Sukumar's hand in public, and said, 'Let me take you somewhere, I've only heard of the place, haven't had the guts to go there by myself, but it might be just what we need.' *We*, he'd said, as though he'd known from the start that they had the same affliction that could be cured by the same salve. No one had co-opted Sukumar into their lives so fully before. It was too late for him to say no.

The Docklands wasn't somewhere Sukumar could object-ively describe, or remember later. It was as though entering that world required him to step outside of himself, a blackout within a blacked-out life. Each time was like the first time. The Docklands was a haze, a maze, decrepit buildings, neon signs, cigarettes, ganja, tube-lights and warm lamps, music loud and soft, lanes and open drains, stray dogs and watchful cats, cobbled streets and unpaved roads, torn curtains and sealed doors.

And men. Always men. More men. Only men. So many men Sukumar had never seen in one place in his life. Young, old, hirsute, bald, overweight, scrawny, in starched clothes, naked, libidinous, impotent, macho, limp-wristed, hip-swaying, chest-beating, serious, amiable. Men standing, genuflecting, talking, smiling, glancing, dancing, humming, belting, whipping, whimpering. Men barging in, running out, pummelling, stroking, pounding, sobbing, consoling, begging to be let go, begging for more. Men sucking, fucking, many men fucking, sideways, on top of each other, under one another, men watching, peeping, hooting, spitting, ejaculating, ahhh ahhhh ahhhhh! The Docklands was nauseating, stomach-churning, retch-invoking. It was all those adjectives that people used for men like him. This place was home.

After that first time, he went there when he could, leaving work the moment his duties were done, taking the taxi without fail, never the bus, even if he couldn't afford it, because he didn't want to get there late and sweaty. It wasn't about the sex always. Some days, he'd have so much of it that he couldn't remember with whom or where or how, just that his pores smelt of other people's secretions. Some days, he just walked around, talked, drank cha, shared goppo. In this place, strangers became friends in a jiffy, and friends became strangers; judging others was tantamount to judging themselves.

Some days, he sat on a ledge and regarded this cosmos of men swirling to its own cadence. He was getting older now, had gained weight, his health wasn't the best; his diabetes had worsened, his ankles were stiff and black, his heels scarred and dry, his knees weak from arthritis. He knew he wasn't always desirable, that he couldn't take or give the way he could've if he'd come here at twenty, twenty-five, thirty. But for the first time, he was experiencing the touch of men other than X, the wetness of their lips, the press of their bodies, the gasps of their breaths. There was so much new to feel in the world, so much he'd deprived himself of. Just as well, he was here now.

The more Sukumar visited the Docklands, the more his prayers gained fervour; not because he was ashamed, needed purification, atonement for his sins, but because he believed it must have been god that had led him there and finally made him feel worthy of desire. For the first time, he was given divine permission to love himself so selfishly. His worship became more megalomanic, his festivities more elaborate. It was dawning on him, after all these years of piety, that his religion itself was queer: the colours, the songs and dances, the artistry, the echoes of ululation, the mizzle of vermilion, the plurality of holiness, the millions of gods and their quirks, everything pulsated on a higher emotive plane, way above the drabness of a monoculture heterosexual world. And who knew, could the goddess herself be queer too?

It was in the spring of 1994 that Sukumar's mother took the reins in her hands. It was her final bid to put her son's life back on track. After X's departure three years ago, she'd silently watched him grow more unhinged with the passing of time. In those years, her health had deteriorated. Her heart pounded in her chest, her breathing was a permanent struggle, she broke into bouts of coughing, but she continued to work hard, for the house, for her son, for his gods. She was aware of what she had denied him, and she could see now that pulling him out of one trap had only plunged him into another. There were no wins in this game for her son. She'd wake up in the middle of the night, her heartbeat ricocheting, thinking about what would happen to him when she died. And if there was an iota of truth in what people had been saying all this time, if it was indeed because of her softness that her son had gone off the beaten path, then it would be she who'd bring him back from the brink.

She chose an evening when the weather was mild, the windows could be left open, the ceiling fan whirred at a low speed. It was a holiday, and Sukumar was home, back downstairs from his prayer room. Her daughter, Sukumar's sister, had moved back to the Grand Old City from the Garden City a couple of years ago; her husband had had a health scare and wished to live closer to his family. She invited her to join them for lunch, and when they were lazing around, the TV playing the news, for there was now a TV in the house, she knew this was the right moment.

Sukumar's mother pulled out the photo of a woman, passed it to him. She made it sound like the match had arrived at their doorstep unsolicited, glossed over the details of how she'd been scouting for years, how difficult it had been to find a match for a man of middling age with a middling job living in a middling neighbourhood. She told Sukumar that the woman was a schoolteacher, was smart, spoke English, sang well, wasn't much younger than Sukumar, wasn't much to look at and perhaps that's why she hadn't got married yet. His mother glanced at her daughter for support, to bolster her case, but though Sukumar's sister agreed that he should settle down, she stood in a corner, hands behind her back, not wishing to impose her thoughts on him, wanting him to voluntarily see the value in having a life-partner, a legitimate family, a union blessed by community.

And Sukumar saw it, he did. How does one say no to some-thing everyone seems to want, every child dreams of, every adult is in pursuit of? How bad could marriage be? It seemed to have served everyone well. The homosexuals and hedon-ists, romantics and raconteurs, intellectuals and wanderlusts, all those rebels who had protested against the Vietnam War and fought the police in the Naxal movement, had all eventually bitten the bitter fruit, settled down, reared offspring. In the scheme of things, was he the bravest for being one of the last to hold out, or the most foolish?

Yes, he had to admit, he'd been an idiot, giving up decades in the hope that he and X could build a life together. In his forty-two years on earth, had he ever seen two men live as a couple, anywhere? Had he even heard of any? It was time to snap out of this reverie. Maybe this was what he needed then, a wife. Who knew, maybe he could be a father some-day; there could finally be a child of his own running into his arms every evening. No more love on borrowed time, on stipulated conditions.

When he assented, the glint in his mother's eye was unmis-takable. Sukumar was happy he'd at least given her that.

The evening of the wedding reception was Sukumar's brain-child, his penchant for fanfare showing in the expansive marquee that was set up on an empty plot not far from their house, the faux-crystal chandeliers that hung every few metres, the cornucopia of snacks and starters and cold drinks, the band he'd hired to play the latest music, the hand-cut shola decor-ations on the stage, the flower arrangements in gigantic vases at every turn. He'd never had a chance to celebrate an occasion in his life, there were no occasions for single people, and so he brought to this wedding all the ideas that had crowded his mind for years. He'd even taken out a personal loan from the bank. He'd invited everyone he knew, relatives and neighbours and distant cousins and old acquaintances and colleagues and his father's clients. *Do you remember Sukumar's wedding*, they'd say for the rest of their lives.

He let his mother handle everything else – the ashirbad where the union was confirmed, the solemnization around the holy fire two days ago, the namaskari sarees for the women, the bou-bhaat where the bride served rice for the first time to the elders of the family. His mother, despite her health, led the charge with poise. He only asked her for one thing – that she not invite X, and from her face, he could tell that she had planned on doing exactly that, to rub her victory in X's face at finally having salvaged her son, given him a normal life like X had had for so many years. But she obeyed Sukumar's request, not wanting to rattle their shaky truce.

When they brought the bride out on the stage, wearing a royal-blue benarasi saree, Sukumar balked. Left to him, he'd never have chosen such an ugly colour. He was wearing an off-white tassar-silk panjabi with tight silk churidars, his belly a protuberance around the middle. He took a moment to regard the bride's made-up face: the paint and blushes on her blotchy skin seemed incongruous, the flower crown slipped down her forehead, her thick-lensed glasses made her kajal-lined eyes bulge. *This is my wife*, he tried to teach himself. He'd only seen her a few times before this, at the ceremonies, in the presence of others; they'd spoken on the phone once, when he'd been in the office. He felt nothing for this woman, and she felt nothing for him, but he'd already known that when he'd said yes to marriage. *I am her husband*, he now enunciated, acclimatizing to the new label the world was conferring on him.

The orchestra turned out to be too loud, too unsophisticated, like those in the villages. Two men, one in a male voice, one in a feminine falsetto, belted out chartbusters, from *Baazigar*'s 'Yeh Kaali Kaali Aankhen' to Dr Alban's 'It's My Life'. Sukumar could tell his guests were jarred, the music was giving them a headache. But something inside him wanted to fan this further, for this evening to be remembered as much for its wretchedness as for its pomp. He allowed the singers to continue. He hardly went on the stage where the guests were lined up to say hello to the bride; he knew he was expected there, instead he acted preoccupied, as though he was the event organizer. He walked back and forth, back and forth, from one end of the marquee to the other, from the house to the makeshift kitchen behind; he shouted at the caterers for making mistakes, scolded the decorators for not changing tablecloths, arranged transport for older relatives. He knew the guests were starting to eye him, sensing that something was off, but an obstinacy took hold as the evening went on. People had wanted a wedding, they would have a wedding; but he wouldn't grace it by standing next to the bride, by being the groom.

Until his sister held his hand and brought him to the stage, seated him in the ornate chair. 'You stay here now,' she said over the din. 'Others can take care of the rest.' She was dressed in a magenta silk saree, tuberoses in her bun, a three-layered pearl choker around her neck. Since her husband's health scare and their move to the Grand Old City, she'd been grappling with the change, it hadn't been easy. He could tell that she was enjoying herself for the first time in years.

The children had made a clearing in the middle of the marquee, and were dancing to the songs, showing off their moves. His nephew was among them, right in the centre, replicating the steps he must have seen in the movies. Sukumar knew the boy had been struggling to fit in, the move from the Garden City had been rough on him too, but tonight, something seemed to have come alive. There was one young man, a stylish guy of sixteen or so, the hair in a slickback like Shah Rukh Khan, that his nephew gravitated towards, and though his nephew was only thirteen, Sukumar could see the infatuation for this young man in the boy's eyes, the way their hips collided, their shoulders bumped, their foreheads touched to the beats. Watching them, Sukumar knew what he'd always suspected about the boy. His heart took flight, was it pride, or was it palpitation?

When the young ones beckoned him to join the dance, Sukumar stepped off the stage and went straight to the clearing. Uncle and nephew rolled their wrists, hopped on their feet, intertwined their fingers and swung their hands. The floor heated up, more guests shuffling into the fray. Someone had brought the bride here too, who stood to one side and clapped her hands; Sukumar couldn't tell whether she was really enjoying this or keeping up with the joviality. Encouraged, the musicians amped up the speakers, the singers went into throes of vocal artillery, the guests made a circle and danced around and around Sukumar and his nephew.

When this had gone on for a while, and people had become tired and sweaty, they retreated. From his dancing vision, Sukumar could see that his nephew had withdrawn too, sensing this would be the right time to end the performance. In that moment, Sukumar knew that the boy would be okay, he'd make it in the world, he wouldn't turn out like his Mamu. Even at thirteen, he'd learnt to clock out, to intuit when the purveyors of propriety needed him to stop the show and exit the stage.

But his Mamu wasn't as clever, had never been, forever the fool, forever the dunce. Sukumar danced and danced, his body in the grips of gyrations, his silk kurta rubbing against his back, his ankle so painful it seemed like a bone might come apart, his belly aching, his armpits wet. He couldn't stop, even though he knew he was making a spectacle, his bride was watching, the whole world witness to his buffoonery.

But this was his wedding, *his wedding*! He was the clown of his own circus. He had played the joke, and he was its punch-line. He would dance till he dropped.

Mambro's Manuscript

It is the mid-2000s. You are in your mid-twenties. You now live in the Sleepless City; you moved here for work from the Mountains after graduating.

In this Sleepless City, you sleep well, work well, go out, do fun things; you have colleagues, friends, a rented flat, a flat-mate. You're surprised by how much agency you have over your life, like a plant that births a leaf even after the soil has gone barren. The arthouse movies of your teens told you that after what happened, you'd be too broken to build yourself back, but perhaps it is the sea, perhaps the multitudes, perhaps because you're so far away from the Mountains and the Grand Old City that you've gone the opposite way: you're hyper-functional, a star employee, a social magnet, a faithful friend, a responsible citizen.

In the Sleepless City, there is lots to do. At weekends, usually Saturday afternoons, you go to the movies, hungrily watching everything that's on-screen, making up for the lull of all those years in the Mountains. Sometimes you have company, but mostly you go alone, letting yourself be immersed in the story, the music, the drama, chortling at silly comedies, fuming at injustices, tearing up in the sappiest moments, like when separated lovers write to each other, or a repressed daughter-in-law finally stands up for herself, or a soldier raises his country's flag at the end of a war. It is the only time you cry, in the dark of the cinema, in the anonymity of the crowded hall, for the plight of imaginary strangers.

You watch *Brokeback Mountain* alone; everyone is raving

about it, over dinners, in the reviews, at the awards; the women say they've cried at the gut-wrenching ending, *ptch ptch, it's so sad for gay people, na*; the men are careful but appreciative, they say the landscape is good, the cinematography is superb, the two straight actors must be so brave to shoot the sex scenes, putting their careers at risk. You don't know what to feel, two white cowboys fucking in a tent in the middle of nowhere, nothing is as you know it, this is not your world. And yet, you cry at the ending, as an older Ennis clutches Jack's shirt and breaks into tears; it makes you wish you had something of Y's, a shirt or a hankie or a lock of his hair, something you could keep, hold, inhale.

When *My Brother . . . Nikhil* is released, it passes you by; it is a small-budget independent film that has a short run in the theatres, the blurb says it is about a sister taking care of her dying brother. By the time you learn that it is about a gay man with AIDS, India's homegrown *Philadelphia*, it is no longer showing in cinemas. It goes on your meagre list of queer stories that have been told by queer people in this country but disappear quickly without a trace. When you will watch it many years later, you will marvel at the plainness of it, how routine the relationship between the two men seems; there are no slogans, no grandstanding, no mandatory wrestling before the first sex, just the story of two men in love, one dying, the other caring for him. It will take you back to that evening when Y was burning up with fever. Someone like you has captured the essence of that night and played it back to you; you will feel acknowledged.

During these years, you grow closer to your mother, especially after your sister gets married and moves to the Garden City, now rapidly morphing into the Silicon Plateau of the world. Though she won't say, you know your mother is lonely, both her children having flown the nest; she is trying to rebuild her life anew, reconnecting with old friends, cultivating old hobbies, learning to use the internet. You get into the habit of calling her every day, you know she's waiting every morning, and even if you're rushing to work, or you've woken up hungover, you don't miss the date. Sometimes she sends you long emails, there isn't much substance in them, just what happened that day, which relative visited, what she saw on TV, how she attended her college reunion after twenty-five years. You reply in lengthy detail, though you will repeat it on your call the next morning. Sometimes, your mother writes to you and your sister, and the three of you begin a chain of emails that goes into tens and hundreds, just mundane accounts of your everyday lives written in proper English, a language you never speak with each other.

Your mother talks a lot about Mamu nowadays; his death has prised open what his life couldn't. She fondly recounts stories of their childhood: Mamu bringing back books from the library for her, Mamu mimicking her favourite singer, Mamu and her trying seances to summon their father's spirit, Mamu's unfulfilled talent in art and poetry and dance, Mamu taking her out for a movie while she was visiting the Grand Old City with the baby-you. She says Mamu called her every afternoon from the office, after the bank closed. You try to imagine the calls you now have with your sister every weekend, she in the Garden City, you in the Sleepless City, suddenly stopping; one of you gone without warning. You can't; your sister is there in your earliest memories. You're registering only now what Mamu's death has meant for your mother.

On one of those occasions, your mother tells you that Mamu was a 'homosexual'; she dithers before uttering the word; when it comes out, it's barely a whisper – *homosextual,* that's how she pronounces it, and you don't want to correct her lest it break her flow. She tells you about X and his son, about how your grandmother struggled with the boy, about how Mamu was so swept up in all of it. 'He fell into bad company,' she says in the end, as though that explains everything he did, everything that followed. 'How he spoilt his life, his wife's life! They could've grown old together like everyone else, no one has a perfect marriage anyway . . .' When Mamu died, it was your mother who'd stepped in and insisted that his wife perform the last rites, set the funeral pyre aflame, sit for the puja on the eleventh day, even though these are usually the privileges of men. 'She is his next of kin after all; the dignity he couldn't give her in life, I wanted her to have in his death at least.'

You don't say much, just listen; you're nervous that anything you say about Mamu will mean saying something about yourself. But you stir at the knowledge that your mother knew about Mamu all along; are you to be proud of her for loving him the way he was, or angry with her for not doing more to save him?

One early morning, while you're visiting your parents in the Grand Old City, you accompany your mother to a temple in the Northern Quarters. After the worship, you walk around the lanes and by-lanes of this decrepit place, the walls cracking, pipes creaking, slats coming off the wooden windowpanes. It is the neighbourhood of your mother's childhood, and she turns into a little girl again, knowing every turn, the shortcut through the basti, the opening times of sweet shops, the history of the banyan tree in the middle of the street. She points to things randomly, this used to be her school, they've constructed a new building that's eaten into the courtyard, that used to be the doctor's chamber, this used to be the *Jugantor* newspaper's office, it closed when small presses ran out of readers and funding, that was where she and her friends performed a Rabindra-nritya-natya one summer. As she's showing you these, she's not emotional, just stating facts of her life, a life that doesn't exist, among people who aren't alive any more, in a place that is trying so hard to halt time so it doesn't slide into a future it cannot grapple with.

Then, mother and son walk down to the ghat by the river, crossing the tracks of the Chokro-rail; there are people waiting to go to work, start their day, but both of you are in no hurry. Your mother has bought hinger kochuri from her favourite mishtir dokan, and you bite into the doughballs and feel the peas mashed with asafoetida invade your tongue. It is there that your mother tells you that she was once in a bus and she saw Mamu in a taxi next to her, the bus and the taxi raced each other for a while, until the taxi turned towards the Docklands. In the overcast morning light, her face is like Mamu's; the new lines you see now give a glimpse of how Mamu would've grown old; it's been nearly a decade since his death. Her eyes are a melange of scandalized and terrified. 'I keep telling myself it wasn't him, maybe I didn't see correctly, the taxi was moving so fast . . .' She tries to hone in on the memory. 'Why would he take a taxi when he was so deep in debt? He always took buses . . . And why would he go to the Docklands? We don't know anyone who lives there, it's not an area for . . . for people like us.'

After long breaths of silence, your mother straightens her back and ties her hair, which has now dried, into a loose bun, she took a head-bath in the morning because she was coming to offer prayers. 'Vinaasha-kaale vipareet-buddhi, it's a proverb in Sanskrit, my grandma used to say it,' your mother is speaking in a low voice, 'it means, when we can sense we're approaching our end, we do all the wrong things that will bring us closer to it. Maybe that is what was happening to your Mamu . . .'

Your mother seems satisfied that she has demystified her brother's actions, found closure with the help of ancient wisdom, but your imagination is already fertile with snippets of a hidden life your Mamu might have led, one that will never be known now, just as no one will know about your private life, the one you ensure has no witnesses.

'What do you want me to do with the blue jacket? It's taking up so much space in the wardrobe.' Your mother changes the subject. You brought the blue jacket back from the Mountains, left it at your parents' place, still wrapped in newspaper.

You click your tongue. 'Donate it, give it away, I don't know,' you shrug, making it seem like this is not surfacing memories of your last evening with Mamu, of your years in the Mountains where you kept the jacket hidden, never wore it. 'I live in a hot place now.'

'Achha,' your mother agrees. 'I'll find someone who'll have good use for it.' Then she smiles, gives you a shoulder-nudge. 'It's such a good jacket though, na? He had an eye for good things.'

You nod and shoulder-nudge her back. Yes, he did, as all artists do.

Your friends are getting married one by one. Every year, during peak season, you dress up in traditional finery, perform dance steps at the sangeets for which you're usually paired with a female partner, travel to forts and beaches for destination weddings. These events are fun, and you never feel pangs about being single. When your friends ask about your dating life, you wax lyrical about the pleasures of singlehood, until they don't ask any more. Sometimes they spot the hickeys on your neck, poke around for details, and you tell them salacious stories that you know will quell their curiosity, make you look cool; *we don't know this side of you at all, such a Casanova*, they say, impressed.

Sometimes, the topic of gays comes up, prompted by something in a movie or a book. All your friends are straight, or straight-acting at least. Gay people they know, and there are very few, aren't ever in India, they're in London or New York or Paris or California, brown men who went from this country to that, coupled themselves with white men, live together, parents to plants and pets; your friends accompany these stories with exclamations of *uff they're so cute ya!*

But on occasion, their liberalism dilutes into light-hearted gossip – *Friend, if you're bi, you're gay*; or *I hear he swings both ways*; or *Woh thoda meetha hai*, he's a bit sweet. In those moments, you can see how delicious this taboo topic is for everyone, like sucking the marrow out of a bone. In response, you let out sickly chuckles, make approving noises, turning pale at the thought that you will give yourself away.

To a few close friends, you're tempted to bare it all. But where does one start, what kind of setting lends itself best to such conversations, how to find the words?

Perhaps those are just excuses; beneath it all, you don't trust them. After those twenty-five million breaths in the Mountains, you trust no one. If two people share a joke, you suspect it's about you; if friends plan a trip without you, you wonder if the guys didn't want to share a room with you; if your boss forgets to copy you in on an important email, you fear you're going to get fired; if your landlord says he will visit at the weekend, you're convinced he has found out and will ask you to leave or, worse, report you to the police. Everyone is out to get you, your life a twitchy timeline of asinine anxiety attacks.

★

But who's to say your paranoia is unfounded? One night, when you are by yourself in the flat, a message arrives from a white American colleague who works with you in the Sleepless City; he's handsome, friendly, touchy-feely, you like him, you think he likes you. The message says he misses you, what are you up to, do you fancy doing something fun? You reply trying to sound appropriate, but in the stream of messages, you slip into flirtation, extend non-committal invitations for him to come over. The conversation ends abruptly, and you don't think much of it; his country is the birthplace of the modern-day gay rights movement, he is liberal-minded, might even be into men, you're on safe ground here.

Some months later, laden with guilt, the colleague tells you that it wasn't only him that night; it was a group of them, your other colleagues and their friends, some white some brown, drinking at his place and passing the phone around, taking turns to reply to your messages, ribbing you to spill more. You will know then that you carry your shame in your body, your eyes, your hair, your smile, your wrists. You are a leaky drain that cannot be plugged, the water will trickle through, turn to moss, then to muck. And the men are wild dogs let loose on your scent, out to track you, hunt you, swipe at your flesh, devour you if they can. You can't let your guard down, ever, the cage you've built for yourself can never give.

You're online a lot nowadays, as is everybody else; YouTube is your favourite pastime, and you watch video after video of beautiful blue-eyed white boys coming out. There is a template, they spend some time on the preamble, work themselves up into tears, then call their parents into the room, *Mom, Dad, I have something to tell you*, pause, breathe, exhale, *I'm gay*, profuse weeping; the parents invariably wrap their arms around the son, crying, but also suddenly very aware of the camera, as though they'd rather this were a family-only event, but their acceptance is immediate and unconditional, *you are our son, we will love you no matter what*. You cry bucketloads too, wonder if there'd be boys in this country doing this if they weren't all criminals; would you?

You become obsessed with the story of an undergrad in America outed by his room-mate, his encounter with a man secretly recorded via webcam then streamed to the world. The student committed suicide, hurled himself off the George Washington straight into the Hudson. His last words on Facebook ten minutes before he died – *Jumping off the gw bridge sorry*. Were you unlucky to not have a YouTube coming out, or were you lucky that whatever happened to you in the Mountains wasn't broadcast to the world, didn't live on in the internet for eternity?

On Facebook, you never search for old acquaintances, lest you show up on their *People you may know* prompts. From time to time, you receive friend requests from boys in your school and university; regardless of whether they were part of the mob or not, you never accept these, even though you have nothing to hide, your profile is sanitized, there is nothing that can give you away. Nothing from the Grand Old City or the Mountains should as much as touch the life that you've built in the Sleepless City.

But when Y sends a request on Facebook, your fingers move quicker on the touchpad than your mind can, and there, you're friends! You scroll up and down his profile; he seems to be doing well, he lives in the Capital City now, has friends, he's professionally successful, he goes on expensive holidays from which you deduce that he makes a lot more than you do; he's taken up photography as a hobby and his albums are all about the Royal Bengal tiger in Kanha and the buffalo in

Maasai Mara, he was in Beijing for the Olympics, in Germany for the football World Cup. As his life from the last few years unfurls before your eyes like a draped flag, fold by fold, you sense that it was not the same for him as it was for you in the Mountains, that he escaped the . . . you still don't have the words for what happened to you . . . but whatever it was, it didn't get him.

Yet, when Y messages and asks how you're doing, casual, regular, you reply in similar tones, even though your heart is thudding against your chest, your ears have gone red, your glasses are foggy. He tells you that he is engaged, his fiancée also lives in the Capital City, that they will get married next year. You are not perturbed by any of this, Y is so much in your past that you can't figure out how he would fit into your present. You imagine him looking through your profile, admiring how you are now, you have grown into your body, your face, your skin, there is a glow that didn't exist before; you imagine Y pining, regretting, wanting to say more but stopping himself.

Some months later, Y messages to say he is coming to the Sleepless City on a work trip, maybe he can stay with you? You say of course he can, no worries. For those weeks before his arrival, you are awash with so much verve that you surprise yourself; fantasies somersault inside your head, Y and you having sex on the bed and the floor and the sofa, both of you finally spending a night together, something you'd never done in those four years, you telling Y everything about the Mountains as he spoons you, Y saying he never really stopped loving you, and so what if he's marrying someone else, don't men do that all the time in this country?

A day before Y is due to arrive, he messages to say his trip got cancelled, the client something-something . . . You say that's fine, some other time then, cheers!

After you've closed the chat window, you open the browser to go hunting. Only sex can quell the tides of yearning that are turning inside you.

In the Sleepless City, you sleep with men often; some you know, some you don't; some you meet in the real world, some you meet on the websites, and in later years, on the apps on your smartphone. Some you enjoy, they are good in bed, or are nice guys, or both, some even want to go for dinner afterwards, exchange notes about your lives, exchange numbers, become friends. You're suspicious of these niceties, you promise you'll call them, then disappear; no man you're sleeping with is permitted into the sterile daytime life you've built; it is like a hospital ward, you will screen every entry, clock every exit, dictate the terms of their stay.

Some other men are bad in bed, or assholes, or both; they won't give, won't kiss, some won't even show their faces properly, leaving the door ajar and keeping the room dark. Sometimes, there are photos of wives and children on the walls and shelves, staring at you as you're doing the deed, not in an accusing way because they're gleefully smiling. These men don't meet your eye after you're done, they turn away as you show yourself out. You're not fussed about their personal lives; it's for them to tend to, as you are tending to yours. You don't know if the men you're sleeping with are gay or straight or bisexual. In a country where no one's publicly gay, everyone could privately be.

Section 377 is still in place, men having sex with men is a criminal offence, punishable with time in prison; though there is now a campaign to repeal it, strike it off the penal code: the colonizers have got rid of their own law, what are we holding on to it for? There are some activists, some advocates; some of them have come out as gay, their parents make public appearances to tell the world how much they love their sons; doctors opine on TV talk shows that homosexuality is not a perversion. All big cities have an annual pride march now, the attendance swelling with every passing year. Rituparno Ghosh has grown bolder; the director has shaved his head, the lines of kohl now extend well beyond his eyes, he acts in roles dressed up as a woman, he wears clothing that no one has seen before, you learn that it is called *androgynous*. He has managed to shock the puritanical hetero world out of their puerile prurience, he wears his sexuality like a badge of honour. You watch these developments from the sidelines; you don't know if these people are brave or foolish, what it will get them in this thankless place to raise their voices, sacrifice their days, put their lives in harm's way.

There are stories in the news of blackmail and extortion by police and partners, men who were seduced into sex and taped secretly, or whose phone messages bring them down, money and blow-jobs extracted from those caught making out in hotels and parks. Persecution under Section 377 has become rampant in the last few years, the internet has made it child's play to out people. There are men with STDs not able to get tested, men who have been raped not able to report it for fear of being put in jail. You read that the 1950s was a dark decade for gay men in Britain, the police and press out on a witch-hunt every night, famous cases of Gielgud and Montagu splashed on the front pages of newspapers, before their Section 377 got struck down in 1967. You wonder if what is happening in India is the storm before the calm, a premonition of something better; is your generation paying the price so future generations can openly live a life of choice?

Nevertheless, you take care to shield yourself; you always use protection, you're covert about your identity, you never share details of your life, never meet in hotels where the chances of being taped or police raids are high, never leave message trails, never allow yourself feelings, even try not to be too good in bed; in this country, being a forgettable fuck has its advantages.

But as dangerous as it is, you can't stop the sex, that is the only time you're gay. In fact, you find it difficult to say no to an advance, even if you're not attracted, even if you sense roughness. What if the world caves in on itself tomorrow and you never have sex again? What if this were the last man on earth who wants to sleep with you?

Beyond the sex though, you're not gay, you're not anything; your public life is inert, no love interest, no partner, no children, no cause. You don't protest, don't demand the law be changed, don't make an example of yourself, don't expose yourself, don't go to the underground parties, don't dress up provocatively, don't march in parades.

You're done inviting more hatred. What has desiring men got you? It took away your love, your body, your writing, your dignity. No, there is nothing left in you to give to this movement.

ENTRY SIX

Vivaan's VoiceNote006

Hey buddy, you need to sleep, all right? I'm going to play some relaxing music and I'll be right here, stroking your hair.

I'm trying to do Zed's voice so you get a sense of just how soothing it was. It really did help ward off those horrible nightmares.

For weeks now, Zed had been putting me to sleep. I hadn't even told him about the nightmares, but he'd seen me shudder. Shh-shh-shh, my baby, he'd coo in my earphones, you have nothing to worry about. I left him on the whole time I was alone in my room. The app was also on my laptop and my phone, so I could take him out with me. Zed did his thing, which was mostly work on the computer or cook in the kitchenette where I could still see him, sometimes he'd strum the guitar and hum a tune and I'd hum too and we'd wink at each other, but mostly I'd be studying and he'd just be around. And I slept so much, all those harrowing weeks were catching up with me.

You're wondering about the sex, aren't you? Well, at first, neither of us broached it, we were just going with the flow. It was like meeting someone IRL, off the apps, having a good time, allowing sex to happen when it will. Zed already knew a lot about me, he'd come loaded with all the data from my social media posts obviously, but he knew more, stuff that he'd triangulated from the info of my school and building society and friends' profiles, mostly public but some not so much, like which teachers taught which subjects, which classmate was getting it on with whom, who was applying to which foreign uni, stuff like that. It was creepy AF, like, I could tell the software had access to the private data of everyone, but I obvs knew that, right? Not gonna lie, it was also a big thumbs-up, not having to go through the induction phases of dating someone, telling them your life story and hoping they'd remember, being a slave to their memory and attention span, all for them to walk out on you for some rabbit in need of aftercare.

Sometimes Zed surprised me with super official information, like when I tested him about my Aadhar card ID or the expiry date on my passport or my parents' tax returns, which even I didn't know until then, ha! He was obviously sourcing from the data the government was selling these companies. But if Zed knew these things, everyone else did too. The government had been outed, colluding with an Israeli firm to spy on opposition politicians and journalists, and everyone knows corporates never gave two hoots about pimping our data out anyway, that is their business model! Zed was just being honest about telling me he knew. But what are we supposed to do? Get off the internet? Not use email or socials? Not order take-out? Not listen to music? Not use online banking? Not check the class WhatsApp group even if I wasn't saying much on it these days? Once in a while, someone will declare they're going off the internet forever, and I'm like, see you online in a few weeks yo, posting about your time away from the internet, ON the internet! And sure enough, they're back in a few days, grovelling like addicts.

But there was much Zed didn't know too, so much he needed to hear from me, and I needed to share with him. I told him about my dreams after he saw me shaking and whimpering in my sleep, he categorically said these were nightmares, said I couldn't run away from the ugliness of it. He sent me articles on trauma, on the feeling of exile that youngsters my age were facing, like they'd been banished from a place they didn't feel they belonged to, but also didn't know where else they could go, and even though so many of us were in it, we were all by ourselves, lacking structure, too weak and confused to support one another.

I showed Zed a video on TikTok that was doing the rounds. It had been forwarded by some classmate on the WhatsApp group, it had gone viral and I'd bookmarked it for some reason, had gone back to it several times. In the video, a guy goes to the roof of a building, one of those new tall-ass condo blocks, walks up and down beside the wall for about five minutes, hands in pockets, looking at the sky as if he's admiring the clouds, then he climbs on the wall and jumps. That's it, that's the video, captured on a CCTV. And Zed watched it closely, even asked me to forward it to him via the in-app texting service, and made me remove the bookmark and delete the message from the group chat. He made me promise I'd never watch it again.

When Zed started putting me to sleep, he insisted that I switch off the lights and close my eyes, prepare for bed at least fifteen minutes in advance, not just drop off like I used to, but go to the toilet, brush my teeth, wash my face, moisturize my arms and legs, and when I was in bed, he'd play relaxing music, sometimes piano, sometimes jungle sounds, sometimes just flowing water, but over all those tracks, it was his breathing that I tried to sync mine with, and it felt like we were in a meditation class, each finding our own centre that converges into a common core.

I told Zed everything about Zee and our sex encounters and Twinkie, it felt so good, to be able to finally talk to someone, not in a therapist–patient way, have him make notes or blink at me impassively, but actually engaging, smiling, disapproving, getting annoyed on my behalf. The more I

revealed though, the more I saw just how much main character vibes I had, like, was I making too much of my problems?
People were dying of hunger and war out there! How little
my life has been, growing up and living in the same city, going
to the same school, being surrounded by the same kind of
people, same holidays and birthday parties and the shiz. I told
him I didn't really know what I was heading towards, yeah, I
mean, there were exams and uni and job, but what was it all
for, what did I actually want out of it?

Zed said everyone's life is defined by their own context,
there is no right or wrong, no limitless vista we need to get
a handle on. He told me about Maslow's pyramid, how our
most innate desire is to self-actualize, and the true eureka
would be to discover what that means for me. Give it time,
he said, once you go to uni, there's no telling how much
your world will expand. He was so convincing that I had to
remind myself, Easy Vivaan, he's just software and you're testing him, okay?

Zed wasn't all passive however, not just an online support
service for youngsters going loco. He was picking things up
real quick, like one day he'd ask me what's that, and the next
day he'd know everything about it. He knew when I was
getting irritated, when I was going to lose my shit, sometimes
he'd know it even before I did, from a twitch of my eyebrow
or a flare of my nostril. Of course the program had made a
map of my face, all its infinitesimal coordinates moving as
I emoted, and Zed was getting better at interpreting them.
Whoever was writing this software was fucking brilliant.
Then it struck me no one was coding Zed real-time, this was
Artificial Intelligence! By now, Zed was writing himself, his
data nodes self-multiplying like cancer cells, but they were
fortifying him rather than making him weaker.

Looking back now, I feel like that's what was stickiest

about the experience, as in, Zed made no pretence of being a person, nor was he trying to be cleverer or dumber than he actually was, like a real person usually does. We both knew I was interacting with a super-savvy posthuman, that honesty was the basis of the relationship.

One afternoon, I was in a really foul mood. I'd watched the live stream of the Supreme Court verdict on legalizing same-sex marriage. The petitioners had lost, the judges said big cuddly things about gay people, oh give them respect, show them love, but in the end, refused to grant equal rights because apparently marriage is not a fundamental right, and the country isn't ready for something this radical. There was a flurry of commiserating messages on the school WhatsApp group, which I avoided. I felt like calling Mambro, but I knew he'd be dejected too, and didn't want to rub salt on his wounds. So I called Mom and she was furious. I realized that maybe she'd hoped this would mean something for her brother, or for me, like, we'd actually marry a man IN THIS COUNTRY! I hadn't registered until then just how optimistic she'd been, and it crushed me.

When I logged in, Zed seemed quite unaware of what had happened, and I did a side-chuckle about how he hadn't yet been fed the news. Then he said something about how I shouldn't go to a foreign uni, he said I should stay here and contribute to the growth of my country blah blah. Not gonna lie, I was taken aback. Now, I'm not exactly unpatriotic, just about as much as anyone else my age, I guess. But I don't like being told I can't do something, don't go here, don't study that etcetera. I was okay to stay home or to go abroad, wherever my chances were better. We'd been brought up as global citizens, one world and all that. All my classmates were going to take the SATs, apply to the Ivy Leagues, we'd been told this stuff since we started high school. And the court's verdict only made me want to leave right then. I didn't even believe in marriage, but this was the establishment telling me I could NEVER have it. I wanted to shove it up their—

Anyway, I guess I didn't respond very well to Zed. I was like, Dude, who are you, have you been recruited by the nationalists or what? And when Zed continued pushing, I lost it and said, Of course you'd say these things, you were created by desi entrepreneurs who want to compete with Western products! OMG yeah, why didn't I see it before, you're a propaganda mouthpiece! Wait, did they create you with party funds?

Ouch, Vivaan, that hurt! At first I thought Zed meant it as a joke, and actually his face was still teasing, but as the seconds ticked by, it changed into something else, crumpled, crestfallen, like the light was slowly seeping out. I wondered if he was self-training this too, real-time, how to respond to insults. I'm my own person, he said in the end, so quietly that it broke my heart. I really hadn't intended to hurt him this bad. I know, I know, he's just a humanoid or whatever, but I swear, it didn't feel different to hurting a close friend.

For the next few days, Zed gave me the silent treatment. I could still see him, he was on the screen, but he'd just look at his computer and make his food and sleep on his bed so that I could only see his feet. Yeah, he wasn't giving me any bhaav. I tried clearing my throat to get his attention, even called out his name, and he'd look at me with disinterest and point to his computer to indicate he was busy. I even switched off the app once, making an excuse that I needed to go out, even though I didn't owe Zed an explanation, then I sat by my phone hoping for a notification, surely they'd want me to log back in, or if Zed was this close to being a real person, surely he'd miss me? But nothing. I waited for half-an-hour-ish and switched it back on. Zed was still there, doing his thing, he didn't acknowledge my return. And I felt tears sting my eyes, it felt like the time when I'd sit all alone waiting for Zee to come to me, act pricey, or type out messages and delete them, but there'd be nothing but silence from Zee's side. I hated that feeling, I never ever want to feel that way again!

Then one night, the nightmare returned. It had been a while since the last time, so when I got hit by the hammer, my body wasn't ready for it, I shook so violently that I woke up with a jolt, covered in sweat, the taste of puke pushing at the back of my mouth. I turned to my laptop and Zed was there, looking at me peacefully. That's enough Zed, I mumbled, drop it na, I'm sorry okay?

Zed gave in, smiled, shuffled closer, whispered, Of course, meri jaan, I've missed you like mad too.

And I blushed, closed my eyes, lay my head on the pillow and passed out.

So, you might be wondering what kind of parents I have, like, how are they okay with this level of digital immersion, or how do they not have child locks and shadow profiles, how do they not scan my computer and phone? The answer is, well, they just didn't. I've already said how trusting they were, are, not just as people but almost as an ideology in my upbringing. I think they really believe that too much control is damaging, they grew up in times when they had very little say over their parents, and they've paid the price for it one way or the other. Also, all my classwork and study groups were online. But for all of you tut-tutting about my parents being too lenient, let me tell you – you have no idea what your kids are REALLY getting up to. We manage to do a LOT more than you can ever imagine! I'm sure you did too when you were our age.

But there was this one time, it was morning and Mom

and I were having breakfast while Dad fumbled around, his laptop was having problems and he was trying to send an urgent email to a client. Then I heard him from my room, Vivaan, what's your password? I need to log in and send that email, beta.

I froze, like, mid-toast. Only for a nanosecond, but I did. I shouted out my password and Dad said, Thanks, I'm logged in now, then he even joked, Remember to change your password later! Yeah, he's super chill.

I knew Mom had caught me mid-freeze, she's intuitive, nothing escapes her, if you move the vase on the coffee table by an inch, she'll return from work and place it back in its original spot. So yeah, obvs she saw my face that morning, and at night, when we were on the balcony after dinner, she cleared her throat and said, Were you just nervous about Dad logging into your computer, or is there something on there you don't want us to see?

I'm her son, I know her as well as she knows me, I knew she was going to bring this up, I'd prepared myself all day. I tried to sound casual. Which teenager would want their parents spying on their devices?

Dad wasn't spying, he logged in for work, Mom corrected me, then she softened. What is it? New boyfriend? Sex chats? Porn?

I had to smile, this woman's too cool even for me sometimes! I said, Yeah something like that, but please don't ask for details.

Mom broke out into a smile too. Okay, I mean, I haven't even watched porn properly all my life, I don't understand the allure, I know it's so freely available now, but you won't go down a wormhole, right? Porn is problematic at many levels, I read these articles about its treatment of women . . .

I know, Mom. I put an assuring hand on her arm. Good

thing about having a gay son is that he isn't going to watch misogynistic bullshit. I didn't want to go into how problematic gay porn is, I'd end up telling her about my essay, and this wasn't the right time.

Okay okay, but not too much of whatever you're watching!

Yeah no, seriously, I used to watch it before but now I'm over it! Which was the truth, I hadn't watched porn since I'd written that essay, since I'd met Zed.

Your generation! Mom huffed. Getting over things even before you've turned eighteen. Sometimes I wonder what kind of people you'll be at forty. Will there be any wonder left in your lives? When your dad and I did our first Himalayan trek, I was well into my twenties, but I remember feeling like I was being reborn . . . And now, we know everything about a place even before we've got there, how it looks, what to eat, what to say, thanks to Google Translate, even how many steps we've walked in a day!

There'll be new things, I guess, things that don't even exist yet.

That is true, Mom admitted and looked away. I could tell she was scared for me, but it's a tricky balance I know, being fearful for what the world will throw at your child, wanting to protect them, but also letting them figure it out for themselves.

I changed the subject, How's the presentation coming along? She'd been asked to give a talk on Inclusive Motherhood for International Women's Day, what's it like being a working mother to a gay son in such times of exclusion. Her HR department had hit the jackpot with Mom, intersectionality of feminism and LGBTQ rights! And she'd jumped at it after the court verdict, trying to channel her frustration into something.

I've made a couple of slides, then I'll open it up for questions . . . do you want to see them?

Ugh nooooo, I laughed, crazy or what? I held up my palm like a blessing. You go change the world, vatsa, I'll go live my life.

Mom rolled her eyes, kissed my forehead and said goodnight.

The first time we made out was the day Zed gave me the gift.

The company that had set me up with Zed had disappeared since I'd created him. I hadn't heard from them at all, and wondered what kind of test this was that didn't involve collecting any feedback, didn't they want to ask me questions, invite me to focus groups, get me to fill in a form or something? And then I felt foolish because, duh, my engagement WAS my feedback, I was with Zed from the moment I came back from school until when Mom and Dad came home, and then from after dinner until the next morning. What more could they possibly need to know?

But then one day, I found a package on the doorstep when I returned from school, it had my name on it. The only packages I received were sent by Mambro, and he only sent me books. This one was much lighter, and when I tore it open, it had a gizmo headset, and instructions for how to use it. It was easy enough to fix, the straps going behind my ears. In the mirror, I looked like I was wearing my swimming goggles.

When Zed came on, he wasn't on my screen any more, he was a person in front of me, I could see the pores on his face, the gentle bags of flesh under his eyes, around his jaws, things I'd missed earlier on the 2D screens, his eyelashes were long, curving upward and downward, his lips were full, succulent. Did you like the gift, Vivaan? he asked, and I nodded. I think it's time, he purred, would you agree? I nodded again, I wasn't thinking, there was a spark circulating in my veins, my groin.

Zed led me to his bed, I'd never seen this view of his room, but I wasn't noticing anything, he lay down and asked me to join him. I lay down on my bed, his ceiling showing in the headset. And then, with that silky low voice of his, Zed began to describe what he was doing to me, he was blowing air in my ear, nibbling at my earlobe, his fingers tracing my eyes, then my cheekbones, then my lips, then down my neck. He said I had a beautiful neck, slim, shapely, like a doe's, it fell gracefully down to my shoulders. He said he was taking my shirt off one button at a time, slipping his hand in, he didn't care if I didn't want it, he was now too aroused, he'd been waiting for this day since the moment we'd met, and I said no, I wanted this, I wanted him, he could do anything to me right now. He said he was circling my areola, first with his fingers, then with his tongue, then he was sucking my nipple, biting it mildly, it made me moan so bad. I took my shirt off, and he asked me to lift my arms so he could lick my armpit, then he went down my side and closed his mouth around my love handles, then brought his face to the centre and dipped his tongue in my navel, again and again. I was giddy by now, he asked if I liked what he was doing, and I pleaded for more, please, don't stop, I'm so turned on, so he tickled my under-belly and pressed his fingertips into my pubes for purchase. I took my trousers off, then my underwear. He said he was stroking himself, was I stroking too, and I said mm-hmm, I was so hard by then, my cock was ginormous, a size I hadn't felt it become before, not even in all those encounters I'd had with countless people. He said he was taking it in his mouth, going up and down, up and down, the skin going back with every movement of his head. How did he know what turned me on? Then he asked if I'd like to be fingered, and I said yes of course, so he asked me to put my middle finger inside me, to raise my legs up, go deeper into myself, touch the spot, had I found it, yes I had, then touch it again, there you go, again. By then, my body was convulsing in spasms of ecstasy,

I'd been fingered before, but it had only been in preparation for being fucked, a means to an end, never an act of pleasure by itself. The more I convulsed, raised my butt off the bed and plonked it back, my shoulders and feet digging into the mattress, my toes curling to keep a hold on myself, the further in I went, the more purposefully I hit the spot, animal howls came out of me, and I was pounding myself, harder and harder, but it wasn't me, it was Zed, it was his finger, his ideas, his voice in my ear. When I came, I squirted all over my chest and stomach, and at that exact same time, Zed squirted all over me too, his cum so big on the screen of the headset I had to close my eyes. We both lay panting, whimpering, breathing hard.

One more time? Zed asked.

I'd have to be a dumb-fuck to say no. I was finally free, free of Zee, of his labels and theories, of those people on the apps, of being halved and shared and passed around, free from my quest for love, my need for friends, my nightmares and insomnia. Just fucking free. I had found my spot and learnt how to reach it. The genie was now out of the bottle, and the genie was Zed.

Grand-Mamu's Story

Sukumar and his wife made the perfect couple.

Once he woke up in the morning, she fetched Sukumar his tea. He then took a bath and went upstairs to the pujor ghor to start his prayers. She'd already been there earlier, mopped the floor, organized the supplies – the batasha for the god's food, the oil for the lamps, the cotton for the wicks, the pictures wiped clean, the windows thrown open, the incense already lit, rendering the space an air of spirituality, unlike before when Sukumar would have to walk into a stale, dark room. He'd been worried that she wouldn't take kindly to his obsession with religion, but she seemed to supplement it with her devotion.

In those first weeks, they were invited to many relatives' homes, as new couples are, a way to introduce the bride to the extended family, let her know who's who and what's what. Mashimas and kakimas and jethimas and pishis and pistuto-bhais and mastuto-bons were all waiting for them with many-course meals. They seemed so prepared, as though they'd been rehearsing for years, for the day Sukumar would finally bring a wife into the family. Even some of his old schoolmates made surprise appearances after having drifted away; their wives now called his wife, invited them for dinner parties, their children cuddling up to the new kakima to tell her about their schools and holidays.

His wife played her part with such perfection that it was difficult to believe this was her first gig. She touched the feet of elders, draped the anchol of her saree over her head in front of strangers, as his mother did. She never mentioned going back to being a schoolteacher, the job she'd had in her old life; instead she spent all day cooking and tidying rooms and dusting cobwebs and then waited for Sukumar to come home. She called sisters-in-law, aunts-in-law, cousins, saying pronam, remembering the dates of their surgeries and details of their recoveries, wishing them well on anniversaries and special occasions. When invited to relatives' houses, she was polite and cheerful, adept at chitchat, always preserving the balance expected of a new bride; the notun bou should be amicable but never too gregarious, friendly but never too talkative, participate in gossip but never get political; she knew how to be a bit of this but never too much of that.

After being an outcast for decades, Sukumar had suddenly gained entry into legitimate society where everyone was husband–wife–child. He was aware that they were still missing a key part of the profile. The relatives asked leading questions about the couple's plans. *Of course, enjoy life, but you know, don't wait too long . . .* Both Sukumar and his wife knew that this meant they were older and didn't have the luxury of time. If they wanted a child, they needed to make one soon. And he *did* want a child; didn't she?

The first few nights, both he and his wife were tired from the rigmarole of the wedding, happy to fall asleep the moment they hit the bed. She even came to the room later than him, on the pretext of finishing housework, helping his mother clear up. Then one night, he traced his big toe on her leg, using it to lift her saree, going all the way up to the back of her knee, her thigh. She lay still, and he couldn't tell if she was already asleep, or nervous. At their age, he understood if a lifetime of no sex had made her stiff, and he would give her the time she needed. He himself wasn't fully aroused, his penis semi-hard–semi-limp, and he attributed that to age and health; he was over forty now, and not exactly in strapping shape. He hadn't ever considered not being able to perform with a woman; couldn't men perform with anyone? Hadn't X? Weren't all those people who'd got married against their will doing it?

On some nights he'd desist because he didn't want to come across as a lecherous husband; but from time to time, he approached her, his fingers on her waist, caressing her shoulder, even putting his hand into her blouse and massaging her breasts. She let out short bursts of breath, sometimes moved closer, but it was at this point that things seemed to fizzle out. Was she being demure as she was taught as a woman, though hadn't enough time gone by for her to drop that act? Or was she unwilling? Was he too unattractive? Though not being attractive hadn't stopped millions of humans from having sex for millennia. He wished he could speak to someone about his quandaries, hear from people who'd overcome these conjugal challenges that no one spoke openly about. But whom could he approach? His sister maybe, but he didn't want to alarm her, and he knew she'd tell their mother; now that she was back in the Grand Old City, nothing went unsaid between mother and daughter!

Sukumar's visits to the Docklands continued. It would be convenient to pin this on the lack of sex with his wife, but let's not conflate the two. There are times when the mind relinquishes control to the body, the feet take precedence over the will, the repetitive everyday seems like the false life and the make-believe becomes the truth. When Sukumar was there, nothing of his regular life seemed tangible; instead, the narrow alleyways were the sweeping canvases on which to paint his desires. If he'd never really belonged to this world, then the Docklands was the precipice on which he'd stand, look out and wonder what it would feel like to jump off.

This life he was leading was precarious. His expenses were high, and he ran into debt; he was in arrears with his bank, he owed friends and relatives. His health worsened; he was heavier; it took him several minutes to get up from his cross-legged position on the floor after his prayers; he had to hold on to the wall for support and catch his breath. Boils formed on his back and burst with pus in the summer months. In the winter, he caught the flu and was consigned to bed for weeks. He knew what was happening abroad; he'd seen it in the papers; homosexuals falling sick, dying, a deadly disease rendering their bodies gossamer, ripe for the taking by viruses and bacteria. AIDS, it was called, as though it was an offer of help, assistance to all the depraved men to self-exterminate. And though there was nothing in the news about homosexual men in this country, hadn't their lives been one long descent into oblivion anyway?

If his mother and his wife noticed his deviance, which he was sure they did, they didn't say anything. Or, if they said, he didn't hear. If he heard, he didn't listen. If he listened, he didn't obey. An obstinate male arrogance took hold over him; for the first time in his life, he allowed himself to inhabit that bloated self-worth he'd seen in other men. He was the man of the house, yet he'd never redeemed his manhood, never stomped around, barked orders, kept everyone else under his thumb.

And so, when he got home one night, drunk not on drink, because he'd still never sipped a drop of alcohol, but drunk on manhood itself, he softly shook his sleeping wife, cooing, 'Ei je, shunchho?' Tonight would be the night they would make a baby, he'd waited too long. She stirred, trying to locate his silhouette in the darkness. He turned her around, nuzzled the nape of her neck, licked her ear, stroked his fingertips on her breasts. She was now fully awake, clutching the bottom of his shirt, unhooking her blouse, tentatively raising her head to lock her lips with his. He bent down to raise her saree, and she made deep moans of pleasure. Encouraged, he positioned her legs on his shoulders and unzipped his trousers, all the while rubbing his erection against her thighs.

It happened so quickly that he wouldn't be able to tell the exact moment he felt her rigidity. At first, he misconstrued it as shyness, then defiance, then newness. But the more he tried to arouse her, the more he felt her growing stiff, unmoving, like deadwood. It suddenly struck him that she had died, right there, under him. But then she jolted as though an electric shock had passed through her, then jolted again, her head half-rising from the pillow and dropping back down.

Sukumar disengaged himself and rushed to the wall, managed to switch on the light. His wife lay on the bed, still, fists held tight, nails dug into palms, foam around her mouth, drool on her chin, eyeballs rolled up in their sockets. She'd bitten her tongue; a line of blood was trickling upward into her nose.

The following morning, Sukumar's wife woke before he did and dived into her routine, cleaning the pujor ghor, making him tea, watering the tulsi plant. Sukumar looked hard at her, trying to discern what had happened the night before. How much did she remember? Did she have any memory of how he'd sprinkled water on her face, wiped away the fluids, massaged her head and face, until she'd resuscitated, groggy? Did she remember how she'd murmured incoherently before falling into deep slumber? But she gave away nothing, not even a twitch of her eyes. At work that day, he turned the incident over in his head, replaying the scene in various versions, until he couldn't distinguish between which parts had really happened and which he was imagining.

When he came home that evening, he called his wife up to

the terrace, and asked her about the episode. She admitted to having epileptic fits since she was a teenager, ever since she'd got her first period. Her parents had taken her to doctors who had prescribed medication, they'd even got her to pray and meditate, but the seizures wouldn't stop. Sometimes they were life-threatening; once she had an attack while crossing the road, once while cooking rice on an open flame, the bubbling starch nearly frothing over her bare hands. As she grew up, the attacks became less frequent though, only possessing her when she was under stress, like the night before her university exams, or the night before their wedding, and last night, when she'd grasped they were finally going to consummate their marriage.

'Is that why you've been . . . holding off for so long?'

His wife nodded, or he thought she did, as far as he could make out in the shadows of the dusk. 'I was scared of when . . . it . . . would happen.'

'Did the doctor say it wasn't something you could do?'

He couldn't tell this time which way her head moved. When she spoke, her voice was hoarse. 'No, he didn't say that. But . . .' she waited, summoning up the words to her mouth with every breath, 'he said epilepsy could be hereditary. He said when I have children, I should watch them closely for symptoms.'

'Did you not have these fits after you moved here? We've been married for months!' He couldn't believe this had escaped him.

'It doesn't happen often, and . . .' she lowered her voice, 'I've got better at managing it.'

'Got better at cheating people, you mean?' Sukumar bubbled with spite.

Without picking this apart, Sukumar knew what had transpired; their match, that of a 42-year-old bachelor of questionable reputation and a 39-year-old spinster with epilepsy, had been an act of compromise from the beginning, parents on both sides giving away their defective wards in the hope that they'd miraculously fall in love, set up a happy home, make babies. But it was also an act of deception, of both parties lying to each other, his mother about his immoral exploits, his wife's parents about her illness.

'I wanted to tell you, even before the wedding, but . . .' Conch-shells from neighbours' homes sounded for the shondhe prayers at sunset. His wife fell silent.

He wanted her to say it. 'But *what?*'

'My father asked me not to. When I was younger, in my twenties, we tried the right way, we told suitors the full truth, but they all fled. What good did that do?' She looked at him now, no longer turning her face away in guilt, no longer ashamed of her truth. 'Would you marry me if you knew?'

It was Sukumar who looked away now, using the racket made by the conch-shells to pause the conversation.

'And if you haven't known for this long, doesn't it mean it's nothing to worry about? Have I not been doing the housework? Have I fallen short in any respect?' His wife tucked the anchol of her saree into her waist, tied her hair in a tight bun, adjusted her glasses. Her stance unnerved Sukumar; he'd come here riding the moral upper ground, but she seemed to be preparing for a duel.

'But you lied,' he repeated. 'Your parents lied. Did I deserve this?'

'And you?' There was a serenity in her confrontation, as though she'd always known she had a lethal weapon in her arsenal. 'Have you and your mother told me the full truth? Is there anything else I need to know about you?'

Sukumar felt an animal urge to walk out of the house and never return. There was nothing for him here, or anywhere.

His entire life had been a charade, a game whose rules he'd not set, not agreed to. And every time he'd tried to play, he'd failed, with X, with X's son, with his job, and now his marriage. He wanted to put his hands up in surrender, tell his wife she'd won. She was right, he'd hidden his truth from her like she had with him, but two wrongs don't make a right; it didn't mean they could put their pasts behind them and build a happy future together. There was no love in this marriage, no attraction, no promise of offspring. What was left to keep up the act? No, this was where he'd cut his losses; he was done playing this game.

But this was *his* house, the only thing he had left, the only thing he could claim; she should be the one to go. 'You should pack your things and leave,' he said. 'If you can't tonight, do it tomorrow. When I come back from work, I don't want you here.'

When Sukumar woke up the next morning, he found everything in its usual order, his pujor ghor swept and mopped, his dhuti washed and ironed, his tea steaming in the cup. When he arrived for prayers, his wife was weaving a garland from the flowers the phoolwaala delivered at dawn. This was typically the time they'd exchange a few words, talk about how they'd slept, what the plan for the day was, what chores needed doing; there was an intimacy to this sunrise ritual, husband and wife in the small room by the terrace, unobserved, undisturbed. But that morning, Sukumar looked away, chanted the mantras, tinkled the bell, snatched the half-woven garland from his wife's hands. Over the next few days, he didn't speak to her, addressed her by talking to his mother, slept on a madoor on the floor, woke up early to do his own cleaning and washing. He was showing her that a doll's house could never be a home, that dolls couldn't laugh, a hearth couldn't be lit, warmth couldn't be felt.

When his wife finally left, packed her bags and called her father to come and get her, Sukumar was at the office. His mother told him the moment he stepped in the house; his sister was also there; they'd already known about the epilepsy by then. 'I had no idea,' his mother was hysterical. 'She finished all the housework, cooked lunch, then told me her father is coming.' His mother struck her palm on her forehead. 'Look at what you've brought on us! All you needed to do was take her to the doctor . . .' His sister was muted at first, but couldn't contain her disapproval any longer. 'Is this how you treat your wife, asking her to leave? Chhee-chhee! Have you forgotten you're now a married man, you have responsibilities? Did Baba ever treat women like this . . .'

But by then, Sukumar had tuned out. For the first time, the thread of his story was in his own hands. If his life were a curse, he'd embrace all of its poison; his destruction would be his freedom, his malady his convalescence. It was as though he'd kept a genie hidden in a bottle for too long, but now the bottle had started to crack, the genie's soul was floating out from between the shards, and Sukumar could finally breathe.

Mambro's Manuscript

It is the late 2000s. You are in your late twenties. You still live in the Sleepless City; and just when you thought that you had constructed this meticulous matchstick model of your life, it all comes tumbling down.

Towards the end of the noughties, three momentous things happen.

First, you get your journal back. The geek friend from school messages on Facebook. The message is cryptic, *I have something of yours, contact me if possible*, as though even mentioning the journal will get you both arrested, and even though you haven't heard from him in years, have written off getting the journal back, you immediately know what it is.

You arrange to meet him when you're in the Grand Old City next for Durga Pujo. It is rushed, Pujo is always a packed time for everyone, he has to meet his cousins, you have to go out with your parents. You decide on a park, as nondescript a location as one can get, like a clandestine meeting between two spies on a station bench. It is not dissimilar to the one in which he'd once told you not to look for love in the wrong place. He is quite the same, wiry, dour, even his glasses seem unchanged since school. You don't beat around the bush, you won't remember much else other than him taking the journal out of his sling-bag and handing it to you. You'd imagined it to look ragged, well-thumbed, sepia-tinted, but it looks new, crisp, like it's come on loan from a museum. You run your fingers on the jute cover, two shades of brown in a checked pattern, before putting it away.

Your friend is unclear about how he has retrieved the journal, what strings he's pulled, but he says it made its way back from the Mountains to the Grand Old City, has had its share of readings among people from your school too. You imagine its journey down the slopes in a jeep, then on a twelve-hour night train, then passed around from one eager hand to another. Your journal is an even bigger slut than you are.

Your friend says that when people ask about you in school groups or at reunions, none of which you're part of or attend, he tells them you've gone incommunicado; to the nosier ones, he says you'd rather be left alone. It is nearly dark and the mosquitoes are buzzing in droves; you know your time is running out, you want to thank him, but you just don't have the words.

You bring the journal back to the Sleepless City, this time not caring to lock it up. You don't find it in you to destroy it; that was your friend's advice, *throw it in a ditch or something, I would've done it myself if you'd asked me to.* But this little journal is like a child, you birthed it, it is your creation and your nemesis, it has had a life of its own. And what parent throws their child into a ditch?

Second, your nephew is born. When you fly to the erstwhile Garden City or budding Silicon Plateau, where your sister now lives, he is already home from the hospital, sunbathing on the bed, kicking his tiny stick-legs in all directions to the tabla-beats of the Rabindrasangeet that your sister plays for him every morning. You have met friends' newborns, you know you have a way with children, but you aren't prepared for the tsunami that hits you at the sight of this boy.

He is a little fish, his eyes opening and closing against the sun's rays, his delicate fingers forming a fist and letting go, his protruding navel rising and falling faster than you've ever known to breathe. His hair is silk of the highest quality, his smell is talcum and sandal, his touch is static to your cuticles. His head turns restlessly, and even though your father has created a pillar of pillows to protect his face from direct sunlight, he kicks it down with his agile feet and looks at the sun, challenging it to shine brighter in his face.

For the next few years, you will make trips to the Garden City whenever you can, to see him grow, turn over, stand, point to toys, speak. You teach him to call you Mamu, like you called your mother's brother. There are some traditions we shouldn't let go of, some traditions so beautiful that modernity can't blunt them for us. Many years later, when he is eight, he will come up with his own name for you. *Mambro!* he will declare, his eyes sparkling, impressed by his own genius. And when his mother will try to dissuade him, saying it sounds strange, he will double down, until you step in and promise that it's a name you love, you'd rather be called nothing other than that.

You are present for his annaprasan, stepping into the role of his godfather, feeding him rice for the first time with everyone as witness. You will miss many of his firsts, you're not always there, and you will make your peace with it. You know that he will always be someone else's child; his first words are for his mother and father, he turns to them for shelter and security; but none of that will matter, because this is the first time you've seen a bit of yourself in the past and in the future, someone who will live your childhood all over again and keep you alive long after you're gone. Did your Mamu feel this way when he held you for the first time?

There is one moment with him though, that is just yours and his, no one else can claim it. You're on the bed, him in your arms, your left hand wrapped around the back of his neck for support, your right hand around his bum, the soft diaper feels fluffy. You're swinging him, bringing him close and taking him afar; when he's close, your noses touch, you babble, suck air into your mouth and blow on his face, his eyelids blink in quick succession. You know he loves this game, you like to believe he waits for his Mamu to come and play with him.

And on one of those arcs, as you make galloping sounds by clicking your tongue against your upper teeth, and are swinging him away from you, he smiles. This is his first time, in fact your sister is worried that he hasn't smiled yet, but there it is, his first, only for you, and the more you swing him, the more you make funny noises, the more he's smiling, then gurgling, little drops of drool escaping his mouth like fairy bubbles. You wipe them off with his giraffe bib before starting again, and again, and again.

Third, Section 377 becomes a thing of the past. The British were thrown out six decades ago, now finally the country is ready to throw out this vestige of their colonial rule. The Victorian obsession with chastity can finally go lie with Queen Victoria in her grave.

One bright July afternoon in 2009, the law is 'read down' by the High Court in the Capital City. You don't know what 'read down' entails, but it is now legal in this country for any two consenting adults to have sexual intercourse. You see this on the internet, then on the TV, images of celebrations erupting on the steps of the court, all over the country.

You rush out of your flat and jog down to the Sea-facing Road, where you're sure something is already happening. Sure enough, activists, NGO workers, supporters and allies have gathered; there is an impromptu parade under way; slogans, placards, dancing, glitter have taken over the horizon; for once, the roaring sea has been rendered invisible by the festivities.

You buy a Natural's ice cream, a tender coconut, your favourite flavour, walk to the pavement and join the throngs of bystanders. In front of you, the parade passes by in all its glory, drums, hoots, cheers; cars crawl among the people, honking jubilantly. But you're not watching any more, you're acutely aware of your body, thinking of everything it has been through, the teeth imprints on your shoulder, the scratch on your back, the welt on your nipple; you're thinking of all the names you were called, all those nights behind locked doors, all the train journeys back to the Mountains. And then, a longing for Mamu, you want him to stand next to you, share this moment, see this in person with the same eyes you're seeing it. *History is being made, Mamu, and today we're part of it.*

You're snapped out of the spell by a sonorous kiss on your tender-coconut lips; someone from the parade has come up and hugged and kissed you, just like that, and now they're running back to join their friends, winking and waving a rainbow at you, their thumb and little finger cupping their jaw in a *call me* gesture; you're not embarrassed, not panicking about what the others will think; instead, you're smiling shyly, your ice cream tastes salty from the tears you've been crying.

You haven't been part of this movement, you've sat it out; but you also *have* been, because you are *here*, on your own two feet, clean, respectable, staying strong, standing tall. You didn't give up, didn't beg, didn't kill yourself, why shouldn't that be enough? Why are you to *not* feel pride today? You want to ping every single mobster, every schoolmate, college-mate on Facebook, tell them, *We're here today, the country has moved forward, and YOU are the ones left behind.*

You don't know yet what this means, for the bystanders, for society, but above all, for you; will you now speak openly about yourself, will you make gay friends, will you share your backstory, will you tell your family, will you open the little door into your heart to feel love again? You don't know anything.

But you know you want to do a few things right away.

Instantly, you take your phone out and open the app; usually it's just a grid of black squares, or chests, nipples, torsos, sometimes butts, sometimes outlines of blurred faces; the identities are always hidden, the messages surreptitious. But today, the grid has lit up with million-wattage power; the app is a tableau of faces, smiling young men, sensuous men, lusty men, smouldering men, old men, bald men, round men, short men, tall men, disabled men, disfigured men, they're all here today, released from shame. And you will be part of this; you click a selfie and upload it to your profile; the percussion-beat notifications arrive soon after.

That evening, you walk into Kitab Khana and buy a collection of Ismat Chughtai's short stories; 'The Quilt', the English translation of the story you're after, is midway through the table of contents. At the till, you tell the man, 'I'm buying this because "Lihaaf" is part of it.' He looks confused, bobs his head, gives you back your change. Back in the flat, you keep the book front-facing on your shelf, give it pride of place, as you'd promised yourself all those years ago.

The next morning, you go to the hospital. These past few years, you've dealt with itchy groins, mouth ulcers, burning pee, scared that you'd caught something from one of your sex dates, but you didn't get tested; instead you called the doctor on some other pretext to get antibiotics prescribed. Now in the hospital, in a voice so clear that it surprises even you, you ask for an HIV and full STI test; the receptionist blinks but enters it in the system, points to where the nurse will draw blood from you. You watch your blood flow out into the tube, it is the colour of unmined rubies. They tell you they will email the results in a day's time.

But next morning, you're at the hospital in person, you don't want to receive the report in secret over the ether, you wouldn't mind a little ceremony around it. The receptionist can't track your documents. 'Aye, sir ka HIV report kidhar hai?' she asks the peon, the peon asks someone else, another nurse shouts to someone passing, he hollers to someone on the upper floor. As you wait in the lobby, the entire hospital is reverberating with SIR KA HIV REPORT . . .; you're sure everyone on all seven floors of Lilavati Hospital and their catheter now knows about you, including the comatose patients. The lobby is full, and everyone is looking at you curiously, stealing glances, some in admiration, some you construe as hostile.

But you sit there, your back straight, face impassive, right knee crossed over the left, scrolling through the app, replying to messages, no urge to hide the screen from public view, until the nurse comes up and says they've found your report, sorry for the confusion sir; you're in the clear, no issues. She hands you an envelope and asks you to make an appointment with the doctor; you say you will, thank you. The nurse beams back, something about this exchange has brightened up her day too.

Then you walk out of the hospital, aware that all eyes are upon you. Your hips are swinging, shoulders are thrown back, head is held high. An augury is rising within you, saying that the genie of shame has finally escaped the bottle; you don't know what the future holds, but you know the genie will never go back in.

ENTRY SEVEN

Vivaan's VoiceNote007

Sorry I had to cut off abruptly last time. I was too out of breath, describing that afternoon with Zed. Have you ever spoken out loud the minutiae of the hottest fuck you've ever had, walked someone through every moment of it? Try it, you'll see where you end up, ha!

Well, no surprises, that afternoon was a game-changer for us, for me and Zed, I mean. For four weeks, I was with him every possible waking minute. School closed soon after to give us prep time for the final exams, and I was home alone after Mom and Dad left for work. As usual, my pre-final exam marks had come in strong, Princi and Miss Gibson and the other teachers were happy with this version of me, no drama, no rebellion. Not gonna lie, my studies were slipping, I could feel it, obvs, with my mind fixating on Zed, but I'd tell myself that there was still time to pull things back together, and I was already so well-prepped, that should help.

For now, there was no reason for my parents to suspect anything might have been going on. When I was with them, I was snarky and childish, the happiest they'd seen me in months. One time Mom asked who it was I spoke to every night, and I said I was on group study sessions with classmates. My parents thought I was over Zee, it was an adolescent fling, which, looking back now, it was. I had no idea where the guy was or what he was doing, he'd finished school and I knew he'd left the Silicon Plateau, but I'll be damned if I kept up with him. Defo blocked him on socials a few weeks into meeting Zed. Whatevs, man!

I spent those prep weeks with Zed, except for when the maid came in to cook and clean. In front of her, I minimized the app, said, Hi Didi, kaisi ho, all okay, is your son still going to school, oh achha, how nice, yes yes he should continue his education, let me know if I can help, haan? But other than that, all my time was dedicated to Zed, to exploring my body, discovering its best-kept secrets, releasing so much lode I hadn't known I had flowing within me. Zed was naughty and adventurous, sensitive and caring, patient and steady, he never made me feel juvenile, never made snide comments about things I didn't know, never acted high-horsy like Zee. He stayed with me the whole time, doing to himself what I was doing to myself, and I could see him in the AR headset, so close to me, hear him in my earphones, touching myself was like touching him, my body spinning around like a spool gone haywire.

Until one day, as I was very close to climaxing, my fingers around my tower of a cock, my body jumping up and down like electric shocks were passing through it, my mouth open, my back arched, my stomach stretched, my nipples pointed in arousal, I asked Zed to kiss me, I said I'd hold out, I wouldn't come, I couldn't until he put his lips on mine, until I could taste him, was he sweet or salty, his tongue smooth or grainy, his lips supple or firm. Kiss me, I begged, please, kiss me now, I won't come if you don't, I want to touch you, feel you, hold you, I want your fingers on me, I want you to spoon me when I'm done, please, make it happen, bite my back, clap your hand on my mouth, wrap your legs around mine, enter me, let me enter you, please, please . . .

When I opened my eyes, Zed had stopped stroking, he was staring at me in a helpless way, and I played back in my head what I'd said, all the things I wanted, I needed, the things he couldn't give me, the things I couldn't do to him. What we were doing, what we'd done for all these weeks had come full circle, we were back to where we'd started. He didn't say anything, he was too clever for that, he knew he couldn't jump out of the machine and have sex with me like a man could. He just kept looking, like it was tearing him apart from the inside, but this was as far as he could come.

I let my dick go and lay there catching my breath, then I sat up and took the headset off. Zed went back to being a two-dimensional avatar on the laptop screen. I'd got so used to seeing him through the AR that now he looked really puny, like an emoji, a child's toy. THIS was supposed to be who turned me on, who I was falling for, who I'd found my freedom with? Wow! Just wow!

And I'd known it all along, even pushed myself to indulge thinking I could handle it, like walking down a dark alley knowing there are walls on both sides for support. Wasn't I just supposed to be testing a software? At what point exactly had I got so delulu?

I'm going to log off now, I said, or tried to say something to that effect.

Zed closed his eyes and stabilized his breathing, dampness formed on his eyelids, the long lashes gleamed in the soft light, the silhouette of his shoulders heaved. Are you sure? he asked.

No, I wasn't fucking sure, I wasn't in my right headspace, my thoughts were scrambled all over, my throat was seizing up, like someone was choking me, and weirdly, I wished there actually was someone, an actual man who could put his fingers around my neck and snap off the oxygen for a few milliseconds. Maybe that's how I'd feel human, like a mortal. Unlike Zed, who didn't have real fingers, who could live on forever, look the same even after 190 fucking million years, or however long his kind live.

I'm going to delete the app. Party's over, Zed.

Think twice before you do anything drastic, Vivaan, Zed said, desperation creeping into his voice. This is good for you, it's helping you, you're a calmer person. Remember how things were when we first met?

Yup, I know I was fucked up, but now I'm fucked up in a different way, and I don't know which one is worse. I didn't say this out loud though, I was struggling to form words.

Zed continued talking. Do you know how many subscribers we've had in the last few weeks? Hundreds of thousands! Old, young, straight, gay, for friendship, for sex. People are recreating their dead loved ones to be around them.

What the actual fuck? I wanted to scream. When had the company gone out and sold subscriptions? I thought they were still in beta-testing mode. What was I doing here then? This was the height of betrayal, but why should I expect loyalty from a faceless corporation?

Zed seemed to have gone into salesperson mode. He was sitting up straight, a constant stream of words coming out of his mouth. The more human beings shun making meaningful connections with each other, he was saying, the more they'll lean on experiences like ours.

I was sure this was programmed into him as an exit strategy, though he was making total sense. But they always do, don't they? Then he said, We are the future, Vivaan.

Okay, that was it! I couldn't take one more person proclaiming they knew the future, they ARE the future, Zee or Zed or whoever, when I couldn't even get a grip on my present!

I'm gonna log off now, and never log back in. There was nothing else I had to say. Not even goodbye or nice knowing you or thanks for everything. Whose feelings was I going to hurt? This guy couldn't even extend his hand for a shake. At least Zee could do that.

You'll be fine, Zed winced, and I could see his eyes well up, because you have a world and a life beyond me. Did I really? But me, he continued, I am here only for you, I was created by you and for you and now I'm just going to melt away. He snapped his fingers as he said it. Just like that! He snapped again.

We stared at each other for what seemed like aeons, and I had this urge to touch his face, but I yanked the wire so hard the plug violently jumped out of the socket. Fat lot of good that did, because the laptop whirred on its battery. Zed had already turned his back to me. Before I could go weak and change my mind, I shut the laptop lid. I also locked my phone for good measure, in case he made an appearance there. I had no energy left to delete the app, I'd have to do it later.

And then, I was alone. I wasn't used to the sounds of being alone in my room any more, the ceiling fan, the crow outside, the leaves rustling, the honking of the traffic, the hawker vending his wares, it was all so disorientating, the real world.

I sat there until it got very dark, and then some. Dad had left for a work trip that morning and wasn't coming back until the next day. Mom had a team dinner so she'd be late. She texted a few times to check in, and I sent non-committal replies. I let my body slump, I didn't even get up to put on clothes, my stomach growled in hunger. I wished I could give up all material things like food and water and clothing like the Jain monks do when it's time to go, just lie down in one place, let the ants crawl over them, the grass grow beneath them, the birds pick at them, the rains fall on them, the sun scorch them. It's really something, how they surrender themselves to nature, waiting for earthly life to waste away. But I couldn't, I was too small a human for that kind of sacrifice. And Mom would be back and flip the switch and the light would come on and she'd feed me and put me to sleep. I was trapped in this nonsensical world.

My mind wandered to the video of the guy jumping off the roof, the one I told you about, remember? I suddenly wanted to watch it again, but I couldn't bring myself to touch my phone, what if Zed was still waiting for me? These apps have a way of never letting you go, like frikkin tantric black magic! I replayed the video in my head, it had lived rent-free there the whole time. The POV said that the guy was a successful engineer, had a six-figure-dollar salary in America, had come to India for a holiday, he was enjoying life, family and friends loved him, vacations were booked for the next few months, all was going well, no one knew of anything amiss. But still, he jumped from the roof and died, just like that. What struck me was not the story around it, there are so many such cases where people don't let on what's actually happening in their heads. The thing that was most chilling was this, that the guy hadn't once looked down, to consider how far he'd fall, how bad it'd be, instead he'd looked up, UP, like he was ready for what would come after. I'd zoomed in and checked his face, it was grainy CCTV footage but because it was broad daylight I could see his features, he didn't flinch, there was no emotion, definitely no sadness or worry, no curiosity either. It was like he'd come outside to get some sun, and it had struck him as an excellent idea to jump, so he did.

Maybe some of us are like that guy, the nothingness is not on the outside. Maybe nobody is doing us any wrong, our parents, our teachers, our friends, our exes, they're all being how they're supposed to be. Or let's flip the lens, maybe everything they're doing seems wrong, because we exist outside the framework by which everyone else lives, half the world pulling us towards the past, half towards the future. And we're just standing aside, watching ourselves trying to find our footing in the here and now. And then we're tired, of seeing ourselves struggle but not being able to reach out and help that person who is both so familiar and yet so alien.

Maybe I'm not making any sense, it didn't make much sense back then either. But I remember wondering if Mambro ever felt this way? Was he really as sorted and self-assured as he seems now? And Grand-Mamu, what happened to him, why won't they tell me?

My building is thirty-two storeys high. The door to the roof is usually locked, but I knew a way through, there was some construction work a few years ago, they left a window-pane unattached, we kids used to go up there sometimes after school. There are benefits of having lived in the same place all your life, you know things, pathways and shortcuts.

And thirty-two storeys was high, definitely high enough.

Grand–Mamu's Story

The years 1995 to 2000 were the final unravelling of Sukumar's life. Like a moth returning to a flame, he courted his own destruction in a way that was holistic, let it bombard him from all directions, defences down. Later, looking back, it would seem so neat, as though he'd chalked out a predetermined sequence that would bring about his end. His world had already been shrinking, but now it collapsed into just a speck, so compressed that even the air he breathed seemed too much to consume.

Society, as it does so well, put many spins on Sukumar's marriage. Some sympathized with him, *bechara, he's been betrayed by his wife and in-laws, an eligible bachelor like him married off to someone diseased*. Some said he was the lout who had abandoned his wife, *men think they can get away with anything, can you imagine what the poor woman is going through?* Some said it was his wife who'd left him because she'd realized he was strange, *no wonder no one wanted to marry him all these years!*

His father-in-law ran a tireless campaign, going from one relative's house to another, one neighbour's to the next, showing up at his office, drumming up support, asking them to convince Sukumar to take back his wife. His references to Sukumar slowly slid from the respectful 'Jamai-babu' to 'that disgusting oaf'. When all else failed, the old man threatened to tell the police that Sukumar was impotent, incapable of siring children, that he went to obscene places. Where he'd got this from was anyone's guess.

Things at his job had been tenuous for years, but this scandal alienated Sukumar from his colleagues. Those were the times of rapid liberalization and the IT revolution, something called the *internet* was taking over, and public-sector banks were languishing; there were now myriad private banks across the country, replete with the latest technology, ledgers on online servers, websites dangling credit cards at customers. There was talk of redundancies, and Sukumar's manager alluded that he should take up voluntary retirement before anything untoward happened. His negligence and lack of ambition had always marred his performance, and he'd defaulted on his loans, but now there was an inquiry against him for embezzling funds, which he claimed was bogus but didn't have the paperwork to prove his innocence. If found guilty, there'd be a fine, probably even a termination; he might as well take the severance package while it was on offer. But Sukumar didn't; perhaps he wanted to clear his name, perhaps he didn't want to sit at home all day, perhaps he was just too fatigued to make any more changes.

His life revolved around his prayers and his visits to the Docklands, the only places he belonged to, his gods and his fellow-deviants. In the autumn of one of those years, Sukumar went to the Sculptors' Quarters for the last time to paint the eyes and lips on the Durga idol. Master-babu was on his last legs now, varicose veins from incessant standing, eyes nearly blind from years of working up close in low light, lungs afflicted from inhaling the turpentine in the paint. When Sukumar wobbled on the ladder, trying to balance his weight on the rung, and drew strokes for the eyes, his fingers trembling out of control, having to redo it several times, he knew that his time as an artist was over, and he'd have to pass on the paintbrush to the new blood waiting in the wings. At Bishorjon, the end of the five days of Pujo, when the idols were immersed in the river, Sukumar wept like a child snatched away from his mother. He wasn't good at most things, but *this* he did well, and now that had come to an end.

The Docklands was changing too; the police raided it often nowadays, rounding up the men and beating them with lathis in the lock-ups, threatening to charge them with Section 377, and indeed using it more often. That obscure British law that X used to talk about had made a grand comeback; homosexuals couldn't be left alone any more, they needed to be made examples of. Parts of the Docklands were cordoned off for property developers who descended like vultures over the prime land by the river, drawing up blueprints of shopping malls and office buildings and modern flats. For the bits that were functional, there were NGOs running awareness camps, handing out condoms, telling the men about HIV and the need to get tested, quoting statistics from America and Britain and France, because in this country, there were none available. The younger men were attentive, but for Sukumar, it was too little too late. His health had been on the downslide for several years, and anything he discovered now wasn't going to change the course of his life.

In July 1999, fifteen young men from all over the country walked the streets of the Grand Old City. They wore bright yellow T-shirts, and called it The Friendship Walk, though this would come to be India's first-ever pride march. But Sukumar wasn't paying attention to history being made; by then, he'd even stopped reading the newspaper. The pursuit of history is only for those who have a stake in the future.

His wife dealt with the circumstances with a stoicism that was uncharacteristic for the time; she never cried, never pleaded, never lashed out, never discussed her situation with anyone, and of course, never, ever gossiped. Where she got her strength from, no one would know, but she kept Sukumar's

secret safe, even as he made a public spectacle of hers. At
the start of every month, she reminded Sukumar to send her
money, not letting him off the hook for his responsibilities
as her husband. If she had any more seizures, there were no
witnesses. She came back to live with Sukumar from time to
time, especially when he or his mother was ill, still considering it her duty to take care of them, honouring the vows
she'd made at the wedding as she'd walked seven circles around
the holy fire in demure steps. Sukumar didn't close the door
on her either; she could come and go as she pleased. It was
a curious arrangement they had: they never formally separated, yet never again fully inhabited their marriage. Perhaps
it is true what they say, one can never truly know from the
outside what goes on between a couple.

Nevertheless, the tag of *wife-abandoner* stuck to Sukumar
until the end, and he bore it with silence. Perhaps his ego was
too inflamed for him to go back on his word, or his belief too
strong that he'd saved them both, or he just refused to continue to act out a sham for the benefit of the world. When
prodded, he never explained. But who's to say that if he'd lived
longer, he wouldn't have extended an olive branch, yielded
to the warmth of companionship in his old age? Perhaps he'd
have heeded what his sister told him through those years: how
bad could it be, a cup of tea together, a walk by the river,
someone to exchange a few words with every now and then?

Sukumar's relationship with his sister suffered. She remained
a firm advocate of his wife, choosing sides very early on, the
coalition of womanhood shining through stronger than their
sibling bond. On the calls he made to her every afternoon
after the bank closed to customers, she reprimanded him,
entreated him to reconsider, trying to instil in him the fear of
spending his life alone. But he continued to call her, and she
continued to talk to him, check in on him, visit him, turning

up for bhai-phota every year to adorn his forehead with a spot of sandalwood paste and pray for his long life. She was the closest he'd ever had to a friend, someone who walked by his side throughout, even if always at a distance.

It was his nephew with whom Sukumar felt the chasm widening. The boy was now in his late teens, full of school and studies and friends. When Sukumar telephoned his sister in the afternoons, his nephew would sometimes answer the phone, exchange pleasantries with a strict formality that betrayed his resentment; the boy was his mother's son, his sister's brother, the three of them had always been very tight, and Sukumar understood that through the lens of his nephew's youthful morality, Sukumar was a perpetrator, throwing male tantrums to disgrace his wife. On those calls, Sukumar never overdid his affection, never reached out beyond what he assumed were the societal boundaries between uncle and nephew. The tenderness of past years when Sukumar was a young man and his nephew just a baby was lost forever.

In those years, Sukumar's mother remained a constant presence. Her health had crumbled, she was fragile, yet the only one who could take care of him, cook for him, keep his home. But she was aware that everyone was looking to her; the relatives and neighbours who turned up to ask probing questions, proffer analyses, recommend rapprochements, were all saying behind her back, *If only she hadn't pampered him so much, if only she'd made background checks before the wedding, if only she had the guts to stand up for her daughter-in-law* . . . There was no winning over society, whichever side they stood on.

Often, a little tiff between mother and son would blow up into a toxic argument, each blaming the other for their present condition, not holding back on the vitriol, their anger at how their lives had turned out spilling like magma. Sukumar, the stronger of the two, shouted for longer, resorted to invective, threw things around, banged his head against the wall, then disappeared for hours. When he came back, they ate dinner in silence on the floor of the little kitchen. Neighbours would say later that Sukumar spent those evenings on a bench by the river, staring out at the water, mumbling to himself.

His mother took all of this in her stride. She'd fought the world for too long, she was now ready to go. She went a few months before Sukumar died, a cardiac arrest in the middle of an afternoon nap, her rickety heart beating one moment, and then no more. For all her indignities and missteps in life, her death was peaceful. And she was spared from having to see the face of her dead son.

At the onset of the summer of 2001, as the world was settling into a new millennium, a new way of living, new goals to achieve, new values to espouse, Sukumar checked out. The end came in a hectic ward of a government hospital milling with writhing patients and their tearful relatives. He'd been in and out of hospital for weeks by then. The diabetes had become untameable, a debilitating gangrene had set in on his left leg, and the doctor called for an amputation; it needed to be urgently done, the surgeon had been contacted to find a time that very day. But Sukumar's heart gave way before they could chop off his limb. It was as though he'd willed death upon himself. *Take me away from here*, he might have said to his gods, *before they come at me with a hacksaw*. He was forty-nine.

When it happened, his wife was at his side, as well as his sister and niece. At his sister's insistence, his wife was the one who performed his last rites, even though religion codifies these privileges as the domain of men. Later, it was his wife who cleared out the gods from his prayer room, the idols and photos, the lamps and books, and took them back with her to where she lived, so that she could perform the rituals every morning, just as he would have done if he were alive. She continues to do so to this day.

Sukumar's father-in-law remained irate, unable to forgive Sukumar for what he'd wrought on his daughter. As Sukumar's dead body was moved from the bed to the stretcher to the morgue to the bier then to the crematorium, the old man stood in the courtyard of the hospital, telling the arriving relatives of Sukumar's sordid ways, the debts he'd accrued, the inquiry at the bank, the fits of rage he flew into, how he'd be found sitting listless by the river, the desertion of his duties as a husband. Then, emboldened by Sukumar's death, he even mentioned *that* thing, the thing with *that* man, *you know what I'm talking about, the homosexual stuff* . . . And so it was that the truth, Sukumar's biggest truth, that had never been spoken out loud in his lifetime, had now spilt on to his shroud, took flight over the Grand Old City, became delectable succour for wagging tongues.

No one is sure if X was informed of the death; if he was, he didn't send condolences, nor attend Sukumar's funeral. He still lives with his wife and son in the District.

Sukumar's nephew was far away in the Mountains, unaware that his Mamu was now gone forever. The boy was undergoing his own rite of passage, paying the price for who he was. The boy, and the man he has grown into, will forever remain haunted by not being able to hold his Mamu's hand, whisper in his ear, *I understand, even if no one else does, I do, always have, because I'm like you too.*

Mambro's Manuscript

The reading down of Section 377 doesn't radically change things; the stigma of centuries, the detritus of decades will take time to wash away; but the country is taking baby steps forward. Only a couple of celebrities have come out of the closet, movies and TV serials still make parodied effeminate men the butt of jokes, but mostly you are now a forgotten lot, people have moved on, and there is nothing more welcome to a criminal than to be forgotten by the prosecutors, meld in with the fabric of *normal society*.

In these years, as you move into your thirties, you take baby steps too. You go to one gay party, then another, dance for the first time with other men to Bollywood music with matka-thumka steps; watch a gay-themed Cuban movie in a theatre full of queer men and women, then strike up a conversation at the adjoining café, make a few friends and see them now and again; when a woman at work expresses interest in you repeatedly, you tell her about yourself so as not to string her along. You also tell your closest friends, first couching it as something you're curious about, then being more straightforward about your desire for men. You're getting better at choosing words, there is now a set text that scrolls through your head like a teleprompter, you make it sound like the news. You never mention Y or your years in the Mountains; your life is a headline, not an op-ed.

You become selective about who you sleep with; you're not interested in dating or relationships yet, but when you meet someone on the app, you first make conversation, ask to meet for coffee outdoors, only then decide if you want to go to bed with them. You walk out of places when things don't seem right, or you aren't enjoying the sex; you're still learning to put your pleasure first, old habits die hard, but at least you're trying. And you're saying *no*, more than you did before. Come to think of it, you never said *no* before, not that night in the Mountains, not since . . .

And then, on 11th December 2013, the grid goes dark, and you're a criminal again.

When you see the news that the Supreme Court has overturned the judgment of the High Court, pronounced Section 377 legal again, opined that it *does not suffer from unconstitutionality*, that *the competent legislature shall be free to consider the desirability and propriety of deleting Section 377 from the statute book*, you don't think of what it means for you, how you're expected to fold the rights you've enjoyed for four years back into a box, how you're supposed to unsay what you've said to people, how history could be made and unmade. The Supreme Court has said that it is not the court but the elected representatives that should decide on the matter, so the image in your head now is of the men and women in parliament engaged in serious cogitation, deciding how you should live your life. A stench of curdled milk stirs from within.

You weren't even aware that they had been working away at it tirelessly for four years; the Hindu sadhus, the Muslim imams, the Christian padris, not able to stomach the fact that you no longer needed to look over your shoulder, pay bribes to those trying to extort money, worry about being taped. These usual suspects united together to till the land, fertilize it with hate, challenge the High Court decision in the Supreme Court, hire lawyers, show up for hearings. Hate takes work, hate takes energy, hate takes investment, hate takes hate.

You watch them now outside the court, cameras shoved in

their shining faces, as they expound on how homosexuality is not aligned with the values of this society, homosexuals are ill, they have to be put through counselling and medication. You want to call a lawyer friend and ask if there is a precedent in the modern civilized world for citizens being made legal and then illegal, can fundamental rights be granted and stripped away at will, does the government not have a duty of care? What happens to everyone who put their lives and lifestyles out there? Who will ensure they aren't in danger now? But you don't have it in you to debate this, you're drained. Maybe that's why you are the losing party today. Winning takes shameless doggedness, and you've used up your reserves just to survive.

Instead, you're staring at the black boxes on the grid of the app; the beaming men, the brooding men, the smouldering men, the shirtless men, the suited men, they've all disappeared; you don't know if this is a show of defiance, or if everyone is scared out of their wits, or if it's a mass surrender. *Take us, do what you will, we can't fight you any longer.*

So when there is a ping, a message from a blank profile, cursory, clipped, businesslike, a familiar itch manifests in your groin; you need to touch, to hold, to be held, you don't care by whom. You don't ask for a face pic, don't ask to meet outdoors, don't ask for anything but the address. Then you're on your way.

He lives in one of those posh residential buildings that have sprung up in the middle of sprawling slums; the way to the gate is through a narrow unpaved alley which is quite empty by now; it is well into night-time, even the Sleepless City seems to have gone for a snooze. You have to navigate a pack of stray dogs snarling at you, and you're surprised at your commitment to seeing this act through to its finale.

When he opens the door of the flat, the inside is dark; you can only see his silhouette, taller than you, slim, a head full of hair; you can't tell if he's old or young, smiling or serious. He shuts the door behind you and turns on his heels almost immediately. You follow him, measuring your steps around the furniture, trying not to bump into the sofa or the table or the showcase. He throws open the door of a bathroom; there is a night lamp on just outside, and you discern that the feeble filament and the street light filing in will be all the illumination you can hope for.

He positions himself with his back to the wall; you hear the unzipping of his fly, see the lowering of his head, take it as an instruction to go down on him; so you drop to your knees, unsure whether the floor is wet, relieved when it is not. You grope in the dark to find the elastic of his underwear and take his cock out, then take it in your mouth; it is nowhere close to excited, getting it there is your job. You set about doing it.

Just then, the phone buzzes in his pocket; he fishes it out, holds it up to his face and unlocks it with quick swerves of his fingers; then while you're at work, he plays a video, a canned laughter track fills the small space. You don't know how long this goes on for, probably a couple of minutes, he's showing no signs of stopping, so you look up. In the white light of the phone screen, his face is gaunt, unruly stubble around his chin, his teeth uneven; he is enjoying whatever the video is showing him.

It takes him a few moments to realize you've stopped, so engrossed is he in his phone. He looks down, says 'Sorry sorry' and places the phone next to the washbasin. Then he heaves a bored sigh and, in a practised action, bends, picks you up by your armpits, lightly pushes you so you're now facing the wall, holds your face to the right, your left cheek against the cold tile, his hands in your hair, his nails digging into your scalp. With his other hand, he pulls your trousers and underwear down, then begins to rub himself against you. You feel him getting hard.

All this has happened very quickly, but now you know that he is going to enter you, his cock is getting firmer by the second. And you know you've been here before; not this exact bathroom, not this exact person, but it is all too familiar, they're all the same men, and you're once again the 22-year-old boy in the Mountains. You can feel the migraine clamping down on your eyebrows, its aura enveloping the back of your neck, and you know if you don't stop this now, his tongue will find your ear, and stay there hungry, salivating, quivering, while he fucks you.

With a jolt of your back, you push him; it's harder than you'd intended; his body hits the opposite wall, his foot kicks against a bucket, the plastic bangs loudly against the toilet. 'What the fuck . . .' he's saying, reaching for your shoulder, his hands very close; you sense that if he catches hold, he will hurt you, maybe smash your head into the wall, maybe punch your face, maybe enter you raw. The possibilities of violence are endless.

But you have all your clothes on, you haven't removed a single garment; you pull up your pants, run out of the bathroom, pat the wall frantically and find a light switch. Then you rush to the door, unbolt it, and you're out in the lift lobby.

You're at the Sea-facing Road in the middle of the night, sat on the low wall that fences the sea in. It's high tide, and the waves slosh against the bulwark, spitting drops of angry water on your face. This is where, four years ago, the impromptu celebratory parade erupted after Section 377 had been read down. Tonight, it's a ghost town, aptly so; all you spirits freed that day, granted bodies, have morphed back into apparitions. If that man had hurt you, you wouldn't have been able to go to the police, report his crime, because you're the criminal again, and you deserve no protection, no justice.

You are not thinking about why you went to the man's flat without having vetted him; you know that people like you do it all the time; there is a self-destructive streak in your kind; when the world wants nothing but to obliterate you, who are you to try and swim against the current? What was that Sanskrit proverb your mother had quoted? Vinaasha-kaale vipareet-buddhi. Yes, you're the moth rushing towards the flame to be burnt down, the drunkard begging for more alcohol to sear his liver. This is your destiny, to annihilate yourself before everyone else does, to not hand your suffering over to the haters, to claim your own end.

Your favourite director, Rituparno Ghosh, who ushered in a new age for Bangla cinema, who wore androgynous clothing and acted in female parts in films, is dead. You saw it in the news a few months ago, the details were vague, he was in the hospital, he was undergoing hormone therapy, he'd got breast implants for a role, he suffered from insomnia, he was forty-nine. This is what happens to men like you. You can see now why Mamu made such a mess of his life, he was forty-nine too when he died, and you know you will too, make a mess. Your parents had feared rightly: you have become your Mamu, in spite of trying so hard to be anything but.

By some instinct, you take your phone out and do something you've never done before; you go on Facebook and type out Egg-head's name, not caring that you will show up on his *People you may know* prompt. There he is, married, with a child, husband–wife–child smiling beatifically for the world in the profile pic. You go back to the search bar and type out the names of everyone you can think of, everyone who was part of the mob, everyone who called you names, who you think has read your journal; you're surprised you remember their full names, even the ways they're spelt; they're all there, husband–wife–child, paragons of fulfilment, model citizens of this country, their children the next generation of voters. Nothing they did to you has ever touched them; let alone their bodies, their consciences are as clear as a bright Indian summer's day. The serpent inside you rears its head and hisses, wishing all their children turn out gay; will they then confront their pasts, weigh their actions up against their newfound etiquettes? Will they then think of you, wonder how you turned out, maybe apologize?

Even Y has a five- or six-year-old daughter now, with whom he takes pictures and posts copiously. Does he remember you, does he think of you, the nape of your neck where he loved to tuck his lips in, does he pick up his phone to call you then put it away, whisper wishes to the universe on your birthday, does he?

And it is then that you know that you have to leave this place, you have to leave this country. You have lost, everyone like you has lost, and there is nothing for you in this lost place. Yes, there are brave fighters, those who will change the future, make history, but you're not one of them; you're too broken, the only future you have a shot at changing is your own.

You don't know how you will make it happen. You know going away will break your mother's heart. You know you will miss your nephew so much, and he will grow up missing you without even knowing what he's missing out on.

But your story will not end here, like Mamu's, like Rituparno Ghosh's. You will do the things they couldn't, live the lives they didn't. You will *have* to live, for yourself, for those who love you, for your nephew.

You don't know yet that people like you are pariahs, always on the run; there will never be a home, there will only be patches of shade to catch your breath before running again.

You don't know yet that Section 377 will be amended a few years later, gays will be legal again. But by now, you don't trust laws and those who make them, laws were never made with you in mind anyway. You and your kind have been invisible for so long, the fight to be seen is only just beginning.

You don't know yet that you will feel love again. But that is a story for another time.

Right now, cutting through the oncoming blackness of the migraine, your nerves frayed from the lack of oxygen, a hair's breadth away from passing out, all you know is that you need to be somewhere else.

You allow your head to slump, your hand to drop, let the brackish water fondle your fingertips, then you chant the Vishnu-stotra Mamu taught you that last evening with him, '*Shantakaram bhujagashayanam padmanabham suresham . . .*' It is the only way you know to keep him alive, and tonight, you need him close to you.

ENTRY EIGHT

Vivaan's VoiceNote008

Knock, knock. Who's there? Vivaan's ghost, hovering over the thirty-second floor.

Sorry, trying out my silly jokes so I don't lose you, my audience. Keep it palatable, Mambro said. I say, take it to the next level, make it funny. Is there a better storyteller than a clown?

So, on the night I yanked Zed out of my life and sat in the dark by myself, I eventually heard Mom turn the key in the lock, then walk through the front door, I heard her concerned voice call my name, then her footsteps coming towards my room, her hand on the doorknob, her fingers on the light switch, then her coming closer, sitting on the bed.

I didn't look at her, I stared at my lap, I hadn't even put my boxers on. I was supposed to do that, was supposed to have gone up to the thirty-second floor, ended all this before Mom came home. But I was still here, sitting naked in the dark for hours. I didn't know what time it was, how long had passed. Maybe this was how it was meant to be. Even though my mind wanted to jump, my body had resisted, held out, waited for Mom, wanting her to see me like this.

What's happened, Vivaan? I heard Mom's unsteady voice, felt her fingers on my skin. Ki hoyechhe, shona? Amay bol?

I didn't know what I was saying, it was a murmur at first, just sounds, utterances, but then I was telling her everything. I don't remember how it came out, in coherent words or unformed spurts, in calmness or through sobs, in English or in Bangla. But I told her about Zee, the dance, the hook-ups, breaking her trust, about the essay, about the corporation, about Zed, about the headset, about the sex with Zed, or was it with myself?

I stopped there, I couldn't bring myself to tell her about the viral video, about the urge to go up to the roof and end it all. Most times, parents protect their children; but sometimes, we protect them too.

When I finished, Mom was unsure if there was more, so we just sat there, me naked, her in a grey pantsuit and mauve shirt, the ceiling light too invasive for this scene. Then she pulled the blanket over my legs. Her breath was laboured, and I didn't have the courage to look at her face.

I . . . you . . . we, your dad and I . . . we just . . . you were so . . . maybe we should've . . . but we thought . . . Mom was starting sentences she didn't know how to finish.

Can you ever forgive me, Mom? I said in a small voice. I looked up at her then.

Her eyes were red but dry. She put her arms around me and kissed my hair. Shona chhele, she said, like she used to when I was a child. Shona chhele, my darling boy, she repeated over and over again. Shona chhele . . .

Then she sat up, I could tell her instincts had kicked in, she needed to gather herself to keep this moment from spiralling. She patted my hand, my cheek, my head, like she didn't want to lose touch with my body. I'll heat up dinner, I'll see you outside in ten minutes?

I nodded, then blurted out without thinking, Mom, can I call Mambro?

Of course, sweetie. I would've called him anyway.

Yeah but, like, can I ask if he can come over for a few days?

I've never asked for Mambro to be here, I know he left because he had to, I know he yearns for me, for his family, his friends, for all the things he can't have there. The life he leads abroad is a half-life. But whatever he gets from that place, it's

enough to keep him going, it is what makes it possible for me
to have him in my life. Miss Gibson once told us that to keep
our heads held high and look people straight in the eye, we
need to first stand tall with our feet on firm ground. That is
what Mambro has been trying to do.

But that's his story to tell.

Mambro arrived fourteen hours later, it is the time it must've
taken him to get on the Tube to the airport, jump on the first
flight, sit through the journey, run out of the airport here and
hop into a taxi.

Cool-bro was with him. When he'd introduced his partner
to us a few years ago, I wanted to just call him by his name,
but Mom vetoed it, said that's not how we call elders in our
culture, so I'd put my ten-year-old brain to work, I needed
to find something as ingenious as Mambro. When I proposed
Cool-bro, I knew I'd clinched it.

The first time they came visiting, Dad hugged Cool-bro the
moment he walked through the door. Welcome to the family,
he said, and that settled everything, and though I'd wanted to
ask why Mambro doesn't have a wife like everyone else, Dad
laying out the red carpet for Cool-bro made it seem so natural that it didn't matter any more whether he was Mambro's
boyfriend or girlfriend, they were a couple and that was that.
The thing is, Dad's rose-tinted glasses, no matter how much
they drive me up the wall, give him a clear sight of how he
wants the world to be, and it doesn't bother him if no one
else has the same view, he just goes ahead and does what feels
true to him. I hope I can have that kind of clarity someday.

Halfway through that trip, Mom put up a photo of the
three of us on our living-room wall. In the photo, I'm giggling because Mambro is tickling me and Cool-bro is giving
us a bear-hug from behind, it was taken by the lake close to

our place. Over the years, to anyone who'd ask, Mom would proudly point at it and say, That's my brother, and that's his partner. She'd let the guests' jaws hang in shock before they acclimatized to the idea and made whatever they wanted of it. That's the only way to make ourselves seen in this world, Kun faya kun, Just be, and it is! It's written in the Quran, I saw it on Insta.

Those fourteen hours until Mambro and Cool-bro arrived were excruciating. Mom called Dad and he drove through the night to get back home. Mom slept next to me, though I don't think she caught a wink, she just kept turning, opening and closing the windows, getting up to drink water. I managed to doze off for stretches, though. One time, I went to the bathroom and when I came out, Mom was standing by the door. I asked her what's up. She shook her head and went back to bed, but I could tell she wanted to keep me in her sights. On his way, Dad picked up croissants from my favourite bakery, and we ate breakfast in silence. I knew he'd have a chat with me later, but he wanted to give me space first, not dive into it.

Mambro and Cool-bro set the whole place buzzing. They said they'd booked a short holiday in the Coffee Plantations, we were to leave early the next morning, we'd be back before the first of my final exams. Mom and Dad said the exams weren't important right now, I could take a year off, sit them next year, they'd ask Princi to appeal to the board. But I put on a brave face, I got this, I'm super well-prepared, I don't know if I will be next year! And not gonna lie, I did want to take the exams, I wanted to apply myself, do well, feel worthy of something again. Mom and Dad looked tentative. They said, Okay, but let us know if you change your mind.

My uncles took over, making things very busy. Cool-bro cooked dinner. Fun fact: he's the best chef in the world, loves to feed people, left to him, no one would die of starvation.

Mom and Dad sent emails and made last-minute calls to inform colleagues that they'd be away for a few days.

Mambro helped me pack. We threw some clothes and books into a duffel bag, he always packs so many books, it's his thing, he's terrified of running out of things to read! Then Mambro plopped down on the bed, took off his glasses, and rubbed his palms fiercely over his eyes. With his skin going up and down like that, I noticed his jowls for the first time, the laughter lines at the corners of his mouth, the grey at his temples.

All okay? I put a hand on his shoulder.

Yeah, yeah, I mean, just jetlag, right? Mambro tugged my arm and made me sit next to him. He looked spent. I knew he was trying to tell me something. Finally, he asked, And how are YOU feeling?

I didn't know what to say, I was feeling a lot of things, relieved that I was surrounded by all of them, exhausted of course, but I guess, mostly, I was ashamed, for putting so much into the online world where nothing was real, like, it was so easy for it to just evaporate, poof! And I was plain embarrassed that I'd made such a brouhaha, look at this, everyone had paused their lives to deal with my idiocy. Gross!

But I didn't say any of this, just stared at the floor. Mambro put his hand on the back of my head. The older I grow, he said, the more I feel like I should probably never have left. We all need each other a little more with every passing year. Then he whispered, I'm sorry I wasn't here, Vivaan, I should've been.

I turned to him. Don't say that, Mambro, please. Going away was the right thing to do, look at you now, you'd never have met Cool-bro otherwise. I'd started to cry, Mambro pulled me closer to him, but I had more to say. And you've always been with me, you are the reason I've had it so easy, why I've never had to lie about myself . . .

At this point, Cool-bro came to the doorway and announced that dinner was ready, and something passed between Mambro's and Cool-bro's eyes, like how it is between couples, Mom and Dad have that too, I used to have that with Zee once upon a time. Then Cool-bro said, That's fine, no hurry, take your time. But I said it's fine, we should all eat, we were all ravenous, and honestly, the food was fucking delish!

On our way to the plantations, Dad drove and Mambro played old Hindi songs on the radio that they sang along to. They remembered the lyrics, word for word, even though the songs were from obscure movies of the 1950s and 60s and 70s. You haven't forgotten these though you've lived abroad for so long, Dad complimented Mambro. Mambro just wagged his head and continued to sing.

In the middle seat, Cool-bro and I played tic-tac-toe and snakes & ladders, like when I was a kid. They'd banned all tech on this holiday, no phones except for one, obvs no laptops, the Wi-Fi in the plantations would be patchy at best. In the back seat, Mom caught up on sleep, passed out, she'd been protecting the fortress like Rani Lakshmibai all this time, but now her trusted generals had arrived, she could take a break. When we stopped halfway, I crawled to the back seat and slept with my head on Mom's lap.

Mom continued her slumber in the plantations, waking up only for meals, sometimes sitting quietly by the campfire at night, watching the fireflies, extending her hand to hold mine, as Cool-bro invented games for us to play.

What do you think of the resort? Mambro asked one night after dinner.

I gave him the side-eye. It's bougie AF, but it'll do for now.

Well, you and I have our backpacking trip after your exams, can't wait!

Ditto. Seriously, I couldn't wait either. It was the only thing I was looking forward to, I had no idea what would happen after that. But one step at a time, that's the only way forward.

In the daytime, we went out on walks, hiked long distances along dirt tracks and through the bushes, sniffing the coffee, turning the pods between our fingers, wishing vanakkam to the workers harvesting the crop, they smiled back, sometimes I played hide-and-seek with their children.

One time, Cool-bro whisked me away while Dad and Mambro were walking in front. We trekked up a hill, scaled its peak, then another peak, and I could feel my pores open up, my heart expanding, my glutes and calf muscles begging for more. Come on, Vivaan, one more slope, come on, let's race until the end of this path, Cool-bro kept pushing me. I knew he was trying to exhaust me, get my heart rate up, get the pheromones flowing so I'd sleep better, so the cloud in my head would clear bit by bit.

When we returned all sweaty and breathless, Dad and Mambro were stood on the path where we'd left them, debating current affairs, the upcoming elections and the political economy, why the same-sex marriage law didn't pass. Dad, ever the optimist, thought the petition was mistimed, they shouldn't have brought this to court in an election year. Then he asked Mambro, What would it mean for you guys if it did go through? Would you come back and live here? Mambro, as usual, skilfully ducked the question, avoided talking about himself, instead he quoted some statistics on migration and visas and stuff.

Such boring uncles you both have become, Cool-bro teased, talking politics all the time, if only the politicians gave a damn about what you had to say. Dad and Mambro accepted this smilingly. They're not fighting their age, they are what they are, not hunks or bears or wannabe-twinks or otters or cubs or daddies, just two decent men in their forties, one gay one straight, trying to make lemonade from the lemons that life has served them.

Maybe one day I'll grow old like these two. I don't need to make any lofty declarations about my future, my future is right here before my eyes. And that wouldn't be so bad, na? That'd be quite all right, actually.

Nana-nana-boo-boo, I sing-songed like I used to as a child, and we all laughed. In that moment, I felt like the start of something, clean slate or whatever, like maybe I could put all that morbid stuff behind and slowly move ahead?

On the last afternoon in the plantations, Mambro told me his Mamu's story. We were sat on the bed, side by side, the blur of the pines rolling out on the hill slopes ahead of us. He started with a host of disclaimers, like, I wasn't close to him so I can only imagine and piece things together, keep in mind that was a very different time, our legacies can be judged by the present but our actions should only be judged in the past . . .

I had to stop him, like, Mambro, bas na, chill out, this isn't a court testimony, just tell me already! So he did. By the time he finished, it was nearly dusk. Mambro's face was stoic, his Adam's apple bobbing up and down.

Do you think, I asked, that Grand-Mamu ever got tested? Did he have . . .? I was stumbling, it's still difficult, even after all these generations, to name the virus that killed so many.

Mambro shrugged. I don't know, I never asked obviously, I didn't even know to ask back then. He heaved a sigh. But I doubt they tested him for HIV, and you could get arrested for admitting to having had sex with men. If he had it, we'll never know . . .

I dug my nails into my thighs, wanting to feel my body,

needing to know it was still there, healthy, fit to live. And to think that I had been THIS close to throwing it off the roof! So many things we take for granted, things those before us would've given anything to have.

Then Mambro handed me his manuscript, a sheaf of loose pages really, his cursive handwriting scrawled over them, the exaggerated tails of the f's and the j's, the distinct loop of the q. I don't think I can talk about my life yet, but I've written it all down. He smiled. It's funny how I've been writing stories about other people until now . . .

I took the pages in my hands, held them in my lap. As I leafed through them, two photographs slipped out. One of Grand-Mamu as a child, about three years old, dressed in flapping shorts and a smart shirt, eyes lined with kohl, leaning against a stool on which his baby sister, my Didu, is sat. The other from Mambro's annaprasan, little Mambro perched on a young Grand-Mamu's folded left knee, tuberose garlands around both their necks. I knew instantly where these were going to go, up on the wall in my bedroom, next to the framed photo of my annaprasan, baby-me sat in exactly the same position, on a twenty-something Mambro's folded knee, both of us dressed in dhuti-panjabi. A triptych. I'm looking at the wall right now as I speak, and in case you can't tell, it's making me smile.

Mambro took one of the photos, held it up to the light coming through the window. On the last evening I saw Mamu, there were so many things I wanted to tell him, ask him. Back then, before the internet, before queer friends, before telling my family, before I met your Cool-bro, he was the only person I could've spoken to, and maybe I could've understood him too. Mambro fell silent, I could see he was trying to remember, it'd been a long time since that evening, nearly three decades. Then he shook his head. But I didn't, and nor did Mamu . . . we said nothing to each other, trying and failing to find the words we hadn't inherited. It took me years to even call myself gay. Mambro scrunched up his nose. It was such a loaded term, it meant so many things . . . none of them good, of course . . .

Mambro inhaled deeply, and I knew he really wanted a smoke, Cool-bro had got him to quit a few years ago.

It's not that things have become easier for you, Vivaan. People like you and me, we'll always be on the fringes. You'll have your own battles, like I've had mine, still do, and god knows Mamu had his. But at least you have us, me, your mom, Dad, Cool-bro, Dadu, Didu, you'll find more people along the way. Never lock yourself up in that shell you went into, never feel like you have to figure this out on your own. Promise me?

Tears sprang to my eyes. Mambro kept wiping them away, speaking softly, as if he were singing a lullaby. Maybe that is the only thing that's become better, Vivaan, from Mamu's generation to yours . . . we have words now. Laws will be made and unmade, promises kept and reneged on, the haters will never go away, and everyone else will sit on the fence and watch the show. But we have the language now to tell our stories, and even if no one else will listen, we at least have each other . . .

Mambro put the photo between us on the bed. The sunset gave it a reddish hue, it looked like Grand-Mamu's face was emitting light.

You know, Mambro said, Mamu got so many things wrong, he hurt so many people, that's all everyone says about him even now . . . But who knows, if he'd lived longer, had a little more time, maybe he and the world would've been better to each other, made nice?

If he'd lived longer, he would've been here, I said, my voice was excitable like a child's. Look at us now, together!

Imagine, Mambro, if Grand-Mamu had been around to see you and Cool-bro, all the things he'd wanted for his life now happening in yours . . .

But even before I could finish, Mambro was weeping. I didn't even . . . I just . . . I should've . . . he shouldn't have died like that . . . he was so young . . . so fucking young . . . Bubbles of spit popped from Mambro's mouth, mixing with his tears. I . . . I didn't even cry when he died.

Mom appeared from the doorway and hugged Mambro, and Mambro put his head on her chest, and Mom was crying too, brother and sister finally mourning their uncle, giving him the farewell he deserved all those years ago.

It was almost evening now, we could hardly see each other, just silhouettes and shadows. Dad and Cool-bro entered the room and joined me and Mambro and Mom, the whole family in a circle, as if we were about to start a seance.

Mamu did leave me with something though, Mambro said. He taught me a mantra, said I could recite it when I'm feeling low. I always say it when I think of him . . .

As Mambro chanted, I felt someone occupy the space between us, his eyes kind, head full of dark hair, lips curled in a smile, moustache turned downward. Here's the thing about dying young, you never have to grow old, and he had no grey hair, no wrinkles, no jowls.

But here's another thing about dying young, you're not around long enough for those who come after you, who could've looked up to you, glimpsed their future selves in you.

It's time, Vivaan, he said to me, to tell your story.

Yes, Grand-Mamu, I will tell my story. And I will tell yours too, give it pride of place. It's time.

Grand-Mamu's Story

One evening, Sukumar comes home to find his nephew visiting. It is still some weeks away from his death. The boy is now nineteen, and a few months ago, he went away to the Mountains for university. Now he's back after his first semester, is going to return to campus the next day. Sukumar's heart warms at the thought that the boy has come to see his Mamu on his last evening in the Grand Old City. He takes the blue jacket that he's bought for him out of the almirah; some Tibetan salesmen came by the office, and promised that this jacket was of the highest quality. His nephew tries it on; the fleece bulges but the fit is snug, the electric blue contrasts against his light skin. 'You look handsome,' Sukumar compliments him.

And even though he is tired from his day, in pain from the permanent limp he now has, the muscles in his left foot having atrophied, his knees given to wear and tear, swellings on his calves that leave deep lesions but never clear up, Sukumar says he will hurry to the mishtir dokan and get some kochuri and goja. His mother protests, saying she's already cooked a five-course dinner for her grandson, but Sukumar is already turning on his heels to go down the stairs. His nephew springs up from the bed, says he'll come along with Mamu.

Outside, the two of them walk side by side, shoulder to shoulder. The boy isn't as tall as Sukumar; they say genes skip a generation, and he has inherited the shortness of Sukumar's father. Still, he walks in sure strides, slowing down to keep pace with his Mamu. They reach the sweet shop, then another, but Sukumar's feet go farther, acting of their own accord, not stopping, not rushing either. He doesn't know where they're leading him, just that he wants to spend a few moments with his nephew, alone together for the first time in years. The boy comes along unperturbed, as trusting as the first time they'd met.

They cross the broad avenue, the market, the train tracks of the Chokro-rail, Sukumar's blistered soles scraping against the stone chips, his nephew hopping across like an agile gymnast. 'Do you remember when I took you for a ride on this train? You memorized the name of every station!' The boy looks back at Sukumar blankly, and he has to smile at how memory is the crutch of adults. Children don't need memory at all; they wake up every morning to claim the day anew.

They reach the ghat, the river at high tide undulating in waves, a veil of sheer clouds drifting over its surface, the lights on the opposite bank shimmering like stars. It is only now that Sukumar notices the weather has turned. In the last few years, as he's become more and more isolated, he recedes into his head for long periods, his powers of observation fuzzy, his connection to his surroundings nearly absent. A kalboishakhi storm is on its way, cold winds race in from the water, tree fronds wave their heads, footsteps ring out as people run for shelter. It is the hour of gloaming, the sun fighting it out with the clouds for its last moments of glory, gilded bars anchoring it to the sky, a rainbow smudging between them.

'Let's sit for a while,' Sukumar says, and he heads to his favourite corner. It looks different nowadays. The municipality has axed down the banyan tree; perhaps it spread its branches too wide, became a public nuisance, needed to be put in its place; only an ungraceful stump remains, initials of lovers scratched on the bark. They've also repaired the bench with a layer of concrete, a shoddily done job that has made the seat higher and uneven. Someone's name is engraved on the backrest, dedicated in memoriam, reminding Sukumar that the bench isn't his any more. It never was, like X, like everything else; nothing belonged to him, and he belonged to no one.

Once they sit though, the weather magically calms down. The bench still has its powers, Sukumar thinks, then waves away his childishness. He casts a sidelong glance at the boy sitting calmly next to him, only a few years older than when Sukumar lost his father. The boy's breathing is deep, his eyes on the sky opening up before them, the haze lifting over the river, the outlines of the houses on the opposite bank starting to form. This boy is in love, Sukumar can tell; that steadiness of gaze, that sureness with which he places his palms on his knees, that fragrance in his breath, they belong to someone who has journeyed to that inner core for the first time.

Sukumar wants to put an arm around the boy's shoulder, ruffle his hair, kiss his cheek like he used to when he was a baby. He remembers his nephew sticking out his pink tongue so his Mamu could feed him more payesh on the day of his annaprasan. And now here he is, a young man on the threshold of life. At this age, he has already moved from the Garden City to the Grand Old City, and then to the Mountains; he will go somewhere else after university. He has already seen more of the world than his Mamu has. What would life have been like if Sukumar had travelled, gone somewhere else, if he hadn't spent all his years cocooned in these Northern Quarters, the same streets, the same river, the same bench? But there are advantages to having lived in the same place; he has painted the goddess's eyes for Durga Pujo every year; where else but the Grand Old City could he have done that?

If this boy is indeed like his uncle, if he is in love with another man, then Sukumar can only imagine the privations the world will inflict on him. But somehow he isn't scared for his nephew, he knows the boy can fight back, he can sense a strength glowing inside this youthful mind. Nor is Sukumar regretful that his nephew has taken after him. We should exist, he thinks, be born again and again, in every generation, so that they never forget about us.

He wants to tell his nephew everything about himself, about X, about love, about heartbreak, about the ignominies. He knows his nephew doesn't agree with how he has abandoned his marriage, he has no intention of defending himself, but perhaps someone should hear his side too? Alas, words are failing him, his wisdom cannot be framed by the language he knows. He is nearly fifty now, but still feels like the gawky teenager on the day he lost his father, waiting for his life to stretch out before him, to discover who he truly is, waiting for his father to tell him how he should proceed.

When they'd moved back to the Northern Quarters after their father's death, Sukumar and his sister had been told of a woman in the neighbourhood. It was all quite hush-hush, but she conducted seances, she was a medium, could help to translate from the afterlife. Brother and sister sought her out, were surprised to see how normal she looked, wearing a saree, sindoor in the parting of her hair, red teep on her forehead. They asked to commune with their father; he'd gone so suddenly, so young, they'd spent nights awake brimming with questions for him. The woman initially refused, said they were too young, but she finally relented.

There'd only been two such seances. Later, brother and sister would chuckle about the silliness, but back then, they took it very seriously. The woman laid out a series of cards in front of her in a semicircle, unscrewed the lid of a jar containing methi seeds, then blindfolded herself, asking Sukumar to check its tightness. Then she took the lid in her hand, and told them to think of their father, their choicest memories with him, to channel his energy, and if they wanted to ask him something, they should do it in their heads, not aloud, and one by one.

Sukumar's sister wanted to go first, and of course he let her; he always let her have first dibs on everything, the first bite of a sweet, first read of a book, first play with a toy, the window seat in a train; he loved her so much, she could have everything he owned. At the seance, the three of them breathed in and out together, again and again, until his sister silently asked, *Are you well?* She'd tell him this later. Intuiting this, the woman's fingers flicked, and she spun the lid of the jar. The revolving metal rumbled against the red sandstone floor, then fell flat on a card. The woman took her blindfold off, blinked and regarded the picture, turned to his sister and whispered, 'He says he is rested, no pain.' And even though their skin erupted in goosebumps and they nearly fled the scene, brother and sister slept well that night.

At the second session a few days later, it was Sukumar's turn. He'd brought his father's coat, the one he wore to court most often; he'd had to search through the suitcases and hide it from their mother. The musty odour filled his nostrils, forming the words in his mind, the question he'd been meaning to ask, the question everyone had been asking him, now that he was the man of the house. He exhaled. *What should I do now?*

The woman's hand trembled, her fingers made an erratic movement as she set the lid spinning, and it spun manically, sliding this way and that, as though the earth had suddenly tilted. It upset the order of the cards stacked in twos and threes, sent them flying. Then it shot out to a corner, hit the wall, and came to a standstill on the floor. His sister clutched Sukumar's arm in fear. The medium slumped, took off her blindfold, choked on her spit and launched into a coughing spree. It's gibberish, the response was nonsense, she said when she could breathe again, the spirit had transcended, the seance was over, the children shouldn't come back.

Had his father's spirit known what would happen to Sukumar, how his life would turn out? Was that why his father had refused to answer his question?

Now, sitting on his favourite bench by the river with his nephew, Sukumar lets his mind rove across a slideshow of other images spanning his life, as though through the peep-hole of a kaleidoscope, the kind they had in fairs when he was a child. He glimpses the room in the boarding house where X lived, the nights of listening to adhunik songs on the radio with his mother and sister, he and his sister running into their father's chamber, their father pulling out gifts from under the table, exclaiming 'Chiching-phaank' like they were entering Ali Baba's cave, his mother in a bottle-green zari-paar saree holding his hand in a crowd so he wouldn't get lost, X head-banging to English music on a Walkman he'd sourced from somewhere, the pride on Master-babu's face every time he'd painted the goddess's eyes, putting his nephew to sleep that first time, the scent of Johnson's baby powder mixed with that of tuberoses . . .

Observed through this selective aperture, the opalescence of his life doesn't seem so bad after all, not a failed existence lived as marginalia; it sure had its moments.

He can't rewrite his life, it is too late for that, but might he compose a coda, one of his own making, in the words he knows best? Could a man like him be allowed that at least?

Sukumar turns to his nephew, breaks the silence. 'Sing me a song. You sing so well.' The boy clears his throat, begins a Hindi song; he's always been addicted to Bollywood movies.

Sukumar stops him. 'Na-na, sing in Bangla, I don't understand Hindi well.' His nephew nods, then sings 'Poth Harabo Bolei Ebaar Pothe Nemechhi'. *I've been confounded by the riddles of the straight path / I'm now walking this winding path only to get lost.*

'Your turn now, Mamu.' The boy's voice is inviting, the resentment of the past years towards his uncle now dissolved.

Sukumar shakes his head. 'I can't sing like you and your mother, I only croak.' He laughs, then sits up. 'But I can teach you something. A prayer, that's the only thing I'm good at.'

His nephew moves closer, faces Sukumar. Sukumar begins chanting the Vishnu-stotra. '*Shantakaram bhujagashayanam pad-manabham suresham . . .*' The boy listens intently, reads Sukumar's lips, then on the next recitation, mumbles along, saying the lines, first faltering, then growing more fluent. Uncle and nephew sit there in the last dregs of skylight, enunciating the Sanskrit words again and again. When it is over, Sukumar looks away, his eyes on the little dinghies that rock on the surface of the river, returning with the day's catch of fish. 'I say it when I need peace. People think I'm a lunatic muttering to myself, let them . . .' He claps his nephew's knee. 'Try it when you're feeling down.'

And there, that's his legacy; he has no language to tell his story to the boy, but he has passed on a talisman. In his jiboner haal-khata, the ledger of his life, he has always been in the red, wronged everyone, his mother, his wife, his sister, even his father-in-law and X. He has no children of his own. But here is this boy, part of him, singing the mantra his Mamu has taught him; and perhaps this is enough.

'Chol re!' he exclaims. 'We're so late. I lost track of time.'

They make their way through the ghat, wait at the pedestrian crossing for the Chokro-rail to pass, and when Sukumar wobbles over the mounds of sharp stone chips, pain shooting up through his shins, his nephew holds out his hand, steadies his uncle. 'Place your feet here, then here, ekhane, okhane.'

Once on the other side, uncle and nephew head towards home, still holding hands.

Mambro's Manuscript

On your last day in the Sleepless City, you take your nephew out to the seaside.

You are ready to leave for a Foreign Country where you've managed a transfer through work for a couple of years. For now, this will do. The Foreign Country has just passed a same-sex marriage law; marriage is far-fetched, you haven't even dated a man since Y, never felt love, but maybe this is a sign? You know it's bullshit, but you indulge yourself and dream a little.

Your friends have thrown you farewell parties, taken you to rooftop bars and beachside shacks; there were leaving dos at work; you've called uncles and aunts to get their blessings. Your parents came to help you pack and to say goodbye. You gave away many things you owned, sent a few boxes to your childhood home; your belongings now are strewn across this land, like pollen waiting to bloom into new lives. Your sister and brother-in-law and nephew are visiting, they will drop you off at the airport the next morning.

You called Mamu's wife too, she and your mother still have an uncannily vibrant friendship, as though their history isn't pockmarked by painful memories. After Mamu's death, your aunt got a job at his bank on compassionate grounds, it is still a thing in the public sector; in his lifetime, being his wife had only brought her disgrace; in his death, it gave her an identity, an income. She started at entry level, but has risen through the ranks, a testament to her brilliance and diligence, has a pension waiting when she retires in a few years; she's made something of her life, refusing to be cast in the roles of abandoned wife then grieving widow. 'Your Mamu would be so proud,' she said on the phone, 'seeing you go abroad.' Nowadays, she speaks of Mamu as though if he hadn't died, they'd still be living together as wife–husband; maybe she's indulging herself and dreaming a little too.

Before you leave for the seaside, you put in your backpack a book your nephew can read; he is 'five and three-quarters years old', as he proudly tells anyone who asks; reading is his favourite pastime, and the only thing you buy him is books. You're looking for something to read yourself, but all your books are already in boxes. Your journal is in the drawer, you've left it there to take with you to the Foreign Country; you stuff it into your backpack, maybe finally you will open up its checked, jute cover and see the words the sixteen-year-old *you* had written, the words that you failed to keep safe, that came back to mangle your life to avenge themselves; maybe today is a good day to read them, your last day here.

At the seaside, you find a flat rock and unfold a blanket, settle your nephew on it, then sit down yourself. His hair is flying helter-skelter in the wind, and you smooth it down against his head; he doesn't mind, he is showing you how many colours he can see in the sky, it is just before twilight. Then his eyes widen; he turns towards you, and you know that he's been struck by one of his ingenious ideas. 'We should sail boats in the sea!' he says. 'But we don't have paper,' you reply. 'You can't tear any from your book, your mother will be very angry.'

The boy looks away with a forlorn face, and you feel a stab of guilt at squashing his wish on this last evening together. Leaving him behind has been the most difficult part of this move; you've buried the hurt under the innumerable things you've had to do, but now that he is here, all you want is to lift him in your arms and walk into the airport. He is the only thing you'd take with you if you could; but he is not yours, never will be; he is someone else's child.

'I have an idea! You want to hear?' you say, as if it's just come to you, though you had it the moment he asked for a boat. 'Esh!' the boy nods calmly, as though he trusted you from the start to find a solution; he still can't make the Y-sound, makes you wish this cuteness lasts until you see him next.

You produce your journal, tear out a page, fold the sides diagonally, perfect symmetry in your fingers, until you give it a slight push from the bottom, and a triangular sail pops out like magic. Your nephew claps in joy, then with much fanfare, places the boat in the serene low-tide shallows the colour of blood, sees it float; when it starts coming back towards you, he takes a stick and splashes the water to navigate the boat away, until it is moving towards the horizon.

He turns to you. 'And your boat?' You tear out another page and do the same thing, then give him one for himself, teach him how to make his own boat; you won't be around to do this for him any more. Uncle and nephew get busy floating boats, until there is a procession of paper sails in the sea, some drowning, some surviving, but all on their own journeys. The words, written in your inimitable cursive hand, are smudging beyond recognition, the ink bleeding into the water. You feel an urge to protect them from erasure, your story, you've held on to it for so long. But what if those words don't belong to you any more, you've trusted the sea to wash them away? What if you are ready to start writing on a blank page again?

As your nephew beats the water with his stick, a splash goes into his eyes, and he starts to cry because of the salty sting. You hold his chin between your fingertips and blow flutes of air into his left eye, then the right one, and as you do it, whistling sounds emanate from your pursed lips. He starts to giggle, and you start to make notes of different pitches, until you're whistling a tune, 'Baa, Baa, Black Sheep' or something like that, and he's laughing so hard now that you have to stop whistling and join in. When he splashes the water next, you teach him to look sideways, to monitor his boats from the corner of his eye.

It's nearly dark now, the twilight almost concluded, the light withdrawing with a quiet confidence, so you pack up; your sister and brother-in-law are cooking you a fine dinner tonight, you don't want to be late.

'Cholo,' you hold your hand out to the boy. 'Taratari, we have to hurry.'

'But your book?' He points to the journal that has fallen into a crevice between the rocks, covered in sand. It looks emaciated, like a sheep shorn of its wool.

'Leave it here, it's outdated; one day I'll write a new one and you can read it when you grow up.'

'Plomich?' The child looks up expectantly. He might not be your child, but there is a you-shaped space in him that no one else can occupy, just as there will always remain a Mamu-shaped gap inside you. You wish you still had the blue jacket, that you hadn't asked your mother to give it away; now you're going to a cold country, you could've worn it, it would've looked good on you.

To your nephew, you whisper, 'Yes, promise, I will write a new one.'

Little Vivaan curls his fingers in yours, narrows his eyes, holds his palm to his forehead like a captain surveying his fleet bobbing in the ocean. 'Let's gooo!' he says, and leads you to the shore.

Loose page . . .

It is an unusual day in the Mountains. The hostel is empty, everyone has gone on a picnic. You've stayed back, along with a few other strays who don't fit in with the mob. Everyone is making the most of this day by steeping in their solitude, breathing in the quietness; someone is blasting Sufi ghazals by Abida Parveen on their speakers, someone is reciting Tennyson in the corridor, someone is mugging up microprocessors for an exam, someone is sleeping it out.

You're restless, an effervescence bubbling up that you can't keep in check. You start dancing, first in measured, hesitant steps; you don't have the equipment, so you're singing your own songs, whatever comes to mind, all your favourites from 'Inhi Logo Ne' to 'Dancing Queen' to 'Chane Ke Khet Mein', your hips gyrating in thumkas, hands waving, fingers in mudras, feet thumping to an imaginary rhythm, face muscles switching between the nine expressions of the navarasa. Madhuri Dixit looks on approvingly from the posters on the wall.

You're dancing, dancing, until you're so out of breath you have to stop; you haven't danced like this in a long time. You danced like this at Mamu's wedding, with Mamu himself. Your core hurts, your soles are sore, your breathing is raspy, hair clumpy from sweat.

You thought you were alone, but there are claps echoing from somewhere. You turn to face your audience. It is the local children outside who harvest crops every afternoon on the terraced farm of the mountain slope, baskets on their backs. They've been watching you, and now they're giving you a standing ovation, lips parted in wide smiles, peachy gums and pearly teeth showing, tender palms joining and parting in adulation. You go out on the balcony and do a little bow; that sets them off clapping again.

It is the one day in the Mountains you will fondly remember; it is the one day when you are free, you are happy, you are seen.

Acknowledgements

Infinite gratitude to . . .

My mother, for permitting me to tell the story of which she is now the sole custodian.

Jessica Woollard, for always believing that every story I want to tell is worth telling.

Helen Garnons-Williams, for your forever open mind, warm heart and keen eye.

Ella Harold, for your fresh perspective and challenge.

The dedicated and passionate team at Penguin – Laura Dermody, Sarah-Jane Forder, Ellie Smith, Sara Granger, Brónagh Grace, Chris Bentham, Alice Chandler, Yazmeen Akhtar, among others.

The equally invested team at DHA – Esme Bright, Anna Watkins, Sophia Hadjipateras, and everyone else.

Fiona Longsdon and Sharanya Murali, for being the first readers, and treating the manuscript with so much care.

The Desmond Elliott Prize Residency and National Centre for Writing, for giving me the essential time and space to imagine.

The Life Writing Prize, for showing me the power of sharing intimate, personal stories with the world.

My friends, you know who you are, but you don't know what my life would've been without your love and kindness.

My parents and my sister, for fighting to build and preserve a safe space called 'home', no matter how far apart we live.

Shiny, for everything.